A Dangerous Game

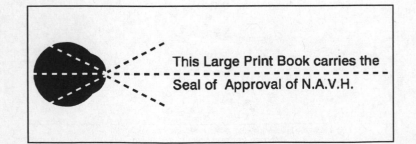

A DANGEROUS GAME

HEATHER GRAHAM

THORNDIKE PRESS

A part of Gale, a Cengage Company

Farmington Hills, Mich • San Francisco • New York • Waterville, Maine
Meriden, Conn • Mason, Ohio • Chicago

Copyright © 2018 by Heather Graham Pozzessere.
New York Confidential.
Thorndike Press, a part of Gale, a Cengage Company.

Thorndike Press® Large Print Core.
The text of this Large Print edition is unabridged.
Other aspects of the book may vary from the original edition.
Set in 16 pt. Plantin.

LIBRARY OF CONGRESS CIP DATA ON FILE.
CATALOGUING IN PUBLICATION FOR THIS BOOK
IS AVAILABLE FROM THE LIBRARY OF CONGRESS.

ISBN-13: 978-1-4328-4846-0 (hardcover)

Published in 2018 by arrangement with Harlequin Books S.A.

Printed in the United States of America
1 2 3 4 5 6 7 22 21 20 19 18

For my beautiful young cousin
Ashley Westermark Stoyanov,
and her husband, Alex Stoyanov,
with love and best wishes
for a lifetime of happiness.

CHAPTER ONE

"Kieran? Kieran Finnegan, right?" The woman asked.

She was wrapped in a black trench coat, wore a black scarf that nearly engulfed her face, and held a dark blanketed bundle against her chest as if it were the greatest treasure in the world.

Kieran wasn't sure when the woman had come in; the offices of psychologists Fuller and Miro were closed for the day, the doctors were gone, and Kieran had just about left herself. The receptionist, Jake, usually locked the office door on his way out, but apparently tonight he had neglected to do so. Then again, Jake might have already left when Kieran's last patient had exited a little while ago. Whether Jake had been gone or he had forgotten to lock up, the door had been left open.

And so this woman accosted Kieran in the reception area of the office just as she was on her way out.

"I am Kieran, but I'm so sorry, I'm the therapist, not one of the doctors. Actually, we are closed for the day. You'll need to come back. Both the doctors are wonderful, and I'm sure they'll be happy to see you another time."

And this woman certainly looked like she needed help. Her eyes were huge and as dark as the clothing she was wearing as she stared at Kieran with a look of despair.

"All right, let me see what I can do. You seem distraught," Kieran said, and winced — wow. Stating the obvious. "I can get you to a hospital. I can call for help —"

"No. No." The woman suddenly thrust the bundle she'd held so closely into Kieran's arms. "Here!"

Kieran instinctively accepted it. Reflex? She wasn't sure why.

It began to cry. And writhe. *Of course.* The bundle was a baby.

"Ma'am, please — Hey!" Kieran protested.

The woman had turned and was fleeing out the door. "Wait! Hey!" Kieran cried. She reached immediately for the phone, hoping that she'd be in time to reach the building's security desk.

Ralph Miller answered the phone at the

8

lobby desk. "Hey, pretty girl. What are you still doing at work? I've got a few hours to go, and then I am out of here. I hear that the Danny Boys are playing at Finnegan's tonight. Can't believe your brother snagged them. I would have thought that you'd have gotten out early —"

"Ralph, listen, please! There's a woman who was just up here, and she ran out. Can you stop her from leaving the building?"

The baby wailed in earnest.

"What?"

"There's a woman in black —"

"In black, yeah. She just left."

"Stop her — catch her! Now."

"I can't hear you, Kieran. I hear a baby crying. A baby! Whose baby is it?"

"Ralph! Get out in the street and get that woman!"

"What?"

"Go catch that woman!"

"Oh! Gotcha! I'm gone."

She hung up, then quickly dialed 9-1-1.

Emergency services probably couldn't move quickly enough to help, since no matter how quickly they arrived, the woman was already on the run.

She was running on the busy streets of New York City where rush hour was a swarm of humanity in which to get com-

9

pletely lost. But Kieran still explained the situation, where she was. The operator was efficient; cops would quickly be out. Child Services would arrive.

But no matter. The woman would get away.

Kieran tried to hold and rock and soothe the baby while dialing Craig Frasier.

If you were living with an FBI agent, it made sense to call him under such circumstances, especially since he — like Ralph — would want to know why she was working so late when the Danny Boys were playing at Finnegan's. To Craig, it was still a normal night — and a Friday night! A nice, normal Friday night — something that would be very nice to enjoy, given their chosen professions.

"Hey, Kieran," Craig said. "Are you already at the pub?"

She apparently wasn't good at rocking and soothing and trying to talk on the phone all at the same time. The baby was still crying. Loudly.

"No, I —"

"Whose kid is that? I can't hear a word you're saying!"

"I'm still at work. Can you come over here, now, please?"

"Uh — yeah, sure."

Kieran hung up the phone. She didn't know what Ralph was doing; she didn't know where the police were. She glanced down at the baby as she hurried from the office, ready to hit the streets herself. How old was the tiny creature? It was so small!

Yet — nice lungs!

Was the woman in black the mother?

She had looked older. Perhaps fifty. Too old for an infant.

Ralph wasn't at the desk; Kieran heard sirens, but as yet no police had arrived.

Bursting out onto the New York City rush hour sidewalk, she looked right and left. There, far down the block, she thought she saw the woman.

"Hey!" Kieran shouted.

Despite the pulsing throng of humanity between them, the woman heard her. She turned.

There was something different about her now.

The way she moved. The way she looked, and the expression on her face.

She didn't try to run. She just stared at Kieran, and then seemed to stagger toward her.

Kieran clutched the screaming infant close to her breast and thrust her way through the people; luckily, she was a New Yorker,

11

and she knew how to push through a rush hour crowd when necessary.

The woman was still staggering forward. Kieran was closing the gap.

"Listen, I'll help you, I'll help the baby! It's all right . . ."

It wasn't in any way all right.

The woman lurched forward, as if she would fall into Kieran's arms, if Kieran had just been close enough.

She wasn't.

The woman fell face-first down onto the sidewalk.

That's when Kieran saw the knife protruding from the woman's back and the rivulets of blood suddenly forming all around her and joining together to create a crimson pool.

Babies tended to be adorable — and this baby was especially so. In fact, Kieran wasn't sure she'd ever seen an ugly baby, but she had been assured by friends that they did exist.

This little girl, though, had a headful of auburn ringlets and huge blue eyes. Kieran had heard that all babies had blue eyes, but she didn't know if that was true or not. Sadly, she just didn't know a lot about babies; she was one in a family of four children herself, yes, but she and her twin brother, Kevin, were only a couple of years behind their older brother and one year older than their younger brother.

Actually, this beautiful baby looked as if she could fit right in with their family. Each of the Finnegan siblings had a form of red hair and blue or green or blue-green eyes. Kieran's own were blue, and her hair was a deep red.

"They say it's the Irish," she said softly to the little one in her arms. "But I don't think that you're Irish!"

Talking to the baby made sense at the moment; FBI Special Agent Craig Frasier, the love of her life and often partner in crime — solving crime, not committing it! — had arrived shortly after the police. The medical examiner had come for the body of the murdered woman. While waiting for Child Services, Kieran was holding the baby, back up in the office.

Drs. Fuller and Miro worked with the police or other law enforcement. While not with the FBI, they were regular profilers and consultants for the NYC office. The Bureau's behavioral science teams were down in DC, and while they could be called in, the city police and FBI often used local help in trying to get a step ahead of a criminal, or in working with criminals and witnesses when psychological assessments were needed, or, sometimes, when a child or a distressed person just needed to be able to speak to someone to ask the right questions and put them at ease. Kieran did a number of those assessments before reporting to the doctors, and she worked with victims of domestic abuse and both parents and children when they wound up within the child welfare system — such as a teenager who had been assaulted by her own father, or a senior citizen who was recovering from gunshot wounds inflicted by his wife. Or Kieran's last patient today, Besa Goga. Besa was a sad case, abused for years when she'd first immigrated to the country, and now quick to strike out. Besa Goga was in court-ordered therapy because she'd bitten a man from her cable company. Kieran had only been seeing her a few weeks.

But the office didn't always work through the police department, FBI or other such agencies. They also handled other cases that fell their way through happenstance or other circumstances — as in the recovering alcoholic who was also a politician and doing very well with Dr. Fuller.

Kieran had called her bosses to let them know what had happened. Both had said they'd come in immediately.

She had assured them that they shouldn't; the police were dealing with the murder, and Child Services was coming for the baby.

Dr. Fuller — who had looks as dreamy as any TV physician — was at an event with his equally beautiful wife and their six-year-old. Dr. Miro was giving a keynote speech at a conference in Southern Jersey.

Kieran had convinced them both that she was fine, that it was just strange and scary.

The poor murdered woman hadn't been scary; she had touched Kieran's heart. She had needed help so badly. But she had called Kieran by name. And that made Kieran wonder.

She sat out in the waiting area of the offices — right where the woman had come up to her, right where the baby had been thrust into her arms. She thought that the baby was bound to cry again soon. That's what babies did. They were hungry or wet or had gas or . . . who knew? She just really didn't have much experience. And she had no clue as to the child's age. But with little else to do — and probably in a bit of shock herself, despite the fact that she'd now thrown herself into the crime-fighting ring for a few years and had seen some shocking things — she talked to the baby. She made

15

soothing noises, discussed her own uncertainty with a cheerful voice, and made a few faces here and there.

She could swear that the baby smiled.

Did babies smile this young?

She knew that those who knew — experienced parents, grandparents, and so on — claimed babies did not smile until a certain age.

This one, she was certain, smiled. She waved her little fists in the air and grinned toothlessly. She even cooed.

"Hey!" Craig had come back up to the offices after checking out the scene on the street.

He nodded to the policeman at the door. Since Kieran had no idea what was going on, and since a woman who had been looking for her had just been stabbed to death, having a policeman standing guard was very reassuring, and Kieran was grateful.

She looked up at Craig, hopeful. Though, of course, she doubted that he or the police or anyone — other than the killer — knew who had stabbed the woman, or why.

"You okay?" he asked her.

"I'm fine. I was handed the baby. I don't think anyone was after me for any reason at all, but . . . oh, Lord. Craig, you don't think it's my fault, do you? I mean, if I hadn't chased after her —"

"Kieran," he said, hunkering down by her. "No." His voice was firm and — as usual — filled with confidence and authority. Craig had been a special agent with the FBI for a good decade. He always seemed to exude a comfortable assurance and strength — things she had to admit she loved about him. Well, along with rock-hard abs, a solid six-three frame and the fact that the term *tall, dark and handsome* might have been conceived just for him. He had hazel eyes that were like marble, seemed to see far too much, and still . . . well, in her mind, they were just beautiful.

"It happened all so fast," Kieran murmured.

Craig adjusted the blanket around the baby. Kieran thought she cooed and smiled for him, too, but it was hard to tell.

Smile . . . maybe gas. Who knew?

"Kieran, that woman was trying to save this child. She brought her to you. You aren't to blame in any way. I have a feeling that she was very heroic — and that she gave her life for the child. She might have stolen the baby from some kind of terrible situation. I don't know — none of us can even begin to figure out what might have gone down yet. But I believe the minute she took the baby away from whoever had it before, her hours were numbered." He was quiet for a moment and looked up at her. "This isn't going to be an FBI case, you know. Whoever your visitor was, she was murdered on the streets of New York. It's an NYPD matter."

"Did you talk to Ralph downstairs?" she asked anxiously. "He should have been on the desk — and you're supposed to sign in to enter this building." So it was with most large office buildings in the city. It had been ever since 9/11.

"Yes, I spoke with him. The police spoke with him. He was a mess. He thinks it's all his fault. UPS was here with a large shipment for the computer tech firm on the eighteenth floor. He thinks she slipped by him when he ran over to help the courier with the elevator," Craig said.

"I can imagine he's upset. Did he ever get out of here? He was planning on seeing the Danny Boys play tonight, too."

"I don't think he went to see the band," Craig said. "The cops let him go about an hour or so ago now."

"Ah," Kieran murmured.

What an end to the week. Ralph Miller was a Monday to Friday, regular hours kind of guy. He looked forward to his Friday nights; he loved music, especially Irish rock bands. He must have been really upset to realize a murder had taken place somewhere just down the street from his front door.

The murder of a woman who had slipped by him.

A woman who had left a baby in Kieran's arms.

A baby. Alone, in her arms.

"Craig, I just . . . I wish I understood. And I'm not sure about the officer handling the case —"

"Kieran, no matter how long we all work in this, murder is hard to understand. That officer needed everything you could give him."

"I know that. I've spoken with him. He wants me to figure out why the woman singled me out. He's more worried about that than the baby!" Kieran said indignantly.

"He's a detective, Kieran. Asking you questions is what he's supposed to do — you know that. *Can* you think of anything?" Craig asked her.

Kieran shook her head. "She probably knew about this office. And it's easy enough to find out all our names."

"Maybe, and then . . ."

"And then what?"

Craig smiled at her. During the diamond

heists case — when they had first met — she had saved a girl from falling onto the subway tracks when a train was coming. When a reporter had caught up with Kieran, she had impatiently said, "Anyone would lend a helping hand."

For quite some time after, she'd been a city heroine.

So she had a feeling she knew what he was going to say.

"Maybe they saw you on TV."

"That was a long time ago."

"Some people have long memories."

There was a tap at the door; the officer who had been standing guard held it open for a stocky woman with a round face and gentle, angelic smile. She was in uniform, and Kieran quickly realized that she was from Child Services.

"Hi, I'm Sandy Cleveland," the woman told her. "Child —"

"Services, yes, of course!" Kieran said.

Kieran realized that she didn't want to hand over the baby. She didn't have a "thing" for babies — her primary goal in life had never been to get married and have children. She did want them — somewhere along the line. But not now. She knew that, eventually, yes, she wanted to marry Craig. She was truly, deeply, kind of even madly in love with him.

But no wedding in the near future. Maybe in a year. They hadn't even really discussed it yet.

She didn't go insane over babies at family picnics, and she was happy for her friends who were pregnant or parents, and she got along fine with kids — little ones and big ones.

But she wasn't in any way *obsessed*.

Here, now, in the office, holding the precious little bundle — who had so recently been tenderly held by a woman who was now *dead* with a knife in her back — Kieran was suddenly loath to give her up. And it wasn't that the woman from Child Services didn't appear to be just about perfect for her job. No one could fake a face that held that much empathy.

"It's okay," Sandy Cleveland said very softly. "I swear she'll be okay with me. We take great care of little ones at my office. I won't just dump her in a crib and let her cry. It's my job — I'm very good at it," she added, as if completely aware of every bit of mixed emotion that was racing through Kieran's heart and mind. She smiled and added, "Miss Finnegan, the street below is teeming with police officers — and reporters. The chief of police is already involved in this situation. This little one will not just have the watchdogs of Child Services looking over her, but a guardian from the police force, as well. She's going to be fine. I personally promise you."

"I'm sure — I'm sure you're good," Kieran said. She smiled at Sandy Cleveland.

"That means you have to give her the baby," Craig said, but she thought he understood, too, somehow.

"Yes, yes, of course," Kieran murmured.

She managed to make herself move, and she handed over the baby.

It was so damned hard to do!

"Miss Cleveland, can you tell me about how old she is?" Kieran asked.

"I think about six weeks based on her motor function. And, please, just call me Sandy," the woman told her. "Her eyes are following you — and when you speak, that's a real smile. It's usually between about six weeks and three months when they really smile, and I think this is a lovely, smart girl. Don't worry! I'll get a smile from her, too, I promise."

The baby did seem to be settling down in Sandy Cleveland's arms.

Craig set an arm around Kieran's shoulders.

"Sandy, I'm with the FBI. Craig Frasier.

22

You won't mind if we check in on this little one?"

"Of course not!" Sandy assured them. She shook her head sadly. "I hear that the woman who handed her to you was murdered. There's no ID on her. I'm just hoping we can find out who this little one is. She's in good shape, though. Someone has been caring for her. Yes! You're so sweet!" She said the last words to the baby, wrinkling her nose and making a face — and drawing a sound that wasn't quite laughter, but darned close to it. "Hopefully, she has a mom or other relatives somewhere. And if not . . ." She hesitated, studying Kieran and Craig. "Well, if not — a precious little infant like this? People will be jockeying to adopt her. Anyway, let me get her out of here and away from . . . from what happened." She held the baby adeptly while using her left hand to dig into her pocket and produce her business card. "Call me anytime," she told them. "I may not answer, but I will get back to you if you leave me a message."

Then she was gone. The cop who had been watching over Kieran went outside.

She and Craig were alone.

Kieran still felt shell-shocked.

"Kieran, hey!" Craig hunkered down by her again as she sank down into one of the

23

comfortably upholstered chairs in the waiting room. He looked at her worriedly. "The cops are good — you know that."

"Craig, you have to be in on this. That detective —"

"Lance. Lance Kendall. Kieran, really, he's all right. He's doing all the right things."

"Yeah! All the right things — grilling me!"

"Okay, I will speak with Egan about it tomorrow, how's that?"

She nodded. "Thank you. Get one of your joint task forces going — at least maybe you can participate?"

"Sure." He hesitated. "I guess . . . um, well."

There was a tap at the door. They both looked up. Craig stood.

A man walked in. It wasn't the first officer who had arrived at the scene — it was the detective who had arrived while others were setting up crime scene tape, handling the rush hour crowd around the body, and urging her to get the baby back up to her offices and out of the street.

Detective Kendall was a well-built African American man. About six feet even, short brown hair, light brown eyes, and features put together pleasantly. He was around forty-five, she thought. He wasn't warm and

24

cuddly, but neither was he rude.

"Detective," Craig said. "Have you wrapped up at the scene for the evening?"

"Yes — a few techs are still down there, but there's nothing more I can accomplish here. Unless you can help, Miss Frasier? You can't think of anything?"

"I have no idea why this lady chose me," Kieran said. "None."

"And you've never seen the woman before?" Kendall asked.

"Never."

"Nor the baby?"

What? Did he think that the infant paid social calls on people, hung out at the pub, or requested help from psychiatrists or a psychologist?

"No," she managed evenly. "I've never seen the infant before. I've never seen the woman before."

"All right, then." He suddenly softened a little. "You must be really shaken. I understand that, and I'm sorry. For now . . . I don't have anything else. But I'm sure you know we may need to question you again."

"I'm not leaving town," she said drily.

He wasn't amused.

Kieran continued. "I've spoken with Dr. Fuller and Dr. Miro. I've told them all that I could, and they will be trying to ascertain

25

if they can think of any reason — other than who they are and what they do — that the woman might have come here."

"I've spoken with the doctors, too," Detective Kendall told her grimly. "And I'm sure we'll speak again."

"I'm sure," Kieran muttered.

"Good night, Special Agent Frasier — Miss Finnegan," the detective said. "You're both, uh, free to go."

He left them. Craig pulled Kieran around and into his arms, looking down into her eyes. "We are free. There's nothing else to do tonight. You want to go home?"

"I know that we both really wanted to see the band play tonight," she told him. "I'm sorry."

"Kieran, it's not your fault. I'm sure you didn't plan for a woman to abandon a baby in your arms and then run downstairs and find herself stabbed to death."

"It's driving me crazy, Craig! We don't know who she was. We don't have a name for her. We don't know about the baby. I think she was too old to be the mom, but I'm not really sure. And if not . . . she was trying to save the baby, not hurt it. But who would hurt a baby?"

"I don't know. Let's get going, shall we?"

"We can still go to the pub. Maybe catch

the last of the Danny Boys?" she said.

"You know you don't want to go anywhere."

Kieran hesitated. "Not true. I do want to go somewhere. I'm starving — and I'm not sure what we've got to eat at the apartment."

"Yep. We've been staying at yours — if there is food at mine, I'm certain we don't want to eat it."

"Then we'll go to the pub," she said quietly.

Kieran hadn't realized just how late it had grown until she and Craig walked out of the building. New York City policemen were still busy on the street, many of them just managing the crowd. The body was gone, but crime scene workers were still putting the pieces together of what might and might not be a clue on the busy street.

It was Midtown, and giant conglomerates mixed with smaller boutiques and shops. Most of the shops were closed and the hour too late for business, but people still walked quickly along the sidewalks, slowing down to watch the police and curious to see what had happened.

Kieran looked up while Craig spoke with a young policewoman for a moment. Her brother had once warned her that she looked up too often — that she looked like a tourist. But she loved the rooftops, the skyline. Old skyscrapers with ornate moldings at the roof sat alongside new giants that towered above them in glass, chrome and steel. And then again, right in the midst of the twentieth- and twenty-first-century buildings, there would be a charming throwback to the 1800s.

From a nearby Chinese restaurant, a tempting aroma laced the air.

Even over murder.

The cops generally knew Craig; he was polite to all of them. They nodded an acknowledgment to Kieran. She'd worked with the police often enough herself.

"Is Detective McBride going to be on the case?" Kieran asked hopefully. They'd worked with Larry McBride before, not even a year ago, and he had been an amazing ally.

Drs. Fuller and Miro worked with city detectives regularly, and nine times out of ten, they were great. Every once in a while, as in any job, there was a total jerk in the mix. Mainly they were professionals, and good at their work, and Kieran knew it. Some were more personable than others. Homicide detectives could be very cut-and-dried. McBride had told her once that

Homicide, while horrible, was also easier than dealing with other crimes. The victims couldn't complain about the way he was working. Of course, the victims had relatives. That was hard.

She had come to really like McBride.

In this case, a baby was involved. A woman had died trying to save that baby, Kieran was certain. So she felt they needed the best.

Craig looked at her quizzically. "You know that there are thousands of detectives in the city, a decent percentage of that in Homicide — and even a decent percentage in Major Case."

"Actually, when you break it all down . . ."

"I don't know who will be working the case — probably more than one detective. For right now, it is Lance Kendall. And he's all right, Kieran. He's good. He was doing all the right things," he added quietly. He looked as if he was going to say something more. He didn't.

He took her hand in his. She held on, letting the warmth of his touch comfort her as they walked down the street.

"Hey, remember, I'm an agent, and you work with psychiatrists who spend most of their time on criminal files. It's the life we've chosen, and we've talked about it. This will be just another case — whatever level of involvement we have with it. You can't let it take over, or neither one of us will be sane."

She nodded. He was right. There were other cases where they found themselves on the fringe, and, frankly, every day of Craig's life had to do with criminal activity in the city of New York. They'd already worked on cases of cruel and brutal murders. This was another. And there was always something that seemed to make it better — at least for the survivors — when a killer was brought to justice.

She couldn't obsess. She knew it.

But this one felt personal!

"Yep." She spoke blithely and smiled.

"You're cool?" She could tell he didn't believe her; it seemed he didn't know whether to push it or not.

But he was right about one thing. There was nothing for them to do right now except try to get their minds around what had happened — and let it go enough to get on with life.

Even figure out how to step back in order to step forward again.

"Yep. I'm fine. Let's get food," Kieran said.

"Sounds good. Thankfully, we always know where to go!"

Chapter Two

Finnegan's on Broadway had been a tavern, inn or den of Irish hospitality since before the Civil War. It was just after the war that the Finnegan family had taken over. Some of the family members were Americans; some were cousins who arrived from Ireland at various times in the pub's history. Whoever wound up in charge knew that they were always purveyors of camaraderie. It was a true center of community, where you brought friends, and if you had none, you found some. To many in the neighborhood it had become a personal place, and they felt as comfortable and welcome there as in their own living room. The taps were extensive and kept spotlessly clean; the kitchen created a flow of Irish, American, and Irish American food that could be rivaled by few pubs — even in a city like New York.

While all of the four Finnegan siblings — Declan, Kieran, Kevin and Daniel — had inherited the pub, it was run by Declan. Kieran had her work, and Kevin was an actor. Danny — after a few false starts due to the death of their mother — had become an exceptional tour guide. Then again, though they all loved their dad, each sibling had acted out in a way when they had lost their mom. Not one member of the family had the least problem waiting tables or tending bar when help was needed, and Kieran still did a lot of the bookkeeping while her brothers kept up with stock and repairs.

Craig and Kieran were greeted by serving staff as soon as they walked in. At the bar — which had a clear view of the front door — Declan saw them enter, and he nodded and raised a hand and looked curiously at Craig.

Kieran had called Declan a few hours ago, to fill him in, but they hadn't really believed at the time they would miss the entire evening. But they had, of course. The band was no longer playing.

It was quiet; the last of the crowd seemed to be paying their tabs, ready to head out.

"Kieran, dear, are you all right?"

Mary Kathleen — Declan's fiancée, who was from Dublin but had been in the States for a few years — rushed up to Kieran.

"Yes, I'm fine, thank you," Kieran said.

32

"I'm going to say hi to Declan," Craig murmured, sliding past the two women. He reached the bar and leaned against it. Declan wiped his hands on a bar rag, shaking his head as he looked at Craig.

"You're a wee bit late. You missed the Danny Boys," Declan said. "They were great."

"Yeah, we missed them. Thanks."

"Ouch. Sorry," Declan said. "That was really rude of me." His jaw was set at an awkward angle. "Kieran is all right? I'm glad she called — knowing we'd freak out if we saw something that close to her place of business and we didn't hear from her. It's been on the news, you know. This time, the media hasn't been using her name — they don't have it, apparently."

"Yes. The police kept pretty good control of the crime scene in the street and got Kieran out of the limelight before the reporters honed in. They know a woman was murdered. They know she gave a child to someone else, and Child Services will be caring for the baby, who will also be under police protection," Craig said. "I guess they want a warning out there that no one should come for the child — unless, of course, they're the rightful parents or guardians. Hopefully, they'd be searching for their baby through the police."

"And here I thought you had the night off. Like it was one of those kinds of normal days for you when you were only going to work ten or twelve hours."

"This one had nothing to do with me."

"Hmm. If they don't have some sick scum of the earth for you to be finding, Kieran will come up with something." He was silent for a minute. "Actually, come to think about it, with what you've got on your hands already, you probably shouldn't have gotten involved with a crazy Irish lass like my sister."

"Yeah. Probably not," Craig agreed.

"A bit too late."

"Yeah, I think so."

"So someone shoved a baby into her arms, and then ran out and got stabbed. That the gist of it?"

"That's the gist of it."

"And it's your case?"

"Not at the moment."

"I know you," Declan said, "and so I also know that I don't really need to be saying this, but . . . watch out for my sister, huh? Even if she's quiet and acts tough, you know she's got to be really shaken tonight."

"I do. And," he added softly, "you know I love your sister."

"I do," Declan said with a slight smile. "I'll go back and see the cook."

"Sounds great."

"Shepherd's pie?"

"Always good."

Declan started to head to the back. "Oh, sorry — you guys want something to drink?"

"I'll get it," Craig said, leaning over the bar for a couple of glasses. As he did so, Kieran came to his side.

"Shepherd's pie. And —"

"Soda water, please," Kieran said softly.

"You okay?"

"I'm fine. Honestly," she assured him.

They sat at the bar. Declan came back with dinner for the two of them; Finnegan's was famous for its shepherd's pie. It was a standard, almost always available.

Declan and Mary Kathleen both came behind the bar as the place began to wind down in earnest. Only a few patrons, just finishing up and paying their checks, remained.

"Anything new?" Mary Kathleen asked Craig.

He arched a brow. "Not since I walked in here."

"Sorry," she murmured. She looked at Kieran. "What was this woman like? Did she say anything at all that would give you a clue about who she was, where she came from — or about why she would leave a baby?"

Kieran frowned. "No. She didn't speak that much. She said my name, and not much more."

"She knew your name?"

"Well, surely no one would choose a random person in any old office and just toss them a baby!" Kieran said.

"But, she didn't ask for Dr. Fuller or Miro, right? She asked for you?" Declan asked, frowning. He glanced at Craig.

Inwardly, Craig groaned.

Now everyone was worried about Kieran.

Naturally, he was worried, too.

"Did you let the doctors know what happened?" Declan asked.

"Of course," Kieran said. "I called them . . . they had to know. The woman came to their office."

"The whole city knows by now, I'm sure," Craig said. "The street was crawling with reporters by the time we headed here. Hopefully, that will be a good thing. Someone out there might know who the woman was — and where to find the baby's mother."

"I hope so," Mary Kathleen whispered.

"Okay, let's clean up and call it a night,"

Kieran said. She stood and started picking plates up from recently vacated tables.

Declan looked at Craig with a shrug.

Craig knew all the Finnegan siblings well — he was pretty sure that he knew what they all might be thinking: *better get involved; make it your case. This is haunting Kieran, and therefore, she will definitely be haunting you!*

Twenty minutes later, they were at Kieran's apartment, which he had mostly been calling home as well for at least the last year. They still used his place now and then. Somehow — though he couldn't remember the last time they'd slept apart — they were still maintaining two apartments. They really needed to get rid of one of them. His apartment was larger — they both actually liked it better. But Kieran's was in the Village, and often more convenient when they'd been out for a night, and they had gotten into the habit of staying there.

More of his things were even at her place, rather than his own.

Not even the sushi bar/karaoke place on the ground floor of Kieran's apartment building was still going, and the streets surrounding St. Mark's Place were quiet, as well.

Kieran seemed really tired as they trudged

up the stairs past the silent bar and to her apartment level. Of course, she was tired. She'd worked some grim cases with him — little could have been much worse than some of what they'd already seen, endured and survived — but it had to have been traumatic for her, having a baby thrust into her arms.

And seeing the woman who had entrusted that baby to her staggering down the street with a knife in her back . . .

He intended to give Kieran whatever space she needed; respecting that might be a need to curl up in bed with her own thoughts, praying for sleep.

He was startled when she turned to him with a grin. "Race you to the shower!" she said, and she was gone.

Racing to the shower.

He'd thought she'd be so exhausted.

Apparently not.

He followed her.

There were, of course, all kinds of ways to deal with strange happenings.

She was already naked, beneath the spray of water. He hesitated at the door, then left his Glock in the bedroom and shed his clothing.

He stepped into the tub. She was instantly in his arms.

Sometimes, people just needed to be held.

And sometimes, they needed more.

Her lips moved over his throat and chest, while her fingers danced down his torso. Her touch . . . the water . . .

He was instantly aroused.

They kissed and teased in the water. They lathered one another, intimately.

Then she laughed and moved away, escaping from the shower.

They'd long ago realized that for a man Craig's size, making love in the shower wasn't particularly erotic. It could be awkward, and slippery in the wrong way.

But heading out of the shower could be completely wonderful, catching up with another with clean flesh, sliding into a damp embrace with token pats from towels, and then falling down into the bed, the coolness of the sheets against the heat of their flesh.

Foreplay quickly became something urgent, something needed, something more and more passionate with each brush of their lips, with the intimacy with which they caressed and kissed one another, with which their eyes met, and they came together at last.

Craig loved Kieran; she loved him. There was no question about that.

It still amazed him how intense their connection could be.

Just as it amazed him that they could live together, sleep together, wake together each morning, and still find it so new and exquisite every time they made love.

He thought that she would want to talk as they both came down after a sweet and wicked climax; she did not.

She curled against him, sighed and seemed to fall asleep almost instantly.

He dozed himself, but woke when she moved. He guessed she hadn't been sleeping at all.

She crawled as silently as she could out of bed, wrapped herself in a terry robe and headed out to the living room.

He followed, and found her looking out the window on what remained of the night.

She didn't hear him at first.

He sighed softly. "Kieran?"

She started and turned to him. "Craig, I'm sorry. I didn't mean to wake you. It's Saturday — and you actually have time off. You can sleep as long as you like."

"I *was* planning on sleeping past four in the morning," he assured her. "Come back to bed."

"I can't forget that woman, Craig. I just can't forget her."

"I know. Come back to bed."

"Kidnapping. That'd be an FBI matter," Kieran told Craig.

"We don't know that it was a kidnapping. Maybe the woman was the baby's mother — or grandmother. Maybe she just wanted the child to be safe. Kieran —"

"Kidnapping," Kieran said. "Craig, you know that poor little girl was taken from somewhere."

"At the moment, the case belongs to the cops. The Bureau might be brought in, but right now, it's not my call. We work hard to keep our relationships between agencies all nice and copacetic. I'm not running down there and demanding that we take the case. I'd be put in my place in two damned seconds," he told her.

"But it must be kidnapping. You can talk to Egan, at least, okay?"

"I will speak with Egan — when it's possible to speak with my director, I promise I will."

"Really?"

"I just told you that I would."

"What if he fights you on it? What if he's dismissive?"

"I'll fight back."

"Really?"

"I'll push and be obnoxious and call in all kinds of favors, okay?"

"Yeah. Okay. I like it."

He led her back into the bedroom and she slipped into his arms. Resting against his chest, she fell asleep.

He thought about his promise.

He hadn't seen the woman, had no connection to the case, and in his life, he'd seen too many murders.

But he would keep his promise, and he was damned determined that they'd get to the bottom of what was going on.

The woman had known Kieran's name, and she had brought the baby straight to her, and that could mean . . . someone out there would be wondering just what Kieran knew about the woman, the baby — and the killer.

And that meant that Kieran might well be in danger now herself.

It was her fault, and she knew it. Craig was up early.

She'd finally fallen asleep. But knowing she'd kept him up meant that guilt riddled her. When he got up to leave and head into the office, she got up to start the coffee.

She pulled out her laptop. She had a desktop computer at work but had it networked with her laptop — it was a good setup. It had often enough saved her from having to go back into the office over a small detail — a note that one of the doctors might need, or even something that she wanted to reread herself to help her with a case they were working on.

She often interviewed and provided therapy for abused women — and occasionally men. It was certainly not in the same number, but there were men who suffered from abuse. One of her recent cases, Harold Lenin, was certainly that man — he'd been given black eyes by his wife, broken bones and tons of bruises. He'd kept silent through the years, a sad, cowed, little man. He was learning how to live again, recovering from his gunshot wounds.

He wouldn't receive any more of them. His wife had shot him while they were up on the roof. She hadn't been familiar with the gun and the kickback had sent her over the roof — and down thirty-five floors.

A lot of the people on the street that day had needed therapy, too.

Oddly and sadly, there were many such cases. They were also working on one case in particular now in which a man had snapped — and killed his wife. An all too common occurrence. As it turned out in depositions from neighbors and his own children, his wife had physically and mentally abused him for years, striking him constantly in the head. Apparently, for a few decades, he — like poor Harold — had just taken it.

His lawyers were still trying to plea bargain his case. Was it self-defense? He had finally slugged her back. He was a big guy; she'd fallen hard across the room, struck the edge of a credenza and dropped dead.

The reports issued by Kieran's office would be incredibly important in what kind of punitive measures the man would face. He had killed his wife, and the prosecution was arguing it hadn't been self-defense, not by the legal definitions that usually set someone free in a courtroom. And women and children were far more often victims of this kind of violence.

Her cases were often very sad, and frustrating. Kieran could usually work really hard and with tremendous empathy and still go home at night. But this thing with the baby . . .

None of the cases in their office at the moment seemed to have anything to do with an infant.

Ah. What about Melanie and Milton Deering?

At the offices of Fuller and Miro, they were also working with a scary pair — a murderer and his bride. The question was just how much the bride knew about the murder — and if she had participated.

Yes, looking at it all, Kieran felt a bit overwhelmed by the number of bad cases on the books right then.

But nothing that might have to do with a baby.

Her newest case was Besa Goga. Her crime had been *biting.* She'd bitten the cable man. At the rate cable men actually showed up in the city of New York, it might be unusual that more people didn't strike out in one way or another.

How had the woman known about their office?

"Who were you?" Kieran wondered aloud. "Why me?"

And then she wondered how the baby was doing.

Fine! The baby was going to be fine!

She looked at her computer again and then emailed Drs. Fuller and Miro, asking them if they could think of anything at all that might help figure this out.

Of course, maybe it wasn't that much of a dilemma. People knew about Fuller and Miro — they were rock stars in their chosen field. Not that being celebrated by your peers meant anything to the general public, but the doctors were known for their talents and the way they helped law enforcement. Word of mouth. In the same way, people knew about Kieran. She had managed to get her name in the paper a few times — she felt lucky the police had helped her avoid the media last night.

The thing was, they weren't out there in the same way as true stars or personalities — actors, musicians, artists, performers — but neither were they any kind of secret.

So what did that mean? Had that woman just known that getting the baby to someone in that office would guarantee police — and help?

Why not just head to a police station?

Kieran yawned.

It was Saturday. She could go back to sleep.

She headed to her room and crawled into her bed.

Two minutes later, she was up again.

She showered and dressed. She was tempted to call Craig, but she absolutely refused to allow herself to do so. No sense driving him crazy at this point, too.

She had the thought that it was too bad that — at this moment — the apartment was almost spotlessly clean. She might start cleaning spotlessly again. No, she would find something else to do.

But it was Saturday. For many places in the downtown area, it was a slow day.

But, Finnegan's was a popular pub, the kind of place people were willing to take the subway or cab to reach, even on a weekend.

Perfect.

She would go to work!

She headed into the bedroom for her jacket and purse and then paused. She'd left the television on.

And she was staring at a reporter who was talking about the murder. And the baby. And she suddenly found herself sitting at the foot of the bed.

Watching.

Even though there was nothing the reporter could say that she didn't already know.

Craig headed into his own office, determined that he'd call his director, Richard Egan, the minute it hit nine o'clock — even though he doubted that Egan ever slept that late, Saturday or no. But nine seemed a respectable hour.

He didn't have to wait, however. Marty Kim — Craig's favorite "kid" in the technical assistance division, stopped by his office, looking in. "Hey!"

"Hey, yourself. Working Saturday?"

"I am. Running some facial recognition programs and the like. I'm not surprised to see you."

"You're not?"

"Nope. Egan just said you'd be in."

"He did, did he?"

Marty grinned. He was tall and thin with a great boyish face. Marty had no desire to be a field agent, but he loved analysis and could coax amazing information from any database.

"He's waiting for you."

"Thanks."

The supervising field director was in his desk chair, swiveled around to study the flat-screen television set up on the wall of his office.

It was tuned to the news. And they were rehashing the story over and over again, as they tended to do. A reporter was standing on the street in front of Kieran's office building in Midtown, telling her audience that as of yet, the police had no identification on either the woman or the infant.

Egan looked at Craig. "It's not a major election year. This poor woman's murder and the abandoned baby have become a media obsession."

"Yes, sir. That's what I've come to talk to you about."

Egan nodded, then shook his head.

"Kieran is involved. Then again, Craig, she's not. The baby was handed to her, but that's where it ends. Child Services has the baby. She's out of it now."

"But she's not. The press doesn't have this, and I hope that they don't wind up with it, but when the murdered woman gave Kieran the baby, she asked for Kieran by name. This woman went up to the offices of Fuller and Miro at a time when she knew they were closing down. And she knew Kieran by name, and possibly knew she was usually the last one out."

Egan turned his attention back to the television. The anchor was showing pictures of the baby, and a sketch that had been done of the dead woman by the NYPD composite artists, showing her as she might have looked in life. Craig figured it was a good idea — getting the picture out there might be their best way and only hope for an identification.

"What do you think? Late forties?" Egan asked. "I don't think she was old — I think she looked older than her years. Poor woman. I'd be willing to bet she lived a hard life before she was murdered. And she was

49

trying to do the right thing by that baby."

"I believe she was. Sir, there's still the baby. The logical assumption is — even if for a good reason, such as saving the child's life — that the child was abducted. And since —"

"Give it up, Craig. Yes, abduction. We can muscle our way in."

"Sir, you know that I don't like to let anything in my personal life —"

"Craig, Kieran Finnegan is your personal life. The woman attracts trouble of the most unusual variety. We work with her employers on a regular basis, though this is hardly the same as most instances. I've already made the calls to set up a joint task force. I've called Mike Dalton. He's glad he had some vacation time lately — he'll be in within the next hour. And what the hell did you think I was doing here today?" Egan shook his head. "It's Saturday. Feel free to say 'thank you' anytime." Egan pushed a folder across his desk toward Craig. "There's what I've got. Joint investigation. Autopsy today — be there by two this afternoon. Obviously, the usual is happening — fingerprints, dental work, and so on. If anything has been discovered about the woman, I don't know it as of yet. We will know more once there's an autopsy, but even that . . ." Egan ended with a shrug. "Ethnicity, maybe. You'd think that in a city of millions of people there would be someone out there who did know something."

"There must be — but they aren't coming forward."

"They don't want knives in their backs," Egan said flatly. "Anyway . . . there's your case. The FBI and the NYPD are pulling information from every source we have — someone has to be missing a baby. And the woman . . . well, we might be looking at someone in the country illegally. That would explain the lack of any ID, driver's license, bank card, anything. Anyway, you're on it."

"Thank you," Craig said, picking up the folder.

"So, in truth, I'm a liar. You don't have to thank me. Word came down today from on high that they want us on this one. US Marshals will be in with us. Fellow from that department will be Hank LeBlanc. He'll meet you at autopsy with a guy from Major Case. They've given it over to a higher division, so that means they're worried about it. I think it's your friend — he got that promotion after the diamond business two years back."

"McBride? That's great," Craig said. "And, hey — thank you, anyway."

51

Egan waved a hand in the air. "You'd be working it no matter what." He looked down at more papers on his desk, as if he'd already moved on. Craig headed to the door.

"Frasier," Egan said.

"Yeah."

"Watch out for Kieran. I don't like it that the dead woman was going for her — not just for someone in the offices of Fuller and Miro. For her specifically."

"Yes, sir. I do watch out for her."

"Three brothers — that should help," Egan said.

"It should," Craig agreed.

In a way, it did. Any of the Finnegan brothers would happily block a bullet for their sister. Then again, it had been Danny trying to help a friend that had gotten Kieran messed up with the diamond heists — when Craig had met her — and her brother Kevin had been dating the most famous victim of the recent "perfect" killings that had plagued the city. Her brothers were wonderful, but they'd grown up rough-and-tumble after their mother had died, and Craig knew that Kieran often worried about what they might do — even in the name of justice and righteousness.

But it was true that they would jump in front of a speeding bullet, train — or anything else — to save her from harm.

"You were there last night. I heard you stuck with Kieran while the cops dealt with the situation. So you already know most of what's in the folder. But there you are. Mike should be in soon — you can read up on what they did get and then . . ."

"Yeah?"

"Nothing like an autopsy on a Saturday afternoon, right? McBride made the call on that one, getting the autopsy a priority on Saturday. Since there's an unidentified baby involved." He was quiet for a minute. "Thank God the baby wasn't killed, too."

"The baby could be our best lead."

Egan shook his head. "We don't know anything about her yet. Thing is . . . you just never know. Historically, children have indeed died for the sins of the parents. When the Russian revolutionaries held the royal family, they determined that they had to do them all in — including the children. Because children grow up. But the baby is safe. Cared for, and guarded, as well. You're talking a beautiful little child — already an American princess in the media. Like I said, McBride is calling the shots on this one. Anyway, there you go. Just what you wanted."

Craig forced a smile. Ah, yeah, sure. *Just*

what he wanted.

Not really at all.

He dreaded what was to come. He knew Kieran. There was just no way he was going to keep her out of it.

Which meant it was really only self-preservation to dive into the whole thing just as deeply as he could.

CHAPTER THREE

So much for waking up early and being so antsy she'd rushed through a shower.

It was frustrating as hell, but Kieran kept watching the news. She couldn't stop herself. It was like the pre-election coverage of the last election. A train wreck. And she'd still felt compelled to watch.

Although, this was different. She had known the woman.

Well, she hadn't *known* her, but she had spoken with her right before she had been murdered.

The more she watched — even though she didn't see anything new reported — the more she began to wonder and try to figure out just what the hell was going on and how the police would try to put it together — try to find a murderer.

So far, they hadn't talked about the knife on the air or in the paper — online or in physical print.

Where had the knife come from? The killer had to have had the knife on them. And if so, wouldn't that mean there would be prints on the knife? Of course, those prints would need to be in the system. And what if the killer had been wearing gloves?

She itched to call Craig again — but she wouldn't.

He would call her.

Would Richard Egan get the FBI on the investigation?

Kieran was well aware sometimes the different agencies working on a situation could be territorial — and not just cops and FBI. New York was filled with different organizations of law enforcement, including the cops and the FBI but extending to the US Marshals Service and Homeland Security. Depending on who found what when, there could be some disputes.

She didn't know anything about the detective who was in charge of the investigation so far on the NYPD side of it all. Drs. Fuller and Miro had a tendency to work amazingly well with all branches — and she knew that Craig and his partner, Mike Dalton, were both the type who worked hard to see that any rivalry was kept to a minimum — that the crime was of upmost importance, no matter who solved it.

She couldn't help worrying about the case. She was on pins and needles, waiting to find out what was going on. And worse, she wanted to see the baby again. Though the child was being cared for by professionals, and Kieran assured herself everything was fine, she couldn't tamp down the urge to see the baby herself — just to make sure.

There was no way she could simply sit in her apartment and wait for Craig.

It was ridiculous that she had started watching the news at the get-go.

She'd known what she really needed to be doing. She forced herself up, forced herself to turn off the television.

Outside, she headed to the subway — finally determined on getting to the venue that was always her cure-all for being as antsy as the proverbial cat on the hot tin roof — without further delay.

The front door to Finnegan's was locked when she arrived. She let herself in with her key.

The pub was getting ready to open for the day. Most of the time, Declan spent a good twelve to fifteen hours a day at the pub; it was easy for him since Mary Kathleen — the love of his life — worked there, as well.

Mary Kathleen had only been in the country about three and a half years. She'd come over to take care of an ailing grandmother, and a family friend had set her up at Finnegan's. She and Declan were a perfect — and beautiful — couple, in Kieran's mind, at least. Declan was tall with very dark auburn hair and the blue-gray-green eyes that characterized their family. Mary Kathleen had eyes that were huge and wide and the color of the sea. Her voice was musical and her accent truly charming — though she had found it funny one day when a patron had told her she didn't need to pretend to be Irish to work in the pub — it was, after all, America.

The alarm had already been turned off when Kieran stepped in. The place was spotless; she was sure that their late-night cleaning crew had been in, one hired just for the weekends when the traffic at the pub was extremely heavy. They had an impressive row of taps; Kieran was proud the place never smelled like stale beer. They maintained it beautifully.

She walked up to the bar, thinking she could put away glasses or do something else useful, but as she was standing there, Declan stepped out from the hallway that led to the offices and the stock room down in the basement. He was wearing a white apron and evidently had been working behind the bar, setting up, and perhaps he'd been in back in the kitchen as well, checking with the chef on the daily specials. On Sundays, Finnegan's always served a traditional roast with a choice of regular mashed potatoes or colcannon — potatoes and cabbage — and a special fresh vegetable. But on Saturdays, Declan and Chef liked to be adventurous — as in "Irish spicy tacos — trust us, the sauce is pure green!" Kieran wondered what delight he'd have prepared for today.

"I figured I'd see you," Declan said.

"I couldn't sit around," she said.

"And you sent Craig off to see his boss, to try to get involved, didn't you? And I know Craig. If he values his peace of mind, he'll see to it that he's involved."

She made a face at her brother. She was glad, though, that Declan — and Kevin and Danny — knew Craig well and really liked him. They'd met Richard Egan, Craig's boss, and Mike Dalton, his partner, too. All them had come into Finnegan's at various times, whether having to do with a case, or simply to have some good Irish pub food.

The pub itself — and her brothers, upon occasion! — had been too involved in deadly activities taking place in the city. She'd actually met Craig in the middle of a diamond heist — a situation Danny had ridiculously gotten her into while attempting to help a friend — and Kevin had recently been a suspect in a murder when an actress he'd been dating had been found dead in the church-turned-nightclub that backed up to the alley just behind the pub. The good thing was that they were all friends with Egan and the FBI. By tradition, of course, they always hosted police officers from the local precinct and firefighters from the fire hall down the street. After all, being a cop had once been a major Irish occupation — and the city had certainly been filled with the Irish!

"It's Saturday — I thought I'd help out around here."

"And you are always a help," he told her. "But as you can see, the cleaning crew was already in. We don't open the doors until eleven thirty. Chef is busy . . . we have a full staff on. In fact, I think we probably have one server too many today. Sounds ridiculous, but if I don't give them all enough tables, they can't make it in their tips."

"Ah, and no worries!" came a cheerful cry. Mary Kathleen came through the tables in the dining room, having just left the kitchen, or so it appeared. She was wearing a light spring jacket and carried a large disposable takeout tray. "Kieran, hello there, me love!" Mary Kathleen paused to kiss Kieran on the cheek. "I'm off to the mission by St. Peter's."

"That's so nice!" Kieran told her. She'd known that — a few times a month, at least — Mary Kathleen volunteered at a mission soup kitchen just down the block off Church Street by old St. Peter's.

The mission concentrated on immigrants who needed support — on seeing that they were fed, first and foremost, and then offering information on citizenship, green cards, work and whatever else might be necessary for someone newly arrived to the country, searching for the American dream.

"Chef has given me a great big dish of shepherd's pie!" Mary Kathleen said, nodding affectionately toward Declan. "Thanks to the generous soul of your brother Declan. Well, actually, thanks to the largesse of all the Finnegan family."

"Oh, no, that's all Declan. He makes the decisions," Kieran said. "But I'm awfully glad. I know that we were all — and different family members have been through the decades — immigrants. I'm delighted we're helping people."

She looked around the spotless, still-empty pub.

"Want some help at the mission or whatever it is?"

"Soup du Jour!" Mary Kathleen told her. "It's great — the Catholics and Anglos and Jewish community and members of several of our NYC mosques came together to fund it. All are truly welcome — and we do mean all. It would be great if you came with me! Super. People will love you. Oh, and don't go thinking they're all dirty, that the people who come in are sleeping in doorways and the like. Many work hard — it's just a difficult thing to come into this country sometimes and instantly make a living, especially in an expensive city like New York."

"Naturally," Kieran said. "And yet we — as Americans, who really have it pretty good — like to whine!"

Mary Kathleen laughed. "There's absolutely nothing wrong with my beautiful adopted homeland. But here's the thing — people come here because we can whine. Complaining is the God-given right of every American! You just have to remember that throughout history, people have come here for a dream. And right here in good old NYC, there used to be notes on the doors of all kinds of businesses that said No Irish! We have to watch out for prejudice against any new group. People still come for the same American dream."

"And even when we think we're a mess, we're still the best kind of mess?" Kieran said. She smiled. Mary Kathleen was going to be a wonderful sister-in-law.

" 'Indeed it has been said that democracy is the worst form of government, except for all those other forms that have been tried from time to time,' " Kieran quoted. "Churchill, 1947, to the House of Commons — if I remember right!"

"Yes, except I've been told that he was quoting a predecessor," Mary Kathleen said. "Anyway, the point is, people do come here for a dream. And sometimes, it's damned hard to realize. In fact, it can be a nightmare for some. They fall on hard times."

"Please, I hope you know me better than thinking I would be dismissive or mean in any way. I wasn't thinking of judging anyone, really," Kieran assured her. "I was just thinking . . ."

Declan suddenly strode directly between the two of them.

"Kieran was thinking she needed to be occupied — or she'd drive us all crazy," Declan said. "Thank the Good Lord, Mary Kathleen. It's a true kindness you can give her something to do! Go on, Kieran — dish out some soup. It is a very good thing to do. And when you're done, if you're still walking around like a caged cat, Kevin has to learn some lines for a guest shot on a cop show. You can give your twin a hand!"

"Cool. Of course, I'll run lines with my twin," Kieran said.

"Ah, yes, poor lass!" Mary Kathleen said. "You do need to be occupied. You canna quit thinking about that poor murdered woman and the wee babe? I don't blame you. So sad. And they still can't find out who the woman was — and they have no idea as to where to find the babe's mother?"

"No, not yet. Not that I've heard about," Kieran said.

"They will," Declan assured her.

"Of course," Kieran said. She took the large dish from Mary Kathleen. "We're out of here!" she told Declan.

"Go forth and be bountiful," Declan said drily.

She made a face at him again.

But he was right, of course. She was very, very glad to have something to do.

The folder that Richard Egan had given Craig didn't yield much more than he already knew; the murdered woman had been found with no identification — no

64

purse, nothing. She'd been wearing clothing with labels from the largest chain retail outlet offering budget-priced brands. There were literally dozens of the shops in the five boroughs alone. Her shoes had been the most common brand of sneaker. The hood she'd had wrapped over her head was a scarf that had most probably been bickered over and bought on the street.

She had been about five foot five inches in height, estimated age about forty.

The baby had been healthy and well kept — also wearing clothing bought at the same bargain-priced chain. The blanket covering the baby, however, had been hand knit. The creator had not signed the work in any way. Still, it was one of a kind.

The knife found in the woman's back was equally common — sold at outlets across the five boroughs, the state and the country. It was a hunting knife with a leather handle and six-inch blade.

The woman had been struck so hard that nearly four of those inches had gone into her back.

There were no fingerprints found on the knife.

The bystanders had been canvassed for information. No one remembered anyone suspicious in the crowd; no one had seen who had thrust the blade into the woman's back.

It was impossible — absolutely impossible, Craig thought. He tried to reimagine the crime, the woman hurrying away . . .

Someone must have seen something. They were afraid. Or it had been so swift an act that they hadn't even understood what they had seen. Maybe, when people thought about it . . .

He set the folder down, frustrated. There was a tap at his open door. He looked up. His partner, Mike Dalton, stood in the doorway.

"So I come back from a glorious vacation to you and Kieran stirring up the neighborhood again," he said drily. "You missed me, huh?"

"I did miss you, Mike. I always miss you when we're apart," Craig said, grinning. "I'm sure you heard about the news-making events."

"I did. Murder and mummies. Creepy!"

Craig pressed his lips into a tight line and nodded. "I worked the case with an old friend, guy named Micah Fox, and one of my cousins — mostly their case. A man they both admired had been killed in Egypt — a mentor. Weird case for sure, but . . . hey, yeah. I'm glad you're back!" Mike was a great partner. Ten years Craig's senior, he'd been the one to really show Craig the ropes. They both had the same sense of moral duty, of right and wrong, and a way of thinking together that had gotten them through many a situation.

"I read all about your mummies," Mike told him. He shuddered. "And saw it all over the news. Mummies! Glad you did that one without me. Actually . . . well, hell, this one sounds pretty bad. A woman stabbed, during rush hour, in the street, and no one saw it, no one can say anything?"

Craig pushed the folder toward him. "This is what they have. Autopsy coming up in a few hours. I was trying to catch up on all the reading first."

"Good, we'll share the reports."

"Thanks for getting here on Saturday — and so damned early."

"Hey, nothing like a good autopsy to get you right back into it all, right?"

Mary Kathleen had been right about the people who arrived at Soup du Jour.

Most were clean and decently clad, and between them, they seemed to speak every language known to man, and yet they all seemed to get on with one another, as well.

The space where the multi-faith organization operated had once been a giant textile factory. The machinery was long gone. Big old windows covered half the wall space — a great early effort in solar power, using daylight to see and work — and they still let in a glow of beautiful, natural light, though, of course, it was now enhanced by electrical power within. The rest of the walls were covered with posters, fliers and more — all to help men and women find apartments, jobs, day care and various other kinds of assistance.

The facility had a massive kitchen and a delivery area that was nearly as large. It had a massive dining hall with wood-plank tables, and on each side of the main room were large hallways that offered restrooms and showers — along with soap and razors and other basic toiletries, donated by various large corporations.

It was really a big enterprise — and it was astonishing the way that it was run.

People of every religion, ethnicity, color, creed, sex — whatever! — seemed to get along and pull together, and do it well.

Those working the food bank seemed to come from all walks of life: there were businessmen and -women, nuns, fathers, rabbis and imams, young and old, every color of humanity.

Kieran had come to give herself something to do. She discovered, instead, that she was in awe of Mary Kathleen and all that the volunteers tried to do at Soup du Jour.

"This is truly just incredible," she told Mary Kathleen. "You've been doing this and I didn't even know. It's wonderful."

"Oh, I do a day a week. That's the great power of the place — they literally have hundreds of people who can come a day or two a week and we'll do our best to cover for each other and that kind of thing," Mary Kathleen said. "I was lucky. I had friends to help me when I arrived here in the city. My family in Ireland knew your family here. I'm actually doing well. But I am an immigrant, and I was able to see how hard life could be for others who didn't have family and friends in the US — especially those fleeing poverty or war-torn countries. Anyway, I'm glad you like it!"

"Like it? I'm amazed. We get so much bad news — this is great!"

"People actually *can* get along working together," Mary Kathleen agreed. She laughed softly. "Okay, so we have police officers among our friends here, too. If anything were to ever get rough or violent in any way, whoever caused trouble would be out on their ears in a flash! But I've been at this about a year and a half. So far, nothing bad has ever happened. People are really just trying to help each other."

Within an hour, Kieran had come to know a ninety-six-year-old nun with a quick wit, salty tongue and empathy that brought people sweeping around her; a striking dancer from a Broadway play — who happened to know Kevin; a Wall Street broker; a stage designer; and a Penobscot Indigenous American girl with the most gentle voice she'd ever heard.

Kieran completely forgot she was there merely to keep herself occupied. She felt honored to be helping out in such a tangible way, and she was fascinated with the people she met working the food bank — and with those who came for food.

They were from the Middle East and the Far East, Russia, the Ukraine, Poland, England, France, Nigeria, Ethiopia, Argentina, Haiti and more. She realized that she was quickly learning a smattering of words — mainly *please* and *thank you* — in French, Creole, Spanish and what she was pretty sure was Russian.

People were grateful — so grateful. She was almost embarrassed; she had done so little.

The shepherd's pie from Finnegan's had

disappeared in the first fifteen minutes, but many chefs and cooks volunteered their time, and there was a constant flow of food.

There were a few unwashed bodies, but Sister Teresa — Kieran's newfound feisty friend — was quick to point out where showers and clothing could — and not *should* but *must* — be found. Sister Teresa fed everyone — they could bathe after they ate, but if they expected to find friends with whom to dine in the future, they had best do so!

Kieran was on her way to the kitchen for a refill on the actual soup pot when she realized that a group of young women was watching her.

Talking about her? They definitely looked at her — and went silent — as she walked by.

They seemed to be of different nationalities — two of the women appeared to be East Indian, three were black, and two were blue-eyed blondes, possibly of Nordic descent. Or Russian. She was friends with some really beautiful light-haired and light-eyed Russian women. Then, of course, the world was a wonderfully mixed-up place, so anyone could be from just about anywhere and have any combination of features: light hair, dark hair, skin, and so on.

She walked by, and then became curious, hurrying back to find them.

At first, she couldn't see them at all. The group had dispersed.

And then she saw one woman moving through a crowd, but turning back now and then to see what was behind her.

Yes, it was one of the women who had been in the group — and now she was watching rather warily for just where Kieran might be.

Kieran was certain then that they had realized she'd noticed them as they had been watching her.

The woman stood still for a moment; she was tall, ebony and regal in her bearing. She made eye contact with Kieran, and then turned away quickly.

"Hey!"

Kieran raced after her, but the woman slipped into the crowd. As Kieran made her way through people, excusing herself, she simply disappeared.

"What the heck?" she murmured.

"Kieran!"

She turned around quickly, aware that Mary Kathleen was calling to her.

"The soup — did you get the soup?"

"No! I'm so sorry. I —"

"They call it a soup kitchen because we

hand out soup. Rich, delicious soup, full of beef and vegetables and good things to help people make it through the day."

"Yes, yes, I know! I will get it, right away. Honestly. Mary Kathleen, do you know that group of young women who were over there?"

"What group?"

"The group that was standing over there."

"Where are they now?" Mary Kathleen asked. "And you didn't get the soup because a group of women was standing over there?"

Mary Kathleen was looking at her with perplexity.

"Sorry, sorry, I told you, I promise — I'll get the soup. Mary Kathleen, I need to know who they were. They were staring at me."

Mary Kathleen looked at Kieran, and then looked down. She was silent for a minute before she met Kieran's eyes again. "Kieran, I'm not meaning to be cruel or rude with these words, but . . . it's just not always about you."

Kieran let out a sigh. "No, no . . . they were really looking at me, talking about me."

"But you don't know where they are now?"

"They scattered."

"Maybe they just left," Mary Kathleen

said softly. "Maybe they actually managed to have some soup — and then they left. It's what people do. We have showers here, but no beds. It's not a hostel. People come, dine, sometimes bathe — and then leave."

"But . . ."

Kieran's voice trailed. Mary Kathleen was staring at her sorrowfully — and worriedly.

"Oh, Kieran!" Mary Kathleen said softly. "Aye, indeed, that woman last night came to you — used your name. But that does not mean that the rest of the world is watching you or whispering about you. You have to know that, right?"

Mary Kathleen was not going to believe her — no matter what she said. And now her almost-sister-in-law was worried about her. And she would tell Declan that she was worried about her. Declan would tell Craig. Craig would try very hard to keep her out of everything.

She let out an inward growl of absolute aggravation.

But she smiled at Mary Kathleen.

"Yeah, you must be right. Crazy, huh?" Kieran assured her.

And maybe she had imagined that she was being watched. Maybe the women had just moved on.

"I'll get the soup," she told Mary Kathleen.

She turned to head into the kitchen and almost plowed into a man.

He was about six foot two in height, sturdy in build. His eyes were almost like coal; his facial hair was dark, as well, though his head was shaved clean.

He appeared to be in his late thirties or early forties. She was certain that he would speak to her in a foreign language.

He did not. When he spoke, his English was perfect. Unaccented.

"I'm so sorry. I believe I nearly knocked you over."

"No, my fault," she said quickly. "Excuse me. I have to get more soup."

"Of course," he said.

She hadn't seen him working the food bank — but neither did he seem like someone who would be in the food line.

But she'd seen other people there today who had come to see about hiring help for restaurants or other venues. There was some job placement support through the organization, who vetted possible employers so that no one was hired illegally or put in a position where they might find themselves deported.

Maybe this guy had a swanky restaurant

somewhere and was looking for servers, cooks, busboys or -girls, and dishwashers.

There were all kinds of agencies to check up on what people were really doing, and they were ready, willing and able to connect people. But at the soup kitchen they only stepped in if their help was requested, since if they asked questions about the hungry men and women who visited, they might be scared off — and then not feel comfortable enough to come back.

Kieran headed into the kitchen, smiling at the mustached chef from a SoHo Italian restaurant, who offered her another big pot of the soup.

They chatted for a minute, then she turned to bring the soup out to be served.

The dark-haired man was watching her. He didn't look away. He smiled, and it wasn't an entirely nice smile. Then he headed out of the facility.

Kieran felt a shiver race through her.

Who the hell was that man? And who were the women? Had they really been whispering about her, watching her?

Should she trust her gut that something was not quite right? Or did she just need to get over herself?

CHAPTER FOUR

The Office of the Chief Medical Examiner, or OCME, for New York City handled thousands of cases a year. Between Manhattan and the other four boroughs of the city, the population was massive, sitting at about eight and a half million, and in a population that size, quite a lot of people died.

Bodies weren't brought in just because of murder; anyone who'd died alone was brought to the OCME, as were those who passed from accidental death or suicide. There were thirty-plus full-time medical examiners working for the OCME, along with another sixty-plus assistants and a multitude of support staff, such as forensic pathology, photography, criminology, lab work, tech, clerical and more.

With that kind of personnel, Craig hadn't been expecting that the ME working the case would be someone he knew well. To his surprise, Dr. Anthony Andrews walked into the reception area to meet with them.

He, Mike and Detective Larry McBride had recently worked together during the "perfect" killings that had gripped the city. Young, energetic, detailed — Dr. Andrews was damned good at his job. Though Craig didn't think there was much that the ME could say that would help catch the killer, he was still glad that this particular doctor was on the job.

"No one saw anything?" Andrews asked after greeting them. "She was stabbed in broad daylight — and no one saw anything?"

"The best I can figure it," Craig said, "she was hurrying down the street. She was heading in an easterly direction. She had just shoved the baby into Kieran's arms and fled the office. Kieran was running after her. She was, at tops, a block behind. Remember, it was rush hour — and that can mean a gridlock of people."

"Someone snuck up behind the victim," Mike said.

"Someone who must have followed her to the offices of Fuller and Miro," Craig said. "The killer moved fast. Partner, you mind?" he asked Mike, taking him by the arm to move him around in front so that Craig could mimic the stabbing as he pictured it had to have happened.

He came up quick, hand strong on his imaginary knife.

"Then," Mike said, arching, as if he had a knife in his back, "she swirled around. Possibly trying to face her killer."

"But," Craig said, "the killer delivered the knife without missing a stride and just kept walking."

"Kieran said there were no screams — not until she reached the woman and screamed herself. She'd already called the cops and me . . . there was an officer in uniform there in a matter of minutes and a detective on the scene within ten. I arrived just about the same time as the detective."

"That would be Lance Kendall — he should arrive momentarily. In the meantime, we'll proceed as scheduled. One would think that the dead would wait patiently — which they do. However, their loved ones tend to be very emotional and impatient, so we do try to keep up. If you'll follow me?" Dr. Andrews requested.

Craig was far too familiar with the OCME. The Manhattan offices were close to the FBI building which, in a way, made it too easy to be present for an autopsy, even when it certainly wasn't always necessary.

Mike must have been thinking along the

same lines.

"You know the French Revolution?" he asked Craig softly.

Craig glanced over at him. "Well, I know something about it. I'm not sure I'd want to teach a course on it."

Mike nodded sagely. "They say that those who had to die, well, they were nobles, and thus they had to behave *nobly* — and so they went *nobly* to the guillotine. Madame du Barry screamed and cried and had a fit, and then the people saw how ugly it was. It was only after that they — the people as a mass — began to protest the sanctioned murders."

"Good thought," Craig murmured. "We've seen enough death. We could have left the autopsy to Lance Kendall."

"No, I know you. We had to be here no matter what. It just always takes me longer than I'd like to get rid of the feel of this place."

That was something Craig understood. They worked hard at the morgue — very, very hard. Every floor, every table, every instrument in the place was cleaned and cleaned again; antibacterial agents ruled.

And still the scent of death was strong.

They were offered paper suits and masks; two minutes later, they were in the room where there were actually two autopsies in process.

Their victim waited for them, tragically naked but clean, ready for the knife.

Anthony Andrews adjusted the mic he wore and cleared his throat. He identified their Jane Doe by date and circumstance and stated the date, his own work as the ME, Jerry Sanders as his assistant, and Mike and Craig as witnesses.

And he set to work.

Y incisions were, to the layman — and to Craig this many years into his work — little less than horrendous. The sound of the ribs breaking seemed extremely brutal.

But Craig was also passionate in his belief that the dead did speak. Autopsy was incredibly important. He believed in God or a higher power, and that when the soul was long gone, the body could no longer be hurt. But, it was still hard to watch sometimes.

The process today was the usual. Andrews and his assistant worked over the body. The organs were studied and weighed; samples of blood and stomach contents were taken.

Lance Kendall arrived sometime soon after the first hour. He stood as Mike and Craig did — still and listening. Craig hadn't met Kendall before he'd arrived at the scene of the murder on Friday, though he did know many of the men with the Major Case Squad of the NYPD. At the crime scene, Kendall had been thorough and detailed — polite to Craig, and making no comments about not needing the FBI for a murder on the street. He was, Craig imagined, ambitious, but didn't seem the kind to put ambition before results. Of course, Craig had no idea how the man felt about it all now that the case had been handed to a task force and the FBI was taking the lead.

"This is something you need to see," Dr. Andrews said.

He was inspecting the corpse's mouth.

They all moved over, one by one, and the ME pointed out the woman's dental work.

Craig had no idea of what he was looking at — only silver fillings here and there.

He knew that Andrews would explain.

"I believe that this woman is approximately forty — though she does look fifty. She has not, however, recently borne a child, so the baby is not hers. What I was showing you, that isn't American dental work, and it isn't new. It was probably done more than ten years ago, and I'd say that it was done somewhere in Eastern Europe — a country that was once part of the Soviet Union or under the Communist bloc, most likely. Russia maybe, the Ukraine . . . but, then again, maybe Albania or somewhere in the former Yugoslavia. In other words, I do believe she's of Eastern European descent, but she's not malnourished. She's healthy — just *worn*. I don't believe she's taken care of herself well — she's probably faced tremendous stress to look ten years older than I believe her age to be. She's worked hard — manually, I believe. Take a look at her hands. Possibly, she worked as a maid. We're trying for an ID, naturally, through fingerprints. We'll search through dental records, but I doubt we'll find local records for her."

"We are testing to see if she was related to the baby," Craig said. It wasn't really a question; it was an obvious action to be taken.

"Of course," Andrews said. He looked at Lance Kendall. "As your FBI team members noted, the one stab wound in the back that killed her most probably occurred swiftly — she didn't know what hit her. She staggered toward Miss Finnegan in the street because you instinctively turn when you're attacked from behind. The attack was planned and fluid — that type of knife isn't just in everyone's daily purse or briefcase."

"So our Jane Doe was followed to the offices of Fuller and Miro. And she went to those offices to hand the baby to Kieran Finnegan. Why?" Kendall asked.

"We don't know," Craig said. Andrews cleared his throat. "Gentlemen, I've given you what I can. I'll make sure you all receive a hard copy of the report. If we discover anything else on our end, of course, you'll be notified."

"What about ethnicity through DNA?" Craig asked.

"Well, we might be able to pinpoint an area of most likely ancestry," Andrews said.

"That will be helpful," Craig said.

"Of course," Andrews said. "I'll keep everyone informed on any information that I get. As soon as I have it, naturally." He stared at them all.

It was their cue to leave. The three of them thanked him and headed toward the building entrance. As they did so, a man was hurrying in. He was very tall and lean, with tawny eyes and sandy hair. He was in a polo shirt and jeans and a jacket. Beneath the jacket, Craig was aware, the man was carrying a weapon.

"LeBlanc?" he asked. "Hank LeBlanc?"

The US Marshal nodded and intros went around. "So we have the whole gang. I imagine we'll get a counterpart from Homeland Security before this is all over," Le-Blanc said.

"Good," Kendall responded, his voice vehement. They all looked at him, and he shrugged. "Maybe we'll get somewhere, working together. As long as we all keep it real — keep the contact going."

"Sure, yeah. Of course," LeBlanc said. "I, uh, I'm trying to see if I recognize our dead woman right now, if she might have been one of ours. Informant or witness. We lose them now and then. Except . . ."

"Except what?" Craig asked.

"She's not one of ours, I'm pretty sure. I'm here because they want every *t* crossed on this thing. If she had been ours, we would have known something. Everyone in every local agency knows about this — we all know enough to know we don't know a damned thing but that someone thinks they're getting away with murder."

"Not this time," Kendall said flatly.

"Nope, not this time," Mike agreed. "Hell, the best of the best, right? We're all on it."

Nods went around.

"We'll keep it tight," Mike said. "I'll be the liaison between agencies — make sure we're always all up to speed on what's going on."

LeBlanc thanked him and headed on in as

they continued out to the street.

"So the woman — our dead woman — knew your girlfriend by name," Kendall said to Craig as they reached the street.

"We established that the other night," Craig said.

"There has to be a reason," Kendall said.

"Yes, we actually figured that, too," Mike said quickly, his tone easy, as if he was afraid that Kendall and Craig might get heated over the facts. "But, as you know, Kieran had never seen the woman before. Of course, we all realize that the woman knew about Kieran somehow — or, perhaps, she knew about Fuller and Miro and knew that Kieran handled a great deal of their therapy and exploratory work. She might have a reputation for having tremendous empathy — as someone who would take care of a baby."

"And Kieran still can't think of anything or anyone who might feel that way about her?" Kendall asked Craig.

"No. And it's driving her crazy."

"Might have to do with that thing in the subway from a couple of years ago now. Miss Finnegan was all over the news then," Kendall said.

Craig wasn't sure why Kendall reminding him of Kieran's *situation* in the subway a few years back disturbed him so much. Actually, she had been meant as a target — but a young girl had wound up being pushed and nearly died a horrible death as a train was speeding into the station.

Kieran had caught her. And when assailed by the press, she just murmured, "Anyone would lend a helping hand."

It became a temporary motto for the city.

Actually, it was a pity it hadn't seemed to have stuck around longer.

"That is possible," Mike said.

Craig knew why he was disturbed.

Damn it. The man was right. Maybe whoever this woman was, she remembered the subway incident, too. And she had heard of Kieran and . . .

If someone could save a baby, maybe it was her?

"I'm not sure it matters how this woman found Kieran. The thing is, she did," he said gruffly. "But, that it was Kieran she found may not mean a thing. What's important is that she was brutally cut down on the street after handing the baby over."

Kendall nodded thoughtfully. "It's a good thing your girlfriend is smart as a whip as well, warning the building security clerk, calling 9-1-1 and you. Because if you think about it — there were cops already on the way when the woman was stabbed. The killer might have seen them milling on the street. If there hadn't been cops around and he saw Kieran with the baby, he might have taken the time to retrieve his weapon and attempt to kill Miss Finnegan, as well. After all, at that point, she had the baby."

Again, Kendall was probably right.

Again, it irritated Craig.

"Yeah. Thank God she's smart," he said evenly.

Mike offered Lance Kendall his hand. "Detective, we'll keep tight on this. The city is in an uproar." He hesitated and shrugged. "A woman murdered on the street in the middle of a crowd, and a baby involved. We'll be on it day and night."

"Ditto. So, we learn anything, we keep one another posted," Kendall said.

"Yes," Mike agreed.

Kendall looked at Craig and offered him his hand.

"Detective," Craig said. He accepted the handshake.

They parted ways. As they started walking, Mike punched Craig in the shoulder.

"Hey!"

"You know, men — and women — in different agencies can be jerks."

"Yeah, they can."

"Don't you be the jerk, huh?"

Craig lowered his head with a half smile on his face. Mike was right.

He was being a jerk. But a jerk doubly convinced that they had to find a killer — and fast.

He looked at Mike. "How's your Russian?" he asked.

"Worse than my Spanish," Mike told him.

"You don't speak Spanish at all," Craig reminded him.

"I rest my case. Actually? I'm kind of lying. I do speak some Russian. Had a Russian great-great-grandma who watched after me when I was a kid. Why?"

"I was thinking we might head out to Brighton Beach," Craig said. They had a friend working at a restaurant out by Brighton Beach pier. Jacob Wolff had been born in America; his mother had been Russian and his dad had been born in Israel. He worked undercover for a division of the FBI linked with Homeland Security — his job was to blend in with the locals so that he could hear all the chatter. Russian mob operations had become a more and more serious factor to the city in the past few years. So far, he'd been able to warn the authorities in time to stop two car bombs and the assassination of a local councilman

— all without giving away his cover.

He listened. And when people were comfortable in a place, they tended to speak a little too openly — dismissing a waiter as a nobody.

"What? You don't think his friends will look at us and think, *Well, hell, they're FBI* right off the bat?"

"Not if we go undercover, too."

Mike groaned. Craig had done a lot of undercover work, changing his look drastically for each assignment. Mike was an upfront, flat-out, find-the-truth kind of a guy.

Dress up wasn't his thing.

"So swim shorts and Crocs, huh? Enough to look like we're wannabe beach boys, huh?"

"No one is ever going to call me a boy," Mike said. He had Craig by a decade and was — as Craig liked to tease him — an old geezer in his midforties.

"Wannabe beach whatevers? Come on, we won't really be working. I'll buy you a fizzy drink with an umbrella," Craig said.

"Don't you dare."

Craig grinned. "We'll head to my apartment."

"Thought you were mainly living at Kieran's apartment."

"Yep, that's why we're heading to my place."

"Think you ought to call her? Let her know that the case is a priority for us and that we're part of the joint task force?" Mike suggested.

"I'll let her know," Craig told him. "I just . . ."

"What?"

"I just need to try to figure out something to tell her that actually suggests we're making headway on solving the case."

"You know you did it. You can't keep lying. You stalked her — you stalked her and then you killed her," Kieran used her fiercest voice, trying to sound like a cop.

Her twin looked at her and arched a brow. He lowered his head, trying to hide a smile. "No," he said simply.

"We can understand how it happened, how you must have felt —"

"No," Kevin said again.

"She rejected you. You felt like an ass."

"No," Kevin said again.

"You were humiliated. In front of so many people."

"No, damn you!"

Kevin looked up at her with fire in his eyes. "You idiots. Don't *you* understand? I

91

loved her. Whether she did or didn't love me, I loved her. I would have never hurt her. I didn't kill her, and when you get your heads out of your asses you'll discover the truth. I'm innocent, and I'm done talking. I want my lawyer — now."

"He's not here yet. We still have time —"

"Get the hell out! I've asked for my lawyer and from here on out, we will wait for him to arrive."

Kieran set the script down and looked at her brother with a smile. "Wow. Did you do it?"

"Nope. I am innocent," he told her, and grimaced. "My character is innocent, at any rate. You see, he's a rock star, and it really does look like he did it at first. The cops believe it was him — until they find a kid who was too terrified to come forward. She was actually killed by her stepfather. Because she totally rejected him!"

"You're really good," she told him, leaning an elbow on the desk. They were in the office at Finnegan's. She was sitting in Declan's chair. She'd returned from the soup kitchen with Mary Kathleen at about three, and Kevin had been there ready to run lines with her.

She'd popped into the back office to eat some fish and chips, and Kevin had joined her. They'd been running his lines for the filming that would take place on Monday and Tuesday.

"You're pretty good at that emoting thing yourself," Kevin told her.

"No, I'm not. You were laughing at me."

"Just because you're not a big black cop who used to be a linebacker," Kevin said.

"Ah, but I love Arnie Westmore!" Kieran said. And she did. The actor who starred as the lead detective on the show Kevin would be filming was both strikingly handsome and definitely talented. He really had been a linebacker, too, with the Jets. She was thrilled that Kevin had scored a role on the show.

There was a tap on the door. Kieran jumped up, hopeful that it was Craig.

She had managed not to call him yet — mainly because she had kept busy all day.

It wasn't Craig. It was Danny. He poked his head in and asked, "Am I interrupting the great flow of dramatic practice?"

"No, you're not interrupting. Kevin knows his lines perfectly," Kieran said, sitting back down. "I do believe he thinks that I'm horrible, and that I overact terribly, emoting here and there and everywhere."

"Come on — she was trying to sound as tough as a linebacker," Kevin said.

"Don't kid yourself — Irish women are supposed to be tougher than linebackers, especially the Irish American kind," Kieran assured him.

"Remember when we were kids?" Kevin asked Danny. "We weren't supposed to hurt our only sister. And then one day Dad said, 'Hey! If she pinches you again, deck her!' "

"Yeah, I remember," Danny said. "But she was older than me — and she grew fast. And I was chicken. I never did deck her."

"None of us did."

"She was too scary," Danny said.

Kieran made a face at them both. "And she's really tired of this story!" Kieran told them firmly. "I was not a terror as a sister!"

"Well, it's a good thing that you're tough," Kevin said. "Seeing you're determined to get into or cause trouble at every turn."

"I am not —"

"Sorry, sorry!" Kevin said. "Okay, trouble finds you. Your boyfriend is an FBI agent and you work with criminal psychologists. But, hey, yeah, trouble finds you."

"This time, it actually did," Danny told Kevin.

"But she's going to let it go, right?" another voice asked.

None of them had noticed Declan when he arrived at the office door, arms crossed over his chest, expression stern as he looked at them all.

"I don't know what you mean!" Kieran protested. "Craig might well be on the case."

"Craig, yes, the guy who wears a Glock and knows how to use it," Declan said. "Kieran, honestly, think about it —"

"Honestly! I am thinking. I'm not doing anything. I handed out food at a soup kitchen with your fiancée, and I've been a sounding board for my twin. I was happy to wait tables, but you were covered for the day. I am being an angel."

"Fallen," Danny muttered.

"I heard that!" she snapped at him.

The phone on the desk rang; it was Mary Kathleen out on the floor — Saturday evening business was picking up. It wasn't crazy, but she could use one of them to help out.

Any one of them.

"I'm going," Kieran said, rising. "It's a hard life to bear the burdens of this family, but I am willing to give my all."

She heard all three of her brothers laughing as she walked out. Shaking her head, Kieran went ahead behind the bar.

Mary Kathleen was hurrying about. She glanced quickly at Kieran. "Terrific, I'm heading out on the floor. You can manage here?"

"God help me, I hope so," Kieran said. She was about to say that she'd grown up in the pub. It wouldn't have sounded quite right. Neither of her parents had been drinkers. Tea had been mom's go-to, and at best, her dad had a pint on a Sunday with his roast.

A pub could be so many things. In the old days, the men had usually enjoyed their whiskey and pints in the main room — women and children had often been banished to another area. But Finnegan's had always been a place where food and camaraderie were the most important aspects of the business. There were hours during certain days when everyone there really did know everyone else.

However you looked at it, she knew how to handle a bar.

She knew a lot of their clientele that day, and it was nice to chat. They all asked her how she was doing, how did she like her "real work." And, of course, she asked back about them and their families as she served up their fare: Larry Adair, whiskey neat and fish and chips. John Martin, a pint of whatever was on special and shepherd's pie. Brian McMann, a soda with lots of lime and corned beef and cabbage. Jillian Boyle, white wine and Guinness stew.

She was moving about quickly and yet easily when the door to the pub opened just as the sun made a powerful streak down Broadway.

For a moment, it was almost like a religious experience. There, in the midst of the tremendous light, was a tall, dark figure with a sweeping cloak around it — as if a presence from above or beyond had arrived with a powerful force.

Kieran blinked, the figure stepped forward, and she saw that it was not a presence from above or beyond — and yet, it was still one containing a powerful force.

Sister Teresa was just outside the pub. She looked at Kieran for a long moment, grinned and turned away.

Astonished, Kieran stared after her. She frowned, wondering why the woman had come — and why she had turned away.

Danny was coming out of the office and heading toward the bar — probably looking for a friend with whom to chat a bit. Danny, realizing that he made one of the most garrulous and charming guides in New York City — if not simply the best, as he assured her he was striving to be — loved to find old-timers at the bar and talk a bit and then listen to all that they had to say.

She couldn't let him get chummy and find a bar chair.

Swinging around the end of the bar — and nearly hopping over the little gate — she hurried to catch him. "I need you — some food coming out, drinks good for now, Brian probably ready for his coffee soon, doesn't need cream!"

She didn't give her baby brother a chance to protest.

She shoved him back, handing him the bar rag as she did so, and raced for the door. Bursting out onto the sidewalk, she was ready to run.

She didn't need to. Sister Teresa — in her complete "penguin" outfit, as they had always called the nuns' traditional habits — was waiting for her, studying the list of fresh smoothies on the menu of the fruit stand just a few feet away.

"What took you?" she asked Kieran.

Kieran's brows shot up in surprise. "I'm sorry! I . . . you . . . I didn't expect to see you. I'm so sorry. I guess you would have been uncomfortable coming in? The pub is quite nice — we have religious groups meet here now and then. Even a few rabbis!"

"Oh, honey, I have no problem going into a pub. Sometimes, when people see us, *they* get uncomfortable. I didn't want to distress any of your customers, child, that's all. Then again, it's best to talk in private sometimes, too," Sister Teresa told her. "And not be terribly conspicuous."

"Yes, certainly," Kieran said, curious — and anxious. She had felt that there was something going on at the soup kitchen. Sister Teresa's presence here now seemed to solidify what she'd believed.

"And yes, sometimes it's good to speak in private," Kieran agreed. But, just how inconspicuous they could be — herself and a fully draped nun in front of the pub door — she wasn't certain.

Sister Teresa waved a hand in the air as if reading her mind. "Never mind — I just don't want people walking out on your lovely place of business. So, anyway, here's the thing — are you going to be coming back to the soup kitchen?"

"Oh, yes. I was very impressed," Kieran told her.

"We are impressive," Sister Teresa said flatly. "But, may I suggest that you return sooner than next Saturday? You are employed Monday through Friday — Mary Kathleen filled me in on you, so I know — but we are open tomorrow, as well."

"And I would come back because . . . ?"

Kieran asked.

"You have a way with a soup ladle?" Sister Teresa retorted sarcastically. "My dear Miss Finnegan! One of our young ladies — a very shy one at that! — asked if I knew you. If you would be back. I assured her that you would be. It is not at all nice to make a liar out of a nun. I am assuming she wishes to speak with you. And — since Mary Kathleen did fill me in on quite a bit — I believe this young woman might be looking to you for assistance, and help in what may be a criminal matter having to do with a beautiful baby girl."

Kieran stared at her and blinked. "Sister Teresa, if you can tell me —"

"I can't tell you anything. I am only suggesting that you come to the facility at about ten tomorrow. We open after the early masses — services and such for some of our partners of other persuasions — and we work until three or four. I'm also going to suggest that you be incredibly discreet — as I said, this young lady is very shy."

"Of course," Kieran said.

Discreet! Like standing with a nun on Broadway!

"Don't dillydally," Sister Teresa said, and for a moment, she felt as if she was dealing with Mary Poppins — had Mary Poppins decided to join a convent. "Get yourself in there early. It's not like anyone has given me a timetable or anything."

"Yes."

"Yes, what, young woman?"

"Of course, yes, I'll be there, Sister Teresa!" Kieran promised.

"Excellent."

The nun nodded sagely, turned and fluttered her way down Broadway.

CHAPTER FIVE

"Hey, what do you think? Maybe we should have gotten some surfboards, eh?" Mike asked Craig.

There were a few boards leaning against the wall in the Cranky Crab. The place was something of a tiki hut, large and sprawling, up on wooden pilings, and actually on the beach. It was large, with a seating capacity of about four hundred.

"Maybe we should have," Craig said.

"I was being a wiseass."

"So was I."

The clientele of the restaurant was intriguing and included young women with cover-ups over scanty bikinis that didn't really cover up much accompanying muscle-bound young males, all the way up to older folks, some of the men with traditional Hasidic locks and facial hair and some of the women in wigs or scarves and long black dresses that concealed them almost entirely.

And there was every mode of apparel in between, as well. And still, the place advertised very importantly that it was completely kosher.

Mike was glad that the two of them hadn't gotten carried away. They were in board shorts and T-shirts, just a couple of guys out to catch one of the first days of nice warm spring sun. It was that time of year when the weather could come and go quickly . . . winter not so far past that it didn't whisper now and then about a return to cold and ice. They ordered light beers and a house specialty — borscht — and kept their conversation to sports. *How about those Jets? And what was going on with the Yankees and the Mets? Of course, then, well, hell, they could talk about the Giants . . .*

Mike went passionately into hockey as their food arrived. It was about then that Craig saw Jacob bussing a table and knew Jacob had seen them, as well. He headed over to their table, clearly ready to join the passionate hockey discussion. If they were noted by others in the restaurant, they were quickly dismissed.

Before Jacob walked away — after vociferously agreeing with every word Mike had to say about hockey, but quietly imparting plans — they knew to meet in an hour in a safe house about two blocks away.

They rose to leave; Craig thanked their pleasant waitress.

"Spasiba," Mike said. *"Do svidaniya."*

He actually sounded damned good. Almost as if he had an edge on the accent.

She smiled and returned his words.

"Thank you and goodbye," Craig said. "A little Russian, huh?"

"It never pays to give away everything you know — haven't I taught you that, kid?" Mike teased.

"A good lesson to remember," Craig assured him.

They wandered the streets for a bit, and as they did so, Craig thought about the city and realized that he was a New Yorker through and through — passionate about his home. Prejudice had probably existed since Homo sapiens had first met another tribe of Homo sapiens. And it had seldom been easy for the different nationalities that had poured into New York, nor was it easy now. So many different nationalities and ethnicities came, and they often came in great waves. At the moment, one of the largest influxes comprised various Asian countries, but that didn't mean that many others weren't coming at tremendous rates, including those from Eastern Europe and many war-ravaged areas of the Middle East.

"Land of dreams and nightmares," Craig murmured under his breath.

"Pardon?" Mike said.

"I keep thinking — I love this city. I love our country. We're a work in progress, always, and we're where you come to escape poverty, war, persecution, and so on. But I have friends working down in the Florida area who in their work have witnessed the tragedy of refugees drowning in the Florida Straits trying to get to the States on rafts made out of anything they can find. Other friends in Texas tell me about Mexicans and other Central Americans and South Americans who are taken for everything they've got by scammers charging impossible fees to get them into the country — and then deserting them.

"And then there are those who manage other rackets — as in selling beautiful brides to American men. Some of the guys are just desperate dudes. Some of them are sick as shit and happy to take in a foreign bride with no papers so that if something bad happens to her, well, she never existed."

"Yeah," Craig agreed. "There's that."

"Life — and dreams — for sale."

"Okay, is it possible that we're dealing with something that has to do with immigration, and God knows, maybe human trafficking or illegal adoption? No one has come forward," Craig pointed out. "What happened has been in the news, on every screen in the city. A woman is dead — and a beautiful baby girl has just been abandoned."

"So people are afraid to speak out. I think that we're on the right track," Mike agreed.

"Okay. So going with that, here's a theory. Someone is trafficking young women. God knows — probably more than one 'someone' in a city the size of New York. Maybe they discovered the baby market on the side. Even good people — desperate for a child — might be willing to go the illegal adoption route."

"But, no one has come for the baby," Craig said.

"Well, not yet, anyway," Mike agreed. "They can't — if they try to claim the baby, there are a million questions. You think the mother is dead?"

"Possibly. I think that the woman who handed the baby to Kieran was trying to save it — and maybe because she believed she could somehow save the mother, as well? I don't know. Maybe it was her way to stop everything that was going on. Hopefully our friend Jacob knows something that can help," Craig said.

Mike shrugged. "I guess we have to start somewhere. But there are a lot of factors to consider, you know."

"As you just said, we have to start somewhere," Craig said. "And Jacob is damned good at his job — he's taken down members of the Russian mob repeatedly without ever being caught. He has his eye on anything coming from Eastern Europe. And — through other contacts — he seems to have a handle on Asian crime and Central and South America, as well. He's definitely our best help for some kind of help on this."

Craig's phone was ringing. He pulled it from his pocket and winced. Kieran. He hadn't talked to her yet. "Hey," he said into the phone.

Mike waved a hand at him dismissively and walked a few steps ahead.

"Sorry — I couldn't wait anymore. I have to know — you're at least on it, right?"

"We're in," Craig said. "I just . . . well, at this moment, we've still got nothing. No, not nothing. The autopsy did give us information. The dental records suggested that the woman grew up in Eastern Europe, probably the former Soviet Union."

"See! That's something already."

"Yes, it gives us a direction, but we need

to move along carefully with open minds. Theories are great. But we can't put on blinders to other ideas — we need a great deal more."

"That's fine. You're in. That's the most major step."

"Yes, so . . . what are you doing? Not going crazy? Not obsessing?"

"Not at all. I promise. I helped Mary Kathleen out at her soup kitchen, ran some lines with Kevin, and then worked the bar for a while. I'm heading home, though. I'll see you there, okay?"

He didn't answer her right away; she sounded far too easy with what was going on.

"Craig? See you at home — that okay with you? Oh, if you and Mike are working . . . did you want me to hang out at the pub and wait for you?" she asked.

"No, no, that's fine. We ate. I'll see you later."

"Great. You . . . really don't have anything, huh?"

"No, but we are working, Kieran. You know that —"

"Cases can take weeks, months, years — and sometimes, they're never solved. I know. But you and Mike won't let that happen."

"Mike and I try not to let it happen. Anyway . . ."

"I'm good. Honestly," Kieran promised.

"I'm checking in with an old friend who works a cop beat. Hopefully, if we put out enough feelers in enough places, someone will pick up on someone. Even in this city, people have neighbors. And sometimes, people are even decent enough to report what they see."

"Yep," she said cheerfully. Too cheerfully. "We'll count on it," she added. "See you soon, huh?"

"Few hours, at least, I think. Lock up, you know, when you're home."

"I will," she promised.

They hung up. Mike walked back over. "What's wrong?" he asked Craig.

"Nothing," Craig said. "Kieran said that she kept busy all afternoon. Everything is fine."

"Yeah, right. And that's what worries you, huh?"

"Exactly."

Kieran sat at her computer again, going through her current client files.

She just couldn't find anything that would lead to someone handing her a baby. At least, nothing that she could figure out.

"Forest for the trees?" she asked herself aloud. Was there something she should be seeing that was so obviously right in front of her face?

There was a faint pounding sound. She smiled — the nightly karaoke was starting up at the restaurant downstairs. Not all the music came through. Someone was singing Aerosmith. One of the top ten songs people picked.

On a whim, she shut the computer and left the apartment, making sure that she did lock her door behind her. She walked downstairs, then slipped into the restaurant, heading for the sushi bar.

Lee Chan — one of the sushi chefs — was a friend of hers. They had a lot in common. His family owned and operated the restaurant. His great-grandparents had been born in China, but every generation since had been born in the USA.

His wife's grandparents, who were Japanese, still remembered being in an internment camp — in the States — during World War II. They'd both been teenagers and they'd suffered a great deal of prejudice, but they had apparently never held it against anyone. Sung Chan — Lee's grandfather, a man who still worked as a waiter in the family business — waved at Kieran as she entered.

Every now and then, he liked to belt out a Sinatra number — with a fine voice and pretty good Ol' Blue Eyes inflection to his lyrics.

"What? You're on your own? Where's tall, dark and lethal?" Lee teased Kieran, handing her a menu, but then lifting it away before she actually touched it. "Wait, you have the menu memorized. What can I get you?"

Actually, sushi did sound good. She'd been too busy at the soup kitchen to eat, and she'd barely touched her food when she'd been helping Kevin.

"How about a sashimi boat — mostly tuna and salmon?" she asked.

"Whatever you want." He winced suddenly as someone screeched out a few notes in an attempt to emulate Whitney Houston. "Except," he added in a whisper, "I'm not allowed to get a hook to pull singers off-stage. Thought about it once. My dad shut me down."

Kieran laughed. "Hey, I always say, if you want to go for a Whitney Houston number, go for it."

"So you really came just to eat?" he asked her, passing her order over to one of his fellow chefs and leaning on the counter.

"I think so. I don't know."

"Did you hear about that murder that happened right on the street in broad daylight? You know, the city gets a bad rap, muggings and pickpockets and that sort of thing. But that murder — I think it happened right by where you work," Lee said. She didn't have to answer. "Oh, you know all about it!" he said.

"I don't know all about it — but I do know that it took place."

"You were there!"

"I was. And here's the thing, Lee — the woman had no identification on her. No one knows who she was. She didn't have much of an accent, but I thought she was foreign."

"This is New York," he noted drily.

"Right. And the medical examiner told Craig that her dental work suggested Eastern Europe. I don't know where she was born, but I can't help wondering if her situation has something to do with her being an immigrant. An illegal immigrant, I think."

"We do get illegals asking for work — my dad has given out lots of food and money," Lee told her. "But we don't do business under the table, you know."

"Of course not!"

"Anyway, you're looking for newcomers.

But not Irish?"

"Correct . . . this woman wasn't Irish."

"Or Japanese, I take it," Lee said.

"Or Japanese," Kieran said, smiling at his gentle stab.

Lee laughed. "I think my family has been in the country longer than yours, though that bar has been around since right before or after the Civil War, from what I understand. But wasn't your grandfather on your dad's side born in Ireland? I thought I read that when the paper did a little write-up on old city pubs."

"Grandfather and grandmother," Kieran added. "Somehow, American Finnegans and Irish Finnegans have stayed in touch. The pub came into the family after the Civil War. The Irish-American who'd actually inherited when they came to the States had been a bachelor and he was glad to see it go to his cousins who were coming in from 'across the pond.' "

Lee grinned. "So I'm more American than you are. And still sometimes people speak to me slowly, hoping that I understand English."

"Well, not everyone learns English to come here. I bet you can get by okay without it in a city like New York."

"Still, it's a foolish assumption. Reveals

113

prejudice." He shrugged. "The American experience isn't always a good one, you know. I have seen good people caught up in bad stuff." He hesitated. "Karaoke can be an intimate experience — I mean, people open up, start talking. And you hear a lot of stories. Too many women come here all starry-eyed and end up falling into strip clubs, and from there into the drug trade or prostitution." He shrugged again. "I guess too many men become criminals."

"Or become strippers and junkies, too — and sometimes prostitutes. It happens to men, too," Kieran reminded him.

"Touché!"

"I'm not on a soapbox, I swear."

"I know, you're just normal about social issues, and we're in a city where we are accepting of race, nationality, sex . . . whatever. I mean, here, if one guy doesn't like you, you've got millions more to choose from! And immigrants also wind up being house-keepers, cabdrivers, busboys, dishwashers — let's face it, you come in, and you take what you can get. But, Kieran, this city is huge, remember. People can hide in plain sight — or disappear down a zillion dark alleys. So what are you thinking?"

"I guess I'm thinking that I do know your family tries to help people and that you hire all kinds of folks new to the States. If you hear anything . . ."

He nodded gravely. "Of course. And I'll try to think if I know of anyone who can help you. But in the meantime, I'll check on your food?"

She laughed. "Yeah, thanks. I'm really hungry."

"Good. We have some amazing tuna tonight. Want to do a Carpenters number with me?" he asked her.

"What?"

"Carpenters — you know. 'We've Only Just Begun?' No, huh. What about Kid Rock and Sheryl Crow?"

Kieran started to laugh. "No!"

"Yes . . . there's nothing like a karaoke song to get people talking."

"Maybe. Except . . . I think that means I'd better have sake with my sashimi boat."

Down a dark alley filled with trash from a number of tenements, and then beneath an archway that led into a half-derelict building, Mike and Craig came to Jacob Wolff's "safe house."

They pushed open the beat-to-hell door; Jacob was waiting directly on the other side.

He was expecting them.

Once they were in, bolts went sliding

against the door. There was no way that they would be surprised in the middle of their meeting.

"Hey, have a seat. This safe house is my apartment while working this operation," Jacob told them.

The room offered a cot, a desk that held a computer and some other office supplies, one dresser, and a little kitchen area with a Formica table, all in about thirty square feet of space. There was also a trunk at the foot of the bed. While Craig was sure that Jacob was armed — even though whatever weapon he was carrying was tucked into the waistband of his jeans, covered with his T and completely hidden from view — he also kept other weapons, and they were most probably stashed in the trunk.

"A little cramped," Craig said.

"A little tawdry," Mike said, making a face. But then he grinned at Jacob. "We've all had worse."

"Yeah? I guess we have," Jacob agreed. He was a tall, wiry man with eyes so blue that they were startling against the darkness of his mustache, beard and long hair, kept somewhat scraggly as befitted his chosen look for the time. A grin touched his lips.

"I heard you're living it up pretty nicely, Frasier," Jacob said.

"Yeah? I haven't moved into the Taj Mahal or anything," Craig assured him.

Jacob laughed. "Oh, my friend. It's not the trappings of grandeur to which I refer. I've heard you've got a lovely thing of some kind going on with a young woman named Kieran Finnegan. I've seen pictures — she's a beauty. And she's a criminal psychologist. And if that weren't enough, she's part-owner of Finnegan's. Not only do you get brains and beauty, you get some of the finest Guinness on tap in the city!"

Mike was already laughing; Craig shrugged and joined in. "And how the hell do you know all that?"

"I actually get by headquarters now and then. Egan had a picture with you all at the pub on his desk. He's pretty impressed with your girl — says you're a lucky stiff who'd best keep his head in place and make it last. When I heard about the murder the other day and how and where it happened, I wondered if she might be connected in some way."

Craig found himself irritated again — not with Jacob, just with life. He was grateful that they'd gotten Kieran and the baby off the sidewalk before reporters had arrived. He was alarmed at the amount of people — even if they weren't average Joes out on the street — who seemed to know that Kieran had been involved.

"So what kind of chatter have you heard?" Craig asked him.

"Questioning," Jacob said. "People have been asking each other if they know who the woman is, if they'd seen her."

"We had a sketch artist work on a likeness," Mike said. "I believe the powers that be have released it. That should help."

"Well, everyone is appalled and asking if they know of anyone missing a baby. Naturally, there are a dozen organized crime families — one for the mother country and one for every satellite that ever existed in any form. Some get together and belong not to just one mob, but two mobs. Thing is, word on the street is that something is going down. Someone is cashing in."

"And every smaller faction is blaming it on every other gang?" Craig asked.

Jacob shook his head. "They say it's a local, American as apple pie. But who he might be, or how he's calling the shots, I don't know. Frankly, I don't even know what this supposed crime boss is actually doing, whether it's illegal gambling, drugs, heists, prostitution or something else. I keep listening. He runs something big, always keeping at a major distance. In other words, he has middlemen, he uses threats, and he's a king who sacrifices pawns as if people were toilet paper. I hear that there is a boss, but, while I'm using the word *he* and I've heard the word *kingpin* used, at this moment, I don't even know if it's a man or a woman."

"Okay. Thanks. This was a long shot," Craig said.

Jacob looked at him earnestly. "I swear, I will do my best to help out. You did save my skin, you know."

Craig was surprised.

He didn't know.

Jacob must have read the confusion on his face. "Five years ago," Jacob elaborated. "That kidnapping detail. The goon nearly stabbed me — you brought him down in one tackle. Thanks."

"No thanks needed, Jacob. It's what we do — and it is damned good to know that we have one another's backs."

"Yeah," Mike put in. "He saved your life. He let me get a bullet — in the butt!"

"Hey!" Craig protested.

"Just kidding — the bullet had my name on it. At least, the way that we do cover, my partner was out there, and I was just grazed."

"See, there you go," Craig said.

119

"Did make for one hell of a sore butt!" Mike said.

Jacob grinned. "Okay, I need you to leave out the front so I can take off out the back. But just let me say — I like your board shorts. Nice legs, Mike."

"Nothing like working with wiseass kids!" Mike said, shaking his head wearily.

"Who said he was being a wiseass?" Craig asked. "You have good legs."

"Pity he injured the ass, huh?" Jacob asked.

"Downer," Craig agreed.

Jacob grinned and then sobered. "I'll get a message to you if I learn anything else."

They thanked him and left. The sun was going down, and Craig knew Jacob Wolff would use the dusk to his advantage. He knew how to move within it.

"Let's hope it was a productive day," Mike said.

"It's going to prove to be," Craig said with certainty. "He's good. He hears things."

"Yeah — and it will be great as long as we don't get mugged on our way out of here."

Kieran didn't hate karaoke. After all, she lived over a karaoke bar. Her brothers could be hysterical at it. Declan tended to be a listener, sitting in a room with an arm around Mary Kathleen. Kevin — naturally, the actor — and Danny — the tour guide, a total performer in his own right — could be very funny. They liked to sing "Barbie Girl" by Aqua, except that neither Kevin nor Danny would sing the part of "Barbie" and as they played it up, even stone-cold sober, people in the room wound up laughing. They also did a wonderfully theatrical rendition of "Purple Rain" by Prince, with Danny falling on his knees to slide across the room, given the space.

Lee waited until Kieran's boat of delicious fresh fish had been delivered and consumed, and then she heard him announce the two of them. He wanted to do Kid Rock and Sheryl Crow; that was fine. She knew the song. And there was no way to grow up Irish American — owning an Irish pub, no less — without being coerced or bullied into singing here and there. The song wasn't funny, but she hoped she did Sheryl Crow some justice.

And, as Lee had suggested, it was an icebreaker.

A couple people complimented her after her performance. One woman walked up to her, grinning.

"That was pretty cool — wouldn't have imagined it! A criminal psychologist, belting away!"

Kieran must have made some kind of a movement or sound of surprise. The young woman quickly went on.

"Sorry, sorry! You probably don't remember me. You worked with a young woman I was helping a few years ago — the husband was a monster. She needed therapy. You were wonderful with her."

"That's great to hear," Kieran noted.

"This place is fun. You know the guys who own it, I take it? It's my first time in the neighborhood."

She offered Kieran a hand, and Kieran took it. "I'm Esperanza Rodriguez."

"Nice to meet you again," Kieran said. "Esperanza — that's a pretty name."

"Thanks. My grandfather is Colombian. But he married a Frenchwoman. She was a huge Victor Hugo fan, but in my family, no one remembers names properly, and that's how it came out by the time my mom named me."

Kieran laughed softly. "French and Colombian is an interesting combination."

"And Dad was from here in New York, but his dad was Puerto Rican and his grandmother was from Mississippi. I'm a big mix, I guess. But it works out well for me."

"How's that?"

"I'm an immigration officer," Esperanza said. "I speak three languages and bits of others. I understand the experience so I'm good with people — and with picking out liars."

Something inside Kieran seemed to go *ting.*

"Immigration. How interesting. And with your background, it does sound perfect. So what's the buzz these days?"

"The same and not the same — as always," Esperanza said. "There's constantly a new wave. Though, this is interesting at the moment, the tide from Central and South America is slowing. By the middle of the century, census reports show that the largest group of immigrants will be Asian. Of course, we're talking about places that have massive populations in their homelands. That affects the statistics."

"And what about undocumented immigration?"

"Inevitable. And sometimes people with good intentions are scammed. I have a friend who came in from Nicaragua when she was a child. Her mother was escaping some horrible circumstances and paid every penny she had to someone to get her legally into the States. The man got them into

123

Texas — and dumped them. She worked two jobs for years to get a proper immigration attorney and make herself and her children legal. So, yes, there are flaws in the system."

"Mail-order brides?" Kieran asked.

"And far worse. 'Nannies' or 'housekeepers' who basically become slave labor, many of them abused."

"Have you heard anything about women being used as surrogate mothers? About babies being taken for sale, or anything like that?"

"You're talking about the incident the other day in Midtown, right?"

"Indirectly. It's . . . heartbreaking. That poor woman. She was stabbed and killed in one violent motion in the street — and no one saw anything."

"Terrible, I agree."

"I can't help but think it has to do with illegal immigration."

"Maybe."

"But you haven't heard anything?"

"I haven't, but I'll ask around," Esperanza told her. She hesitated. "Sometimes, you know, people who aren't involved but who do know something keep quiet because they're afraid."

"Isn't that often the case with anything,"

Kieran said lightly.

Esperanza produced a card from her bag and handed it to Kieran. It had her name, her title, email and other pertinent business information.

"Thank you," Kieran said. "I'm sorry, I don't have my card. I left my purse — I can write down my phone number for you . . ."

"Oh, it's okay. I think I remember. Are you still with Fuller and Miro?"

"I am. Your memory is amazing."

Esperanza smiled.

They said goodbye.

Lee, grinning with an annoying I-told-you-so expression, swept by her. "See. You must always do karaoke with me when you're at a crossroads in life."

"I'm not actually at a crossroads."

"Ah, but a wise man said that karaoke is good for the soul."

"And which wise man was that?"

"I consider myself a very wise man."

She laughed, shook her head, and asked for her bill. He wouldn't give her one.

She gave up and headed out and back up to her apartment. She wondered if she would learn anything from Esperanza Rodriguez. At the least, she now had two contacts on her own, Sister Teresa and Esperanza Rodriguez. And she knew the woman with Child Services.

Kieran wanted to see the baby. Little Baby Doe. She wasn't sure why; there was just something about that little girl. Maybe it was because Kieran had been trusted with the baby when her life might have been threatened.

She could just ask Craig.

No. She didn't want Craig worrying about her and thinking that she was getting too personally involved.

She'd deal with it in the morning. She very badly wanted him working the case, wanted to know what was going on.

But she wasn't obsessing.

Was she?

If so, she couldn't help it.

Craig thought Kieran was an amazing woman. Spectacular in so many ways.

She was always a sensual lover, her very smile something erotic enough to create an instant burst of heat within him. They had been together awhile now, and somehow, it was always fresh and exciting.

That night, however, she seemed on fire.

When he first arrived at the apartment, he thought that she was sleeping. And he meant to leave her undisturbed.

But she turned to him in the darkness,

arms outstretched. When he moved to her, she curled against him, as sleek as a cat. Simply moving her body against his, she could awaken every ounce of desire within him into an ache, an agony and finally ecstasy.

Her lips, teeth and tongue over his body were magic. She had a gift for a light touch mixed with a rougher brush of lips and tongue that was completely delicious, and a way of moving the length of her that was vibrant and wicked.

Tonight, she teased, they laughed, they grew passionate. Afterward, they lay tangled together.

It was incredibly late when he murmured, "And I thought you'd be distracted."

"Me? About what?" Her whisper was nearly a kiss.

"The case."

"Oh. No. You're working it, and I know you'll tell me when you find something, right?"

"Of course."

"So?"

"So?"

"What can you tell me?"

"Kieran." He rolled her over and looked down at her in the dim illumination seeping in from the hallway light. "I'm looking into it, I swear. We've got some contacts kind of in the underbelly of the city — they're investigating."

"You won't stop just because it's a weekend?"

"Of course not."

"Oh, I just remembered — I told one of the nuns I met that I'd help her again tomorrow."

"You're going to help a nun?" he asked skeptically.

"You don't believe I'd help a nun?" She was definitely indignant.

"No, no. I just . . ."

"I didn't realize what Mary Kathleen's volunteering was about before. It's pretty amazing."

"You know you need time off, too. Time to breathe. Kieran, it's barely been a day since that woman was killed."

"Forty-eight hours means a lot, right? At least they say so on television."

"It means a lot, but not everything," he said quietly. "You've been working with Fuller and Miro a long time — you've seen that justice can take years."

"Justice, yes. But this killer . . . he has to be caught!" she said passionately.

"Hmm."

"What?"

"And I thought you had just been missing me!" he teased her.

Even in the shadows, he knew that she blushed.

"I will leave it all alone and just dish out soup with my new nun friend, okay?"

"Gotcha," he said, and then he added seriously, "Kieran, I won't let it go."

"I know," she said. She curled up against his chest.

Eventually, he felt her ease beside him, asleep at last.

Then he allowed himself to drift off, as well.

CHAPTER SIX

"Well, as I'm sure you're aware, we can narrow down DNA to a certain extent," Dr. Andrews said. "A DNA profile can take weeks to be processed — often because of backlogs in the system, but not just that. Obviously, it is imperative that all instruments and lab equipment be maintained in excellent condition. Then generally, the process involves finding the sample or samples of human material to be tested, ascertaining that they are separate and that the exact sample itself is not complicated by other factors. Just to get started, at the best of times it requires about twenty-four hours' worth of careful and tedious laboratory work, and, usually nearly fifty-four hours. It can be days and maybe weeks or months on some cases because of the massive accumulation of work. You need to have the facilities to do all this and the technicians who have been trained to prepare and find results."

It was Sunday morning, but Mike and Craig were back in the morgue.

The body of their Jane Doe lay before them. Andrews had a look on his face that clearly displayed the fact that they should understand — and be excited by — every word that he was saying.

"DNA — amazing," Craig said enthusiastically, elbowing Mike. "The amount of cases it has solved — the amazing way it has helped not just in court, but on the streets. Not just helping to find the guilty, but showing us just as clearly who was innocent of a charge."

"Not to mention telling curious people in America that they should be wearing kilts instead of lederhosen," Andrews said, shaking his head. "The technology of DNA can be complex, but in this case, at the very least — and for whatever good it may do you — I've been able to find out exactly where this woman came from originally."

"Exactly? I didn't realize that markers could be so exact. I thought it was a broad strokes kind of thing." Mike paused. "Okay, I know nothing. Just what I've seen in commercials for various ancestral DNA testing companies," he added.

"Yes, because when we, mankind, began

131

to move about in prehistoric times, country borders weren't what they are today. As we all know, many of them have changed even during our lifetimes. But what can be done is narrowing it down to certain geographic areas," Andrews explained.

"And are you planning to share the info about Jane Doe here with us?" Craig asked, his tone light.

Luckily, Andrews grinned. "So this poor woman hailed from Transylvania."

"Transylvania? As in, vampires? That Transylvania?"

"You've done more than just a country," Craig said curiously. "That's a specific section of a country."

Andrews nodded. "I'm good, right?"

"You're good."

"She does come from a country filled with lore and superstition, though whether that will help you any, I don't know. Transylvanians are not vampires. Vampires are myth and legend and lore, helped along by novels such as *Varney the Vampire,* created by James Malcolm Rymer and Thomas Peckett Prest, and first published as a series of pamphlets between 1845 and 1847, and then published in book form in 1847 as a penny dreadful. Bram Stoker went on to perpetuate the legend with his 1897 novel,

Dracula. Actually, 1897 was a big year for vampires — artist Philip Burne-Jones unveiled his painting *The Vampire,* displaying an evil and yet seductive woman over the prone body of a man. Others, like Rudyard Kipling —"

"You missed your calling!" Mike interrupted. "Doc, you should have been an English professor," he added.

Craig shook his head. "We didn't think she was a vampire, sir. She was a victim. Romania is a beautiful country. The thing is, Dr. Andrews — how do you know? How can you know so specifically where she came from?"

"Ah-ha! You law enforcers tease and taunt me cruelly," Andrews said. "The fact that I am fascinated by world culture has given me what you need. I am — and God knows why, with what I do daily — a fan of myth and legend and even horror novels. In that vein, of course, I find many countries especially interesting. Romania happens to be one. We have a tendency to think of ourselves as the best educated, the most advanced population in the world. Well, we are ego prone."

Mike looked at Craig a little helplessly.

Craig smiled. "Okay, so the Romanians are up on us in some kind of science?"

"Not exactly. But they — like *many* countries — have excellent scientists and doctors, who have specific ways of doing things. Gentlemen, with this woman — voilà — her teeth. She had some dental work done, probably at least thirty years ago, that wasn't just specific to Romania, but to Transylvania. Once her initial DNA results had narrowed my search down to the rather broad spectrum of *Eastern European,* I went through my resources to find a more exact location."

"Phenomenal," Mike said.

"An incredible help, thank you," Craig told him.

"My pleasure. I put a call in for Detective Kendall. I guess he takes his Sundays off," Andrews said.

"Go figure," Mike said drily, giving Craig an evil glare.

"Yep, go figure," Craig agreed.

They thanked Dr. Andrews and left. When they were out of the morgue, Mike turned to Craig and said, "He couldn't have done that with a phone call?"

"Maybe MEs get lonely and need some appreciation for their work."

Mike made a grunting sound. "Yeah, he wants to feel a part of the footwork. Still — Detective Kendall will just call him and get the info in two minutes. We're the ones who probably have the ongoing problem."

"The ongoing problem — what's that?" Craig asked.

"He likes you. Andrews really likes you." Mike sighed. "As if we don't already spend enough time at the morgue."

Mary Kathleen was needed at the pub, so Kieran was solo at the soup kitchen. Kieran wasn't worried — she was accustomed to doing things on her own, even if in situations like this, it was always more fun to be with a friend.

She had, however, acquired a number of friends the last time she'd worked there.

The chefs, cooks and people working in the kitchen were great; the volunteers on the soup line were equally nice.

She'd arrived at the soup kitchen at 10:00 a.m. Manual labor didn't bother her a bit. Once when they'd been kids, one of her brothers had complained about helping unload supply boxes, and their father had reminded him to thank God that he was *capable* of moving boxes. Health and wellness were some of the most precious gifts in life and were to be cherished. Since her dad had said those words, she'd been happy to pick up any box. There were people in wheelchairs or otherwise disabled who could not.

By 11:00 a.m., she was on the line.

As guests came through, some people were talkative. She saw an older man again whom she'd seen the other day; he was excited and ready to talk to her. He'd come from the Gaza Strip; he spoke fluent Arabic and fluent Hebrew. He'd been hired the day before as a tutor for a businessman in the garment district. Kieran told him how happy for him she was. He assured her that he was on his way. He was going to become a citizen of America — in his opinion, the greatest country on earth.

On a break, Kieran spoke with a major-league attorney with a large maritime firm in New York; on the side, he worked with immigrants pro bono. Andy was in his early thirties and good-looking, and the younger women in the soup kitchen flocked to him.

"My father was a rich man when I was born — a high-priced criminal attorney," Andy told her. "My mom was a Polish immigrant, and the way for her and members of her family wasn't at all easy. That's why I do this."

"People love you," Kieran assured him.

He flashed her a smile. "Yeah, I like that part, too. Doesn't always matter what kind of an attorney you are — people have a tendency to think of us as walking sharks. Not that maritime law tends to be so terrible, but . . . anyway, I'm happy to be here. My pro bono clients all know that I won't take them for everything they have — and that every step I take will be within the law. Having had a family member who lived the experience, it just means a little more."

"I understand," Kieran told him. She realized that no member of her family had ever had a problem when immigrating — but then, the Finnegans had always been helped along, sponsored and supported by others already in the States.

By 1:00 p.m., she was wondering if Sister Teresa wasn't one of the most cunning nuns out there, luring her to work with the promise of information. She acknowledged Kieran with a small nod and knowing smile, but didn't say anything else.

But Kieran didn't mind being of service. She enjoyed interacting with the people who came through.

Some were lonely. Or they came in couples, or sometimes in families.

Going through a rough patch or battling homelessness could happen to anyone.

One girl let Kieran practice Spanish on her.

A man complimented her — her French accent wasn't entirely *horrible.*

People came and went.

But no shy girl. No one with anything to say about a murdered woman and a beautiful infant.

It was nearly 2:00 p.m. when Sister Teresa — while chiding a man for not speaking up that he'd missed out on a great piece of cheese bread — stopped mid-rant and elbowed Kieran in the ribs. "Eleven o'clock," she announced, as if they were in the military. "Yes, over there. Somebody, please give this good man a piece of Chef Rosello's cheese bread."

Kieran looked across the large central room, trying to determine just where eleven o'clock to Sister Teresa might be.

She thought she honed in on the right person.

The woman was tiny — perhaps five feet even and ninety pounds. Her hair wasn't just blond, but rather like a soft and shimmering platinum. Her face was lovely, a little gamine face with wide cheekbones, a pursed red bow for lips and giant eyes. She was chatting with another woman, and yet it seemed that she looked around nervously as she did so.

She suddenly looked directly at Kieran, staring.

And then she turned and walked away — toward the rear exit of the facility. Kieran was holding a soup ladle. She wasn't sure just how rude and uncouth it would be to drop the ladle and take off after the stranger.

The petite blonde paused at the exit. She stared pointedly at Kieran again.

At her side, Kieran felt Sister Teresa reach for her ladle. "What? Did you need an engraved invitation? Go on. I've got this. She's the one you want to talk to. And she's also the one who was here with a very pregnant woman . . . I'd say that was just about four or five months ago. Get going. She'll be out of here — afraid of who else may follow her."

Kieran released the ladle without a word.

The young woman was out the door.

Kieran ripped off her apron and followed just as quickly as she could.

Detective Lance Kendall arrived at the FBI offices almost at the same time that Mike and Craig made it back from the downtown morgue.

Craig was pleased to see that he was with McBride, a detective he had worked with on the case when he'd first met Kieran.

Kieran would be happy.

"McBride," he said, and Mike echoed his enthusiasm.

"Yeah, my fed friends, it's me. Lance was told he had to partner up on this. He asked our lieutenant about me, and I said, those feds are a pain in the ass, but, hey, I know how to work with them. Sure, use me!"

"It's good to see you — seriously," Craig told him, and he looked over at Lance Kendall.

Kendall shrugged. "I thought you guys might like me better if I pulled in an old friend."

"I liked you just fine," Mike said. "My partner here, Frasier — he's an ass sometimes."

"Kieran was involved," McBride said, and Craig nodded.

"Egan got us a conference room. Let's head up," Craig said.

In the office, a large board held the information they had acquired thus far: pictures of the dead woman, and of the baby. Beneath those, the police report from the responding officer, and then the notes Lance Kendall had taken.

There were four folders at seats around the table — each was filled with information on known criminal activities involving immigration, both legal and illegal.

Mike droned out loud about a few of the investigations that the NYC office of the FBI had handled.

Twenty women from mainland Mexico, smuggled across the border in a meat truck, intending to work in an underground sweatshop for a clothing manufacturer.

A Russian bride, basically sold into sexual slavery.

A Latvian woman rescued — along with many others — from a "gentlemen's" club.

An Eastern European cartel broken; the women brought in had not just been intended for use in high-priced brothels — they'd been used as mules and carried in bags of cocaine. *Swallowed* so that they wouldn't be caught with it on them.

And there were more.

Despite any politics from 1776 on, the American dream remained strong.

"Because no matter what, they believe they'll be better off here than in the poverty and oppression they face elsewhere," Craig murmured. He was studying his folder. "Here!" he said, looking up at the others. "In 2012, the Brooklyn police arrested a man named Michel Marcus. He was suspected of being a broker in an illegal adoption operation. A woman was found bleeding to death in an alley in the Vinegar Hill area of Brooklyn. She named Marcus and whispered *Baggatella* — which turned out to be the name of a restaurant — before dying. The medical examiner found that she had given birth just hours before and her death was caused by a severe hemorrhage. Had she just been in a hospital, it would have been stopped in time. The baby was never found, but . . ." He paused and looked up at the others. "Michel Marcus was found, right where the woman said — in the restaurant."

"What happened to Marcus? He couldn't have been working alone," McBride asked.

"Right — but nothing happened. Because he killed himself in his cell before ever going to trial," Craig told them. "Police at the time staked out the restaurant, searched, questioned and kept a task force going for a year. They never found another thing — not another baby, nothing. And because legal adoptions are so protected, it can be a very difficult maneuver to look for illegal adoptions."

"It's something," Kendall said.

"It's more than anything else," Mike agreed.

"Hell, this has to be it. Michel Marcus couldn't have been acting alone. That poor woman escaped the house, apartment, abandoned warehouse — wherever she gave birth — in order to stop them. I'm sure she hoped to get her baby back. I doubt if she intended to die, but maybe she was willing to die to stop them."

"According to the records, though," Mike said, flipping through his folder, "she only ever gave one name — that of Michel Marcus — and one place, the restaurant. The cops never even knew the name of the deceased woman — no one came forward to claim her body and no one ever found the baby."

"The restaurant looks like it's along the lines of a diner — breakfast, lunch and dinner. A pancake place," Mike said.

Craig stood. "How should we do this? McBride, Kendall? You want to try the restaurant? We'll talk to the cops who worked the case before. That way it's the FBI and not Major Crimes asking if they missed something."

"Oh, great — the feds horning in!" McBride said. "But, yeah, let's start that way. We can swoop in as sympathetic saviors if you come off as asses!" He grinned and turned to Kendall. "Guess we're all heading on out to Brooklyn."

"I'll let Egan know what we're doing,"

Craig said.

"Text him. The man isn't a fool — it's Sunday, so he's not in his office. I did get a message from him about keeping in touch," Mike said.

"We'll all keep in touch," McBride said grimly. "You want a ride over?"

"We'll take our own transport — we may be moving around," Craig said.

Kendall and McBride preceded them out of the office.

Mike collected the folders and told Craig, "Got another message from Egan, too."

"Yeah?"

"He said to watch you — personal involvements can be dangerous."

"We're just going to see some cops. Nothing dangerous about that," Craig assured him.

"I think he might have been referring to *you* being dangerous," Mike said. "So watch the pounding on the guys, huh?"

"I'll be as good as gold," Craig promised.

"Oh, yeah. That's a long shot. Just don't be an asshole, okay?"

Kieran rushed to the back entrance — if it could be called rushing. She wove through the crowded room, excusing herself as she pushed by.

When she reached the door, the young woman was gone. For a moment Kieran stood there, frustrated.

And then she thought she saw the woman heading toward Church Street. She raced after her.

She reached the end of the block and paused, inhaling hard to catch her breath. Again, she thought she saw the woman just turning a corner up ahead, except that it seemed the corner was in the middle of the block, and when Kieran reached it, she realized that the young woman had disappeared down an alley.

She hesitated.

It was broad daylight, of course. The alley wasn't shadowed — there was no reason to believe that dark characters might be lurking there.

But Kieran knew that she needed to be careful. In this case, a woman had been murdered — *in broad daylight in the midst of a crowd.*

Only an idiot would go down that alley.

Kieran liked to think she wasn't an idiot.

She had a true feeling — gut intuition — that she was being approached because someone wanted help. They didn't plan to hurt her.

They needed her to help them.

Of course, *Craig* would kill her. Not literally — he'd just be disgusted with her lack of common sense and restraint. But she couldn't worry about that now.

She stepped into the alley.

The old buildings were close together. One was an office building that had probably been erected in the 1890s. The one on the other side had been a residence of some kind. It had been built circa the Civil War, she thought, either right before or right after.

A true treasure — a beautiful little building. Overtaken now by T-shirt shops and possibly apartments, it had a Victorian facade that was absolutely charming and probably seldom noticed.

She came to the end of the alley; four buildings backed onto the narrow space, creating a kind of courtyard. Fire escapes ran down the walls, but there was only one other way out — another alley across the way. A large group of trash and recycling containers were shoved together at odd angles, creating some patches where the homeless had created little houses, lining the hard ground with cardboard boxes and newspapers.

As Kieran blinked against a sudden flare of the sun, she saw that the petite blonde woman was standing at the entrance to the other alleyway.

Right in front of her, there was another woman: taller, about five-eight, and perhaps twenty-five years old. Her hair was a true flaming red — a color Kieran had seldom seen in anyone who wasn't Irish or of Irish descent. Or, of course, who had bought the color in a box.

She frowned, not thinking that she needed to be afraid in any way, and yet she knew that she had been led to this woman.

"Are you Kieran Finnegan?" the woman said.

Irish. By the inflection of her voice, she was definitely Irish.

"Yes," Kieran said softly. "And you are?"

"Riley McDonnough, Miss Finnegan. How do you do?" She extended her arms, indicating the trash containers and the makeshift cardboard beds on the ground. "Welcome to my home."

Kieran hesitated before speaking.

People sometimes came to Finnegan's from the mother country when they were looking for jobs. Declan was always willing to help — legally. If this woman just needed work . . .

She swallowed, not wanting to be disappointed. It wasn't that she — and her family — didn't want to help newcomers. That was how Declan had met — and fallen in love with — Mary Kathleen.

But this wouldn't bring her any closer to figuring out who the beautiful baby belonged to.

"You know who I am. You must know, then, that if you just came to Finnegan's —"

"Oh, no, no. It's not like that. I am Irish, of course — I suppose you've noticed?" Riley McDonnough said, her tone dry. It was impossible not to notice. She had a beautiful brogue.

"Yes, well . . . If you came to the pub — even as an illegal — we could set things in motion to help you."

"I'm illegal, but, trust me, there are people out there looking for me, and I would not bring them to your pub."

Kieran shook her head. "Okay, please explain. I admit to being at a complete loss."

The tiny blonde woman watching the back alley said something — she spoke in Russian, Kieran thought, recognizing the sound of the language, but not the words.

Riley, however, apparently spoke Russian, as well. She replied in kind.

"Tanya is nervous and wants me to get to the point," Riley said.

"Yes, which is . . . ?"

"We knew her," Riley said, and she sounded as if she was choking.

"Knew who?"

"Her name was Alexandra Callas. She was a dear friend. She cared. She tried so hard to help. We tried to get her to leave. She just wouldn't . . . There were others, you see?"

"No — I don't see. Exactly what are you telling me?"

"The woman who came to you, Miss Finnegan," Riley announced, her brogue growing exceptionally strong. "The poor woman murdered with a knife in her back, right there on the streets of New York. We knew her — she was our friend. And she believed in you!"

David Beard had been the lead detective on the case when Michel Marcus had been arrested and later died by his own hand in jail.

Beard was about six foot even with close-cropped dark hair, a square man with big shoulders and rough hands — the kind of guy Mike referred to as an "in the trenches" kind of cop. Beard would never wait for backup, Craig thought — he'd plow right in.

The man agreed easily enough to meet

with Mike and Craig; he was off duty and hanging out at a neighborhood pool hall that was frequented by cops.

Sitting with the two agents, he told them about a civilian being horrified when they'd seen the young woman bleeding to death in an alley — she'd been found by the early morning employee of a diner who had come out to dump trash. He told them that it had all seemed too easy — before dying, the victim had given them a name.

They'd gotten the guy, all right.

And then Marcus had died without saying a word against another soul.

"I can't begin to tell you how many man-hours went into the hunt. There was a baby somewhere — we were all passionate. We owed it to the victim to find that baby. You should have heard about it on the news." Beard shook his head and leaned forward on the table; he had arms like an old-time sailor, full muscles straining at his shirt.

"We probably did," Mike said, a long breath escaping him. "But whatever we were into at the time was probably pretty heavy, too."

"Probably," David Beard said. He had a haggard face, worn from years on the job, but a good smile when he chose to use it. At the moment, he was reflective. "We had to give up. We had nothing but dead ends. Every officer in Brooklyn had been apprised of the case, and nothing. We got nothing."

"We're just wondering if you ever took the angle that this woman was illegal, or a refugee, if she'd been smuggled in. We have to keep pursuing that now, since it's the only lead we've got."

"It's very possible," said Beard. "When you have people willing to come here outside the law, they can end up on the wrong side of everything. It isn't easy getting refugee status."

One of the guys playing pool had apparently overheard them. Holding his stick while his opponent played, he joined in, saying, "The refugee thing is ongoing. You know, some of the things people are escaping . . . we can't even picture. Dictators — including guys we almost never hear about. Or Islam Karimov from Uzbekistan. He's taken all kinds of prisoners, given them no trial and executed them. There's even sound evidence that he *boiled* two prisoners alive. The Gambia's leader has been known to *decapitate* gay citizens. Eritrea's leader — total dictator — known for torturing his prisoners. Hey, there's a long list out there. People have to come to the States. They're desperate."

"And because they're desperate," David Beard continued, "they are far too often victims. There are those out there — some who even came from that kind of misery themselves — ready to take advantage of them."

The waiting pool player added, "We knew that Michel Marcus was just the sprout of the plant on the surface — that there was a system somewhere going really deep. Any of us will gladly help at any time, let me say that. Oh, I'm Holmes, by the way. Detective Holmes. Believe that? It's my real name. Randy Holmes."

"Guys, meet my new partner," David Beard explained. "My previous partner — who I worked with before, on the Marcus case — is retired now. Moved to Arizona. Or somewhere hot. Wherever. Cases like this — still gnawing at my insides — make me want to follow in his footsteps fast."

Craig glanced over at Mike. It wouldn't be easy to get in touch with Beard's old partner and get a second opinion or memory on anything that had happened.

"We all knew there was much more to it. And we were close," Randy Holmes said, nodding grimly. "I wasn't a detective yet, but I was with the officers on the ground. We came to a building — a warehouse —

right smack on the main street of the Vinegar Hill district, right near where they found the victim. They got a search warrant through some blood found on the door. When we opened it up, though, the place was as clean as a sterile chamber."

"Who did it belong to?" Craig asked.

"Absentee owner, hadn't been in the States in two years. He inherited the property from his family, apparently. Wealthy guy."

"Absentee owner . . . a foreigner? Does he have a name?" Craig asked.

Beard sniffed loudly. "Foreign? Hell, no. The guy's name is Smith. James . . . Jim Smith," David Beard said. "American as apple pie, so it sounded — or as American as any of us can be. Just rich as Midas. Anyway, there was nothing found — nothing whatsoever. We looked like idiots. His attorney said that his rights had been violated. I'm telling you, though, there was something going on with that place."

"What is it now? Still an empty warehouse?" Mike asked.

"Hey, Holmes!" another pool player shouted. "Your shot!"

"Excuse me," Holmes said.

They watched him walk over to the table. He was emotional, worked up from the memory he was sharing, but it seemed to add to his expertise. He made his shot. Balls — the right balls, they noted — flew across the table and into the pockets.

"You play?" Mike asked Craig. "I've never seen you play."

"I'm no shark," Craig said. He glanced at Mike and shrugged. "Then again, I don't entirely suck, either."

"Don't worry — he'll clean up the table and come back," Beard said. "This whole thing is really getting to him. Don't get me wrong, he's a really good cop. But, as they say sometimes with the guys who don't have a people way about them, Homicide is really a good place for him. The victims can't give him their opinions on the world."

"He has hot opinions, huh?" Mike asked.

"Don't we all?" Beard asked quietly. There was silence for a minute, and then he said, "Poor kid forgets sometimes that I was lead on it and that it hurt like a son of a gun when we kept coming up against stone walls. It was my case, yeah, but it belonged to every cop in Brooklyn, too, really. We hated it — really hated it — that we couldn't solve that poor woman's murder. And that someone did it almost as easily as swatting at a fly and walked away free."

Observing the pool game, Beard contin-ued.

"We kept an eye on the warehouse — all of us — for a long time. It was used once as a staging house for a parade. And once there were a pack of sailboats stored for a while for a regatta. Apparently, Mr. Smith rents it out for occasions that intrigue him. Kind of disgusting, really," Detective Beard said. "The kind of money you'd need to own a hunk of property like that in Brooklyn *and leave it empty half the time.* But the powers that be have kept at it. We tried the old catch-him-on-taxes thing, too. Jim Smith keeps his nose clean — and he stays out of the country and hires exceptional attor-neys."

They spoke for a while longer; Beard promised to have the complete files and anything that he could add sent to their of-fice in Manhattan.

Holmes had cleaned up the pool table.

He headed back over, grabbing Mike and Craig before they could leave.

"You call us and let us know if you need us, day or night," Detective Holmes said passionately. He handed Craig a card. "I mean it." He shrugged suddenly, and his tone changed. "I'm one of those lucky guys who knows his family history. Mine came over right around 1900, and my great-granny was a hooker. Most of them died by the time they were forty. Anyway, people using other people and squeezing the life out of them? Pisses me off. And using desperate women for God knows what, and taking their babies? Maybe so that their infants can be sold? Even worse."

"Some of those kids wind up in rich households, though," Beard said. "Maybe better off than they would have been."

Craig thought Holmes was going to explode.

"Adoption is great. When it's legal. And when the birth mother really intends for the kid to be adopted — not when a baby has practically been ripped from her womb."

"Thank you both," Craig said. He looked at Mike, and Mike widened his eyes before nodding.

Yes, let's get out of here before those two wind up in a full-blown fight!

Out on the street, Mike asked, "You want to go check out the restaurant? See if they missed something? Not that those guys aren't fully competent, but I know you."

"Sure. I want to see the restaurant," Craig said. "Maybe we can join McBride and Kendall for meat loaf. But, first . . ."

Mike groaned.

"Yep, it's a trip to Vinegar Hill — to stare at a warehouse."

"Hopefully we can do more than stare at it."

"Craig, we can't get anything thrown out in court on this."

"Me? You know me. I'd never dream of doing anything except by the book," Craig said.

Mike groaned again.

"What?" Craig demanded.

"You're by the book as long as you think you could possibly be caught!"

"The law is a marvelous tool — one just has to be careful how one uses it," Craig said. "Let's go. I don't care how squeaky clean this Jim Smith appears to be. There's something up with him, and with that warehouse. We just have to figure out what."

CHAPTER SEVEN

"I'm so confused. The woman — Alexandra Callas — who came to me, was a friend of yours. Her English barely had an accent. I couldn't even begin to tell where she came from. She had to have been in the United States for some time. Was she . . . was she with some kind of an agency? They tried to identify her with her fingerprints, but —"

"Illegal," Riley told her.

"But . . ."

Riley lifted a hand and looked over at the pretty young Russian woman, Tanya, who was still guarding the narrow alleyway.

The woman made an okay sign with her fingers and thumb, showing Riley that they were still safe.

"Your friend here — is she Russian? How did you all come to be together? How the hell did you learn Russian so quickly?"

"Yes, Tanya is Russian. She is Tanya Petrofskya," Riley said. "We met once we came to the States. But that's all part of the same story."

"About the murdered woman," Kieran said.

"Alexandra Callas," Riley said softly. "That was her name. She came to the United States as a child — her parents spent a great deal of money to escape the oppression of her country at the time. Her mother, she told me, dreamed of being a ballerina. Her father had been arrested — they heard he died in prison. How, they never knew. Her mother trusted a man who took all their money when they reached America, and so they went into hiding. Alexandra was able to go to school — her mother just kept moving and moving and moving. And when her mother died, Alexandra took over her mother's jobs, cleaning toilets. She met a man who promised he was going to help her gain her legal status here. He had a job for her — a great job for her. Caring for infants."

"Oh!" Kieran suddenly felt the need to sit.

There were no chairs. She forced herself to stand still.

"The man — the man who killed her? A man who is forcing illegal immigrants to give up their infants — and then selling them illegally?"

Riley nodded. "I figured you'd be quick," she said drily.

"Riley, I can help you. I can help you and Tanya. And anyone else. I don't know how Alexandra Callas knew to come to me — maybe she saw something in the paper."

"Yes, possibly."

"Because that's how you know me?"

"No — I wasn't in the country when you saved that girl in the subway, when your name was everywhere. I know because others explained to me why Alexandra might have been downtown when she was murdered."

"Were you with her when . . . when she took the baby?" Kieran asked.

Riley shook her head. She whispered. Her brogue was heavy, and it took even Kieran a minute to understand. "We've been on the run, don't ye ken? And then . . . we heard. We saw the news."

"You're hiding. You ran away. From where?" Kieran asked.

Riley shook her head. She had seemed so brave, but there was suddenly a look of terror in her eyes. "I don't know, I . . . We ran . . . we ran and we ran . . . there was a truck . . . we hopped in. We slept in a different alley. We heard about . . . about the kitchen, and we were hungry and desperate.

And someone there pointed out who you were."

Too many people knew who she was!

"Okay, you ran. But why didn't you go to the police?"

"We can't just go to the police."

"The police will protect you."

"Really? No, years ago, a friend was on her way to the police. She never made it. *They* have eyes everywhere. He is everywhere. That's how he . . . how he killed Alexandra."

"Who is *he*?" Kieran asked.

"He calls himself 'the King.' Sometimes, when he is feeling cruel, we have to call him 'Your Majesty.' He . . ." She hesitated. "You come here, and he owns you, and that's the way that it is. He has other enforcers, of course. And drugs. They like to get girls addicted. They're obedient and malleable that way. And there are others like Alexandra who stay, who help."

"What about the baby? Does that precious child belong to either of you?"

Riley shook her head. "No — he has her. The mother. Yulia Decebel. She is Romanian. The man who calls himself the King has her, and we're so afraid. She wants the baby, of course — it is her baby. But no one will help her, or go near the baby now.

161

Because the entire operation could explode if they're caught going after that baby, do you see? I know that Yulia must be pretending to our handlers that she has just let it go. Because he will be watching her, and he will kill her if she tries to escape. Another woman died, you see, escaping. The King — he sees everything, he finds everyone. Because others work for him, and then sometimes, they die, too. He sees everything."

"We're in an alley in Lower Manhattan," Kieran said flatly. "He's not here. You didn't go to the police, and I understand your fear. But these people really can't be everywhere. The police will protect you. And if not the police, then the FBI. I'm dating an FBI agent," she explained. "Please, honest to God, I understand your fear of being killed, but —"

"Not just of dying, lass. It wouldn't be so bad for me, but for Tanya . . . she's terrified of being deported. She can't go back. She'd be arrested. She fought with an officer — it's a long story. She'd go to prison. And worse."

"Okay, but I have people as friends who can see to it that nothing bad happens to you. First, you'll be protected because we protect people from crime in this country.

Plus, you'll be helping with an investigation, which means everyone will want to help you all the more. There is legal entry to this country — we can make it happen. My family will help. Special Agents Craig Frasier and Mike Dalton and even their boss, Richard Egan, will help. And the cops. Please, let me help you! Let me call Craig. Let me call him right now."

Tanya suddenly came rushing over to Riley. She spoke in rapid Russian, leaving Kieran unable to understand a single word.

"We have to go," Riley said.

"No, no, you can't go —"

"You go, too! Do you want a knife in your back?" Riley demanded.

"Come with me. I'll stand up with you —"

"Against them? Listen to me, quickly, comprehend," Riley snapped. "Wait for the nun. She'll contact you. Now get the hell out of here!"

Tanya was grasping desperately at Riley's hand. Riley let the young Russian woman pull her hard toward the other alley, back the way Kieran had come from.

They were almost out of the alley when Riley shouted back to Kieran again. "Run!"

It was daylight, a bright day. A beautiful spring day with a powder blue sky and bril-

163

liant sun.

And yet it appeared that the largest, darkest shadow suddenly appeared at the top of the alley across the courtyard.

Kieran's heart thudded.

The killer? Killers?

Riley had warned her; she had to go. She was standing in a small, deserted alleyway, and these people had already killed in the midst of a crowd. They wouldn't hesitate to leave her dead among the sad cardboard "houses" and rubbish of the alley.

She turned and ran.

The warehouse in Vinegar Hill was just that — a squat, ugly building with a main entry in the middle of the block and its giant arms reaching out to just about the ends of the block on both sides. Only one quaint old residence ruined the building holding court on all of the address; it was a colonial with a historical marker on it — the kind that made you happy someone had tried to preserve something of the past somewhere along the line.

There was a small gap of space — enough for two slim people to walk abreast — between the walls of the house and the warehouse. The rear of the warehouse backed to a broader alley with broken pavement and bracken coming through what had been — or could still be — a delivery entrance.

Mike and Craig walked around the warehouse several times.

Craig was surprised that the place offered ground-floor windows; peering in through one of the filthy panes in the front, he surmised that the bottom floor had been something of a machine shop. A few of the machines remained.

There were broken windows here and there — no one had cared much for the property in a long time.

"So we think that at one time, our killers were keeping women here? Illegal immigrants, pregnant women among them," Craig said thoughtfully, looking up at the massive building.

"This just doesn't look like a place where anyone could keep anyone else alive," Mike murmured.

"Let's see if they're paying electric and water bills," Craig suggested, starting to reach for his phone.

"I'm on it — calling our number one tech boy," Mike said. He was referring to Marty Kim.

"On a Sunday?" Craig asked.

"It's Marty — he'll answer," Mike assured him.

Marty did. "Hey, Marty! It's Mike Dalton. Yeah, actually, I know you know by the caller ID, but, you know, thought it might be polite to identify myself."

Craig walked up and down the street, studying the building. A young woman — bleeding to death from childbirth, unattended by any physician — had died right by the place.

Something had gone on here.

Absentee owner. Jim Smith. Out of the country — could claim he hadn't been involved in anything. If criminals had used his property, he could say he didn't know. He hadn't been in the States. People break in. Why hadn't the cops been on it?

Craig hurried back to Mike. "Ask Marty to do a thorough search for us on Jim Smith — the guy who owns the property."

"The absentee owner?"

"Yes."

Mike repeated Craig's request to Marty. He listened to Marty's reply and then looked at Craig and said, "He wants you to know that there are probably hundreds of men named Jim Smith."

"He just wants us to appreciate him. I know Marty. He can narrow it down in a matter of seconds — the owner of this building. Talk nice to him. Tell him we owe him dinner."

"We owe him overtime," Mike muttered, but repeated Craig's offer.

Craig walked past the front of the warehouse building while Mike waited on the phone. It was fronted by a storage facility and an office building. Across the street kitty-corner to his left was a gas station; to his right, there was a parking facility.

Few people would be in the office building on a Sunday, he reasoned, but checking with some workers might not be a bad idea.

"The building is under Boswell Management Corporation — they handle all rentals for Jim Smith. Yes, electric and water bills are paid — promptly and on time." Mike spoke a little breathlessly, after chasing to catch up with Craig.

"I want to get into this building," Craig said.

"The cops served a search warrant here. They brought all kinds of personnel and crime scene technicians. They didn't find anything. It's ego to think that we might do better."

"I'm not thinking about doing better," Craig said. "I want to put my mind in the head of whoever is running all this — figure out the real plan, the main plan — or where the hell they went from here."

"I don't see any reason . . ."

"I do. Broken window — the pane there really smashed. We thought we saw someone slipping into the building, maybe hiding out or trespassing."

"Craig, there's nothing going on in there now," Mike said. "We can't lose this one when it gets to the courts."

"Right."

Mike's phone rang. He answered it quickly. "Yeah, yeah, yeah . . . wow. Go figure. We're going to have to work on getting down to the truth on that one. All right. Thanks, Marty. You are a true scholar and gentleman, however that saying goes. And yes, we owe you dinner."

Mike hung up and looked at Craig. "Our Mr. Smith was part of a bank inquiry a few months ago. Apparently, he supposedly arrived in his private jet and headed into his bank to get something out of his vault. One of the employees was disturbed by the way he looked and acted — he was pushy and rude and in a real hurry — but by the time she got her manager, Smith was gone. They reviewed the security footage, but when they tracked him down to verify his appearance at the bank, he was already out of the country, out of contact."

"And where did he go?" Craig asked.

"Cuba. From Cuba, he wrote in and swore that he had been the one to arrive at the bank. Naturally, they wanted him in person, and he was indignant. He's a busy man. He'd be happy to remove all of his business from their bank. Since it was just the assertion of one teller, it was at that point that they all decided to let it go. People studied the surveillance footage, and the man's face, and apparently they came to the conclusion that he was one and the same. The teller was let go — hey, we all know that money talks. Of course, if someone had wanted to pursue it, they would have hit a stone wall."

"Cuba. Getting to find out if the real Jim Smith is there might be difficult. Or impossible. Doesn't mean we can't see that his assets are frozen," Craig said.

"Not going to happen. According to the powers that be, he proved himself real. Call Egan. I'll drive. I want to get on this Jim Smith thing."

"Right."

Craig called Egan.

Then, realizing the time that had gone by, he put through a call to Kieran. Her phone rang and rang. She didn't answer.

Worried, he called the pub.

Mary Kathleen answered. "Ah, hello there, Craig. And how are you doing this fine day?"

"I'm good, Mary Kathleen. Is Kieran there?"

"She's at the soup kitchen."

"Yes, I know she went there, but she's not back yet?"

"I'm not expecting her for maybe another hour. It's wonderful that she's helping, Craig. Just wonderful. They needed me today, but we had a reservation for a group of Shriners coming in, and while Kieran may be an owner, I'm way better on the floor than she is, so I'm grateful she took my place."

"I'm sure she's happy to be doing it," Craig said. He still wished that he could speak with her. "If you see her, have her call me."

"Indeed. Ah, and the roast is especially fine today, my friend! Hope you're coming around when the day is done!"

He assured her that he would. And hoped he'd find Kieran there.

He hung up.

"Buddy," Mike said.

"Yeah?" Craig looked over at his partner.

"She's a very smart, savvy woman who

has handled many a situation brilliantly before," Mike assured him.

Kieran was all those things. That's why he worried. She could have been a detective. She knew people, too. Better than he did sometimes, though he prided himself — silently, of course — on his ability to read lies from the truth.

She really had a lot of intuition and curiosity . . .

Enough to get herself into all kinds of dangerous situations.

There were times when a situation just called for it — a time to run.

Kieran ran.

She burst out of the opposite alleyway, not sure where she wound up at first, but familiar enough with the neighborhood to head straight toward Broadway. Once she reached Broadway, all she had to do was get to Finnegan's.

She turned around to look behind her on the street.

She saw a woman with a stroller, and a man walking along hand-in-hand with a little boy.

A pair of young lovers laughed and teased as they held hands, too, bumping into one another as they walked, pausing for a kiss.

An older woman with a veil on seemed to be headed for church.

No one appeared to be the least bit dangerous.

Was there really a baby in the stroller?

Were the young lovers really lovers — or assassins?

Okay, it was crazy if she was going to start suspecting everyone on the street. For that matter, she'd never be able to go out again. The paranoia had to end.

She forced herself to slow her gait.

There was indeed a baby in the stroller.

The lovers seemed to be in love.

She dashed along the street, panting.

People barely noticed her. It was New York City, after all.

She reached the pub and raced into it, and then closed the door and leaned against it, desperate to regain some of her breath.

She wasn't sure what to do.

Call Craig right away. Tell him.

What if the nun didn't call her? What if she never heard from either of the women again?

Mary Kathleen saw her by the door and hurried over to her. "All done for the day at Soup du Jour? Was it busy? Are you enjoying it?"

"Ah — yes! Very much. Sister Teresa is really something, isn't she?" she asked.

"She is a force of nature, that she is," Mary Kathleen said. "Well, it's at a nice low roar here. The roast is really fine today. Are you hungry?"

Actually, she was starving.

"I am, but I guess I should wait. I assume that Craig will be coming. He isn't here already, is he?"

"No, but he called. Please call him right away. Table eleven needs a check — I've got to be running it over. Call Craig. Now, please! He'll think I forgot to tell you. Well, I did forget to tell you right away, but . . ."

She waved a hand in the air and went on to take table eleven their check.

Kieran whipped out her phone and noticed that she'd missed a call from Craig just a little while earlier. She quickly dialed.

He answered on the first ring and guilt riddled through her. The tone of his voice was filled with worry.

"You okay?" he asked.

"Fine. Absolutely fine," she assured him. She was going to tell him — just maybe not the whole thing. Maybe she would say that Riley and Tanya had run off quickly and she hadn't been able to stop them. That had been true. She certainly didn't have the physical power to tackle both women. But she didn't want to lie to Craig. What she needed was a moment to process what had just happened. Better to tell him in person, anyway.

"I'm hungry, though. I hear this pub has an exceptional roast today. When do you think you're going to get here?"

"Soon, but don't wait for me if you're hungry. Go ahead and get something to eat. Mike will probably come with me. Save us some food, eh?"

"Yep — I'll see we have a couple of servings kept aside," she told him.

"We won't be too long." He hesitated on the other end. "I may have a few things to tell you. I mean, I don't know where we are yet, but I think we're actually on a very old case. Tell you about it when we get there."

"Great. I have some things to tell you, too," she said, and then added quickly, "See you soon."

She hung up before he could reply.

She threaded her way through the tables to the back, eager to reach the kitchen.

In charge in back was Chef Rory O'Bannon, a tall, red-cheeked, white-haired, powerhouse of determination who had arrived in the country about ten years earlier, hailing from County Cork. Kieran's dad had hired Rory; he was like family now.

Working with him were the grill cooks

he'd hired, brothers named Pedro and Javier Marcos, and they hailed from where they considered to be the "very far south of Ireland — Puerto Rico." Pedro and Javier had been there for over five years, and everyone loved the brothers. No, they weren't even a little Irish. Declan thought that the combo was absolutely perfect — it made Finnegan's a truly Irish *American* pub. The cooks kept their customers very happy. Any of the three would happily make a change on a plate for a customer with an allergy, a diet or a simple dislike of something. After all, their menu wasn't for *surgery,* Rory was quick to remind them all. It was quite all right to change things up.

She hurried on into the kitchen and was startled when Rory swept her up in a hug. "Hav'na seen you back here in a wee bit, Kieran, lass. What would you like?"

"Roast, of course!" she told him. "And I need a favor. Craig is coming and bringing Mike. If it looks like we're starting to run out, hold a couple of servings, please."

"A pleasure for the lads. How are they doing on that murdered woman?" Chef asked her. "They must be investigatin', right? Else the lad would be with you on a Sunday, girl, eh?"

"They're working it. We'll find out soon

175

enough how they're doing," Kieran said.

Chef Rory was moving about, fixing her a plate with far too much food. There was no way out of it; she accepted the loaded plate.

Pedro and Javier swept by quickly to give her hugs. They chided her, telling her that she didn't stop in the kitchen often enough, though it was all right. They knew she had work.

It was good to be part-owner of a pub, and she usually loved the camaraderie. But since she was really hungry and needed some space to think about her encounter with Riley and Tanya, she thanked the cooks, swept by the bar to deliver a peck on Declan's cheek and grab a soda, and then headed into the solitary quiet of the back office.

She opened Declan's office computer. She had no plan in mind at the moment — she just had to figure out how she was going to tell Craig everything she knew without sounding as if she had ever put herself in danger. And also wait for Sister Teresa to call her.

She wondered if Sister Teresa knew that she was supposed to be getting in touch with her. Maybe she should finish up and hurry back to the soup kitchen. Kieran didn't actually know the address of Sister

Teresa's convent, though she doubted that it would be difficult to find.

She wondered, too, just how much Sister Teresa knew about Tanya, Riley, the imprisoned Yulia and the poor dead woman, Alexandra.

Kieran decided not to use the computer, but she drew out a notepad and started writing, hurriedly eating with her other hand. She began with the baby being thrust into her arms. She created a picture, with the King as a stick figure, minions beneath him on one side, and his prisoners on the other.

She thought of so many more questions she should have asked.

The King: What did he look like? Did he speak with an accent? Did he have a real business, or was he exclusively a criminal?

She stood up.

She had to see Sister Teresa and find out exactly what, if anything, she knew.

Hurrying out to the dining room, she saw that Mary Kathleen was with Declan at the bar; all seemed quiet and in control for the moment.

She wished that Mary Kathleen wasn't standing next to Declan. There was something about her brother. Maybe it was just that he was the oldest. She found it very hard to lie in front of him.

"Craig is still out working on a Sunday?" Declan asked. "You have him running ragged."

Kieran forced a smile. "Hey, the man chose to be an agent. Anyway, I figure the soup kitchen is closed now, Mary Kathleen, but I'm pretty sure I left my scarf there, and I'm willing to bet that Sister Teresa picked it up for me. Can you tell me where to find her now?"

"She might be at mass, but you can head to the convent. It's within walking distance — for the young and energetic, anyway — not far off Church Street. Here . . ." Mary Kathleen scribbled the address on a cocktail napkin and handed it to Kieran.

"Don't go getting into trouble," Declan warned as she turned to hurry out.

She paused to look back and smile at him reassuringly. "Trouble? I'm headed to a convent. Just how much trouble can I get into?"

"I went to Catholic school, too, remember. You? Tons of it."

She made a face at him.

"Craig should be here soon. Tell him I'll be right back!"

She didn't let him say more. He was already looking at her suspiciously.

She was headed to a convent, for God's sake!

And yet, the minute she was on the street again, she remembered her fear when she'd left the alley.

She remembered just how quickly a man on the street had slammed a knife into the woman's back.

The FBI agents weren't magicians, but there were times when Richard Egan had the power to do things that otherwise might seem impossible.

Craig had wanted the surveillance video from the bank and the contact information for the teller who had been fired.

Her name was Kathy Miller. Craig was pretty sure that the fact that Richard Egan had tracked her down in an hour on a Sunday was proof that the man was as close to a law-enforcing magician as anyone was going to get.

He'd managed to get the footage in question, as well.

Marty Kim had arrived at the NYC offices of the FBI by the time Craig and Mike made it back from Brooklyn. He was already setting up in the one of the conference rooms.

Egan introduced them to the twentysomething former bank teller.

"We think that you might well have been right — and that, I'm afraid, a corporation's eagerness to maintain assets probably hurt you. We're truly sorry — one way or the other. You were certainly trying to do your job," Craig told her.

A large screen was set up and Marty was hooking up the computer. Egan just sat, patiently watching and waiting.

"It turned out to be one of the best things that ever happened to me," Kathy said. She was a pretty brunette, tiny as could be, with huge brown eyes. "I was a gymnast once upon a time. And thanks to being fired, I was desperate. I applied for work as an instructor, and now I get to work with wonderful children who might be our future Olympians."

"That's great to hear!" Mike said.

"Yes, absolutely," Craig agreed.

"Okay, guys," Marty informed them. "Here's the last known picture of Jim Smith — his driver's license renewal, about nine years ago."

The image went up on the screen. Smith had a slender face, pale blue eyes and white hair. His cheekbones allowed for a fair amount of sunken flesh.

"Ghoul," Mike muttered. They all looked

at him. "Well, I mean, honestly, he looks like he could find great work at a Halloween horror park!"

Craig tried to hide a smile.

Egan didn't bother, but he said, "Please. We don't know the real fate of this man. Let's have some dignity here," he protested. "We have a guest," he reminded them.

"He does — he did or he does — look like a ghoul," Kathy said. "That's the thing. He signed up for all his accounts with Benjamin Osterly. Ben retired about four years ago and sadly — he was a great guy — succumbed to cancer just last March. I don't think that anyone else at the bank really remembered Jim Smith, even though he kept a lot of money in the bank and has a box in the vault. I met him because I was Benjamin's assistant at the time. And, yes, it had been years since I had seen him, but, still . . . he was just different!"

Marty shifted the license picture to the left side of the screen. Then, on the right, he played the surveillance video. They watched the man come in, stop at the desk, and enter the vault with a clerk. Next, he was seen leaving. He paused by the door, next to a poster that advertised the way to save for a growing child.

It was difficult to get a real view of the

man's face.

He wore a sweater and a cap, and he kept his head lowered.

He was, however, tall — and gaunt. Yes, someone else who resembled a ghoul.

"You really can't tell," Mike murmured.

"If there was just a full-on face shot, it would help," Marty said. "I've played with it, worked with it — I'm giving it the best I can."

"You see, that's it," Kathy said quietly. "I did see his face. And it just wasn't him. But I wasn't in any position of power and the man who could have helped was . . . well, he's passed away."

"Run it again, please," Craig said.

The men could have been the same.

But there was just something . . .

And when Craig saw it; the difference was so staggering that Craig was amazed that they all missed it. Or that anyone had missed it. But then, looking at an ID was far too often a casual formality, done very quickly. Rather than studying IDs, most people just gave them a glance.

"How tall does Jim Smith's license say he was?" Craig asked.

Marty shifted the picture on the screen. "Five-eight," he said. "Oh, yeah, wow . . ."

The man claiming to have been Jim Smith

was much taller. At least six foot one.

"I always thought a man shrank as he grew older," Egan said. "I do believe that our fellow gained over four inches."

"How can you tell?" Kathy asked.

"Marty, if you will?" Craig asked.

He hit the proper buttons and the security footage played again.

"Stop!" Craig said. And he rose and pointed to the screen. "There — Savings that grow as your children grow!"

A smiling, benign father was patting the head of a little boy in the poster on the wall. Behind the two was a measuring rod — clearly delineating feet and inches, all the way from one inch up to six foot six.

The little boy was about four foot ten.

The father was about six foot one.

And so was the man walking by the poster — the man claiming to be Jim Smith, multimillionaire.

CHAPTER EIGHT

It was stretching probability to assume that whoever had killed Alexandra Callas also had the foresight to hang around Finnegan's pub on Broadway to wait for Kieran to leave so that she could be attacked on the street.

And still . . . Kieran found herself turning around and heading back into the pub.

Luckily, Declan was engaged in conversation with someone else at the bar. Mary Kathleen had moved on and wasn't to be seen. Danny was walking through the dining room, and Kieran immediately grabbed his arm.

"Danny!"

"Kieran!"

"I need your help," she told him. She looked at him earnestly, searching his eyes, wondering how much she could explain and how quickly. Danny had always been the most mischievous of their foursome of siblings. He would never hurt anyone, but he had done many foolish things over time in the defense of others.

Kieran had actually met Craig because Danny had tried to help out their very good friend Julie when she'd been at the worst end of a sad divorce — a situation that had led them into the realm of diamond heists and murder.

If anyone should understand now, it was Danny.

"Come with me — I need you. And I need you to be really careful," she said.

"Kieran, I know that poor woman was murdered on the street, but —"

"There's much more to it now. I'll try to explain. Come with me."

"Wait — you want me to get stabbed in the back?"

"No, of course not. But if there are two of us, we can keep a better watch of the people around. Come on. We're not going far. Just a few blocks to the convent."

"You need Craig for this."

"He's not here right now. I'll fill him in just as soon as I see him."

She really had to at this point. She was becoming ridiculously paranoid.

"Why are we going to a convent?" Danny asked.

"To see a nun."

"Surely, you haven't done anything that bad!"

"A nun, Danny, not a priest. I'm not going to confession. I'll explain while we walk." She hesitated. "Oh, and, um, just kind of keep your eyes open, okay?"

There was one interesting thing about the US and money: when it was time to freeze assets, it could be done quickly.

Everything was set in motion to freeze Jim Smith's assets at the bank, and to allow federal agents access to his safe-deposit box.

The box, however, had been emptied. Whatever treasures it had held were gone.

As it happened, the number of men named James Smith in NYC was staggering; the FBI tech crews would work on figuring out which might have been the Jim Smith they were searching for, or where else the imposter might have struck.

For the moment, Craig was done. Wiped out, tired and done.

Mike made a point of reporting all that they had learned to their counterparts with the NYPD.

Craig drove and found street parking not far from Finnegan's, and they headed into the pub to be greeted by Mary Kathleen.

"We've been waiting for you, Craig — aye,

and you, too, Mike!" she added, seeing Mike enter the pub behind him. "Kieran was just starving, so she said, and she's eaten, but we've roast put aside for you. Have a seat, lads — you look quite plumb tuckered!"

"Long day," Mike told her.

"Dinner will be wonderful," Craig said. "But where is Kieran?"

"Why, she just headed to the convent. Had to get something back from Sister Teresa. Amazing woman — she's ninety-plus and moves like a bat out of hell!"

"We just missed her?"

"A minute or so ago," Mary Kathleen assured him. Declan had come up behind her. She turned to look at him, "Right, luv?"

"Yep. Someone told me that she came back in — Danny is with her," Declan said.

Kieran wasn't alone. Craig wasn't sure why he was so glad of that fact — especially since Danny Finnegan had a penchant for trouble like no one else he knew. Great guy, Danny — though sometimes his view on helping others was a little off. Especially when it came to the law.

"Seriously, just left? Maybe I can catch her," Craig said.

"Just minutes," Mary Kathleen assured him.

"Where does one go to find this nun?" Craig asked.

"Two turns!" Mary Kathleen said, rattling off the address. He knew it.

"Thanks," he told her, and turned to Mike. "Take a seat — have your food. I'll be right back."

"And if you're not, at least one of us will have eaten," Mike said, sighing.

"Aye, Mike, have a seat. I'll get your plate," Mary Kathleen said.

Craig hurried from the pub and out to the street. It was about a five- or six-block walk to the convent where Sister Teresa lived — three long and a few short. He didn't see Kieran and Danny ahead of him, but at least he'd walk back with them.

He was anxious to see Kieran after the day. So much had happened in a very few hours, and he knew the first forty-eight hours after a homicide were crucial to any investigation.

And now they knew that it was likely they were looking at more than one homicide. It was more than possible that the man responsible for stabbing their Jane Doe was the same man — or under the employ of the same man — who had caused the death of the young woman years before, the case that was still haunting Detectives Beard and

Holmes. The operation had been going on for many years; he was certain that the real James Smith was dead and that his identity had been stolen. Most likely, this group was using the identities of other deceased persons. Whether they died of natural causes or were helped into their graves was yet to be seen.

He reached the convent without catching up to Kieran and Danny. Inside, he was met at a front desk by a nun who seemed to be holding the fort much like the desk sergeant at a police station. She was friendly and smiling, a giant penguin with bright green eyes and a quick smile.

"Ah, Sister Teresa is popular today — and always. Moves like a speeding bullet — and she's well over the age of ninety! So much for the good dying young. Anyway, I just sent that young couple over there by our beautiful *Pieta* to wait. Sister Nan has gone for Teresa."

He looked over at the young couple.

Yes, Kieran and Danny.

He headed over to them, smiling.

Kieran looked at him with pleasure — and a little wariness, he thought. A small tremor shook through him. He knew that look.

Just what exactly were they doing here, looking for a nun?

189

"You had a productive day?" she asked him anxiously.

"Yes, and you?"

Danny groaned, shook his head and rolled his eyes.

"Very productive," Kieran murmured, trying to discreetly step on her brother's toe. "I'm not even sure where to start, except that I don't know how much of Sister Teresa's time we can take, so as soon as we've seen her —"

She didn't get to finish; she was interrupted when someone let out a blood-curdling scream.

Craig pushed ahead as they all raced down a hallway toward the sound of the scream, his hand on his Glock. The sister who had been sitting at the desk followed, as well.

He burst into one of the small rooms. It held nothing but a single bed, a wardrobe and a desk with a chair up against one wall.

There was a sister sitting in the chair. Her hands were folded on the desk in front of her. She leaned against the wall.

Her eyes were closed.

Her face was white.

Her lips held an equal pallor.

Dead.

He touched her throat, to be certain, checking for a pulse, for any sign of life.

She was cold as ice.

"No!"

He turned. Kieran stood in the doorway of the little room, gripping the doorframe. She cried with a wail of agony, rushing forward. "No!"

Craig caught her before she could reach the sister, pulling her tightly into his arms and crushing her face to his chest. He spoke over her head, feeling the tease of her hair against his chin. "No, Kieran, please, you can see, she's gone, and you can't touch her. The medical examiner will have to come out here, Kieran. She's — gone. I'm sorry."

She struggled in his arms. "They got to her! The King — the King and his men — they got to her!"

"Oh, dear Lord, dear Lord," the sister who had greeted them at the desk said over and over, her fingers moving over her chest in the sign of the cross. "Dear Lord, dear Lord . . ."

"Go fetch the mother superior," said Sister Nan — the nun who had gone to fetch Sister Teresa and found her as she was. She bustled the other sister out of the room. "Oh! Teresa was . . . so wonderful. We did think that she'd live forever." She turned to look at Kieran, as if she'd realized what she had said. "My dear, no one did this. Teresa was blessed with an amazing long life. But she was in her nineties. And look how sweetly she died, just sitting here!"

Craig had to agree with the nun — the dead woman looked entirely peaceful and at rest.

"Kieran, why would someone come in and kill an old nun?" he whispered.

One way or the other, though, Sister Teresa had died alone. That could mean an autopsy, even if her regular doctor arrived to say she had suffered from a bad heart or some other ailment that could have taken her life. He doubted foul play.

Craig pulled his phone out, though.

He called Egan. Since they were already working with Dr. Andrews, Craig asked if there was any way they could get the medical examiner to come out for this.

Kieran was watching him. Her eyes seemed truly enormous, and she nodded. At the very least, he was pleasing her. At the worst, he was doing a good job of ruining the evening for Dr. Andrews. Then again, the weekend had already sucked, so . . .

"I have a medical examiner coming," he told Sister Nan, who remained in the room.

Another nun arrived at the doorway; she

appeared to be sixtysomething — and her look was stern, that of a formidable battle-ax.

"Ah, so the time has come. Our dear sister has gone on to join our Heavenly Father," she said. "I'm sure you people were friends. But, please, if you could just leave now and let us handle the doctor and the details and arrangements, we'd be so appreciative."

"I'm so sorry — Sister Teresa was alone. The medical examiner is on his way," Craig said.

"What?" the battle-ax demanded. "I am Sister Margaret, Mother Superior here, and I won't have you making a mountain out of this. Who are you, anyway?"

Craig produced his credentials.

"I'm sorry," he told her again.

"Mother Superior," Danny said, stepping up and smiling gently. "This is such a beautiful place. Sister Teresa must have led a wonderful life here with you all. But, please, understand — I know that you do —" He paused to cross himself. "There are God's laws, and man's laws, and Jesus did tell us that we must always deliver to Caesar what is Caesar's — obey the laws of man."

She studied Danny and seemed somewhat mollified. "And who are you?" she demanded.

"Um, a friend. A friend of a friend," he said.

Kieran jumped in quickly. "I did not know Sister Teresa long, but long enough to know that she was a wonderful and giving woman who tried to help us — perhaps help others to the extent that she put herself in danger."

"So it's your fault they want to chop our dear sister to pieces," Sister Nan said.

Kieran could be quite a power herself when she chose.

She spun on Nan.

"It's my *fault* that I will see justice done — that if anyone harmed her in any way, they will face man's laws, no matter what forgiveness they might find elsewhere!" she announced.

The mother superior turned on her heel and walked away.

So did Sister Nan.

Danny, Kieran and Craig were left alone with the body. They could hear sirens approaching.

"I guess we don't have time for you two to tell me just exactly what is going on right now," Craig said. "But you're going to, right?"

"Hey — I just tagged along!" Danny said, shaking his head.

Craig stared at Kieran. "A lot has happened," she said quietly.

"And you didn't tell me?"

"I didn't see you," Kieran reminded him evenly.

Touché. He was off digging — it seems she found something right on the surface.

The sirens were growing louder. He was going to need a reason to explain why he had called for an autopsy on a ninety-plus-year-old woman who looked as peaceful as a babe.

He could hear people at the entrance.

"I need *something*!" Craig demanded.

"Two illegal immigrants terrified of some man they call the King found me through Sister Teresa and the soup kitchen. They talked to me and then became convinced that someone was after them. They ran, telling me that they'd find me again through the nun. I came to tell Sister Teresa that they would be trying to reach me again through her," Kieran said quickly. "And to see if she knew anything else."

"And that's when we all arrived," Danny said.

There were voices at the entry and then the sounds of people coming through.

The very irate mother superior led the way like a bulldozer.

Two officers came behind and then — to

Craig's incredulity and gratification — Dr. Andrews.

"So . . . you think you can special request who looks after your bodies, hmm?" Andrews asked him softy. He looked up at the large wooden crucifix on the wall of Sister Teresa's tiny room and moved his fingers over his chest in the sign of the cross.

He glanced at Craig and flushed. "Habit — um, sorry, no pun intended. Anyway . . . let me see what I can see here. Then we'll get her moved."

"She was ninetysomething, right? That's what we were told," one of the cops was saying to the mother superior.

"Yes," the mother superior said, casting Craig a glare that would have melted stone.

He was actually tempted to smile. He didn't allow himself to do so. He glanced at Kieran instead; she stood straight and still and silent at Danny's side.

The officers looked over at Craig skeptically; they had been informed he was FBI.

Maybe taking his work just a little too seriously.

Then, in a moment almost as miraculous as Dr. Andrews having arrived, Richard Egan came striding into the room.

Craig could have kissed him.

He stepped forward. "Sir!" he said to

Egan. "Officers . . . detectives? Mother Superior, if you will listen, you'll understand." He kept speaking, explaining that Sister Teresa, being the essence of goodness and kindness, had befriended two truly lost — and terrified — souls who had confided in her that they needed help. They'd then dared to reach out to Kieran Finnegan, but ran again in fear when they thought that their one-time captors were upon them. They had told Kieran to find the nun, and thus Kieran had come tonight to let Sister Teresa know that the women would be contacting her again.

Only to find her thus. And so, with the possibility that truly heinous and experienced killers might have come upon her, he was asking that her death be investigated.

"Perfect call, Special Agent Frasier," Egan said. "Thank you. Dr. Andrews, if you will see to the dear woman."

There was more talk and some confusion. The room was too small for everyone at once. Dr. Andrews performed his initial examination, and asked that Sister Teresa be brought to the morgue. Crime scene technicians arrived, further horrifying the mother superior.

Then Mike Dalton arrived — Craig had been busy, but Egan had seen to it that he had been brought up to speed. Mike had let everyone at Finnegan's know what had happened, though all they really knew was that Kieran and Danny had arrived to find the elderly nun deceased, and so natural confusion and speculation followed.

It wasn't until eleven that they finally returned to Finnegan's. The pub closed early on Sundays, and it was almost empty when they arrived — other than for Mary Kathleen, Declan and Kevin, who were all waiting anxiously for them to arrive.

"Your roast is a wee bit dried out," Mary Kathleen told Craig. "But I can try heating it."

Craig realized that he hadn't eaten. Of course, Mary Kathleen had spoken like that in a somewhat sharp tone because she didn't want to sound worried.

Food was always a good cover.

"Dried out will be fine," he assured her. "Mike?"

"Buddy, I already ate. I was hungry. And it was delicious," Mike said apologetically.

"Mr. Egan," Declan said, "if you're here, I'm assuming that we're having a meeting in the pub. Glad that we're just about closed, sir, and you can have your choice of meeting space."

"Excellent. I'm going to suggest that span

of cocktail tables between the entry and the bar, Declan, sir — and that we all share everything gleaned today."

"Yes, that will be very interesting," Craig said, looking at Kieran.

"Indeed it will," she shot back.

"One moment," Mary Kathleen murmured, smiling brilliantly as she walked to the front door, saying good evening and locking the last customer out.

As he heard the bolts clicking, Craig turned to Kieran. "So this was all new today? You just met Sister Teresa today?"

"Of course not! I helped out yesterday. I just met the immigrant women today," she said.

"Shall we sit?" Egan said firmly.

"Yes, please. I'll bring the coffee and the cups," Declan announced.

In a matter of minutes, they were all around the tables — Egan, Mike, Craig and the Finnegan crew: Kieran, Danny, Declan, Kevin and Mary Kathleen.

"I'm going to need the gaps filled in," Egan said. "But since they're going to come from two sides, let me get started with the story up to now." He looked around the table with the steely gray look in his eyes that had surely helped get him into his position. "Someone is dealing in human trafficking. Now, we all pretty much can imagine how that works. Most of the time, you pay a scam artist a fortune, they get you into the country with promises of a better life, but once you've arrived — illegally — you're at their mercy. Then they use you for slave labor, prostitution, or both, I'm assuming. They're probably using people in drug deals and gambling operations, as well. Those who come from war-torn countries, who were on the wrong side, who maybe had some kind of even minor skirmish with the law in their country might be terrified of going back. I'm not sure how they'd control them. Usually drugs — probably threats. This situation has been going on for a long time. There was a murder five years ago — a woman who had just given birth was found bleeding to death in an alley in Brooklyn, where Craig and Mike spent most of the day."

"The woman who gave me the baby was trying to save her from an illegal adoption," Kieran said. "She wasn't wrenched from her mother the moment she was born, though. I believe the baby is about three months old."

"Maybe after they lost the young woman a few years back," Craig said, "they've started making the babies be a bit older for adoption. Maybe it was an unusual case."

"I don't know about that," Kieran said quietly. "I do know that the woman who was killed was brought to the States and turned into slave labor. I believe she loved a lot of the girls that she was forced to look after — and their babies. I know that her name was Alexandra Callas —"

"You know her name?" Craig demanded, startled, his voice rough. "Sorry," he added quickly, but he was afraid that even his apology was rough.

Kieran was silent just a moment, and then she nodded. "I know what the young women today told me. Or what the *one* told me. She is Irish and her name is Riley McDonnough. The other was Tanya — Tanya Petrofskya. Russian. They know the mother of the baby, too — Yulia Decebel, who is Romanian. They don't know the name of the man running the whole thing, but he makes them call him the King. It is one man. They knew about the woman who died years ago," she added. "Although, I believe that's all they know. Riley hasn't been in the United States that long. I'm not sure about Tanya. Her English is poor. And somehow Riley has learned enough Russian for the two of them to communicate, at any rate. The thing is, I was trying to get them to come in. They are really terrified. I don't think that just one man can be running this whole thing, but there is a boss, or what have you — the man who they call King, or, sometimes, Riley told me, they even have to call him Your Majesty."

"And now Sister Teresa has passed away," Egan said. "Her passing tonight might, of course, be coincidence. Sad coincidence. I just looked up the dear lady a few moments back — she was ninety-six . . . four years short of a one hundredth birthday. We'll see what Dr. Andrews discovers. That's all beside the point."

"These women saw you at the soup kitchen, right?" Craig asked. He hoped his voice sounded more normal.

"The soup kitchen is a very good place, and it shouldn't be darkened by the likes of these people!" Mary Kathleen said.

"I always thought of the pub as a good place," Declan said. "And that sure as hell didn't stop criminals from meeting here — but, neither did it stop us from going on as we were. Lucky, of course," he added, nodding toward Craig, "that the FBI was in on it."

"Bad things happen in good places all the time," Craig assured him. "And," he added, glancing around the table, "good people do bad things because they think they're doing the right thing or the right thing for the situation. That's all beside the point. This time, we're not letting go. The cops had a bad time when that poor girl was murdered in that Brooklyn warehouse — they hit some walls because they just didn't have enough power behind them. Now, the FBI is in on it and there will be help from the US Marshals and Homeland Security, too. We won't let these deaths — or this horrible example of man's inhumanity to man — go on."

"Kieran," Egan said, "thanks to you, we have a great deal more to work with now."

"Thanks to Mary Kathleen," Kieran murmured.

"Ah, well, sister, no one wanted to come to me," Mary Kathleen said. "They didn't ask for anything — didn't show themselves at all — until you came."

"Just as the dead woman — Alexandra Callas — knew to come to you," Craig said thoughtfully.

"It's probably not that great a dilemma," Mike said. "Kieran was in the news a while back, but she's also been associated with the law and helping victims and other vulnerable people in distress."

"What about you all?" Kieran demanded,

turning to Craig.

"We've frozen the assets of a man we believe to be dead," Craig told her. He looked at Egan and Egan nodded; he was free to share what they had discovered. Which wasn't much.

Especially when compared with all the names Kieran had managed to acquire!

"We believe there's an extensive network that's been operating for quite some time. We are all but certain that the same man — this *King* — is head of it all. The whole operation is probably fairly large, and well funded, for this man to have gotten away with so much for so long. Anyone who looks as if they might speak at all probably winds up in the river. For this kind of enterprise, there have to be enforcers. Many levels of involvement. I believe that they're bringing vulnerable young women in and then forcing them into prostitution. If they do become pregnant, the babies are sold in underground adoptions."

"But, how many people would do that?" Kieran whispered. "Someone else's baby — a baby stolen from the mother?"

"Kieran, no one is told, 'Hey, I kidnapped an immigrant, held her prisoner, and made her give birth and, so, hey, cool, here you go, your perfect beautiful child,' " Craig said.

Kieran flushed. "Of course not, but wouldn't they know something wasn't quite right?" she asked in a whisper.

"They might know," Egan said. "In their hearts, they might know. But the adoption process isn't easy. For years, most Caucasian applicants wanted white infants — and there just weren't enough to go around. And then, your whole life is checked out — background, income, all that. Legal adoption can be very intrusive — there are tons of older kids who need good homes, but people want infants. No baggage. Between red tape and supply and demand, it's tough. People often have to travel abroad. When you want a baby badly enough, you're probably willing to overlook a lot. They're likely told that these babies were rescued from a foreign orphanage. The parents who might be receiving these babies want to believe that they're making a better world for the infants, and that it's all one big happy story."

Mike reached across the table and took her hand. "Kieran, we've spoken with one of the officers — David Beard — who was originally on the case. His partner now is a young guy named Detective Holmes —"

"Detective Holmes?" Danny asked.

"As in . . . Sherlock Holmes?" Kevin asked skeptically.

"The dude's first name is Randy, and I don't guess you lie to become a cop, so his name is really Randy Holmes. But, that's beside the point. He's furious and avid about catching these guys and he's among Brooklyn's finest," Mike said.

Kieran nodded. "That's good to hear."

"And we have a great undercover guy working in Brooklyn, too," Craig said.

"From Major Crimes, we have Lance Kendall and now Larry McBride working with him," Egan added. "We're moving in the right direction. What we need now is . . . hell, we all need to call it a night and get some sleep."

"But what about Riley McDonnough and Tanya Petrofskya?" Kieran asked.

"That's a tough one," Egan said quietly. "We can't put their names or pictures out there, Kieran. We could lead the killers to them just as easily as we might find them ourselves."

"So what do we do?" she asked. "Whether they — whoever 'they' are — killed Sister Teresa or not, she is dead. They won't be able to come to her."

"They knew her through the soup kitchen, just the same way they came to see you,"

Craig reminded her.

"Yes, but they wouldn't stay with me. They ran."

"They will find a way," Egan said.

"Or we'll find their bodies," she said morosely.

Craig didn't correct her.

Neither did anyone else.

They all knew that it was possible.

Craig was quiet when they left Finnegan's and headed for Kieran's apartment.

He was aggravated with her — if not out-and-out furious.

She could always tell when he was the maddest — he was the quietest.

"You should just explode," she said. "It's not healthy to be so silent."

The look he gave her, she was certain it would cause a hardened criminal to shiver.

She swallowed and tried again. "I don't get it. I don't understand why you're so angry with me."

"I love you," he said simply.

"Yep, I can see it in your eyes!"

He didn't respond.

"I didn't do anything dangerous or anything —"

"What?"

It wasn't exactly an explosion. It was a

word stated so precisely with such vehemence that she paused and took a deep breath before she tried to speak again.

"I went to a soup kitchen!" Okay, so she was explosive. She shouted the words. She wanted to hit him — to thunder against him. To make him react.

He shook his head. "Yep. You just went to a soup kitchen. And all this happened, and you didn't think it was important to tell me right away."

"Kind of like you — I was waiting for something to say!"

He remained quiet.

"Look, this is the truth, the absolute truth, I swear it. I went there with Mary Kathleen yesterday just to be helpful. Okay, so the nun came to me and suggested that I come back today — so I did. But, you have to believe me, I didn't know anything. There was nothing to tell you."

"Except that you might have been in danger there — since evidently, people do know you."

"Craig, any of us can be in danger walking down the street. Look how they killed Alexandra Callas! These people have to be found and stopped. They've been at this for years. God alone knows how many people they might have killed and how many lives they might have destroyed."

He let out a long breath and looked over at her. "Yes, I know."

And, of course, he did.

She didn't say anything more.

They reached her place at last, parked and headed up the steps. She still wanted to hit him. She didn't, of course.

"They killed her. I know it," she said quietly opening the door. "They got to her. Somehow. Yes, she was very, very old. But to die so suddenly — right now? No way!"

She was stunned when Craig suddenly grabbed her and backed her against the wall. His hands were on her shoulders. His eyes seemed to gleam like fires from hell.

"Don't you ever put yourself purposely into danger again — and keep it from me on top of all else!"

"You do it all the time!"

"It's different, and you know that! I can't handle you being involved in this if you're going to act irresponsibly!" he warned her.

And she did hit him; she slapped her palms on his chest, and then leaned against him and said, "It's just such a mess, and I'm so sorry, and I cared for Sister Teresa so very much, and . . ."

"Kieran, this really bothers me." He tried a smile and said, "Hey. Come on. I'm scared. And when I'm scared, well . . ."

She had to smile back at him. She sagged into him with a sigh.

"It's all right. We are going to get them. Especially if you start talking to me," he told her.

She nodded. "I just . . ."

"There's no *just.* Kieran, seriously, you're not a trained agent. Or cop. Please."

"Yes, yes," she whispered.

They stared at each other for a moment.

He let out a breath of serious frustration.

Then he suddenly swept her up into his arms.

She smiled wider and held on tight.

Make-up sex after an argument seemed like a damned good way to make sure they'd really made up.

CHAPTER NINE

Kevin Finnegan — a fine and respected actor in the community, as well as part-time pub-keeper — had once told Craig that if the law-enforcement thing hadn't worked out for him, he might have joined the ranks of entertainers.

Craig wasn't so sure about that, but he'd never been against going undercover and in disguise. In fact, when he'd first met Kieran, he'd had a good dose of her infamous Irish temper when he'd worked in disguise.

Thankfully, his disguise had been instrumental in breaking the case.

A disguise for a soup kitchen wasn't difficult. He was exceptionally good with whiskers, mustaches, beards and spirit gum. He could look like the dregs of the earth — or just like someone who had fallen on really hard times. The kind of person who would try to get a toothbrush and a bar of soap over a bottle of whiskey.

Or not.

Mike was joining the other workers on the soup line — just doling out food and chatting, much like any other volunteer.

Not that he would have been needed that day.

Sister Teresa had been really loved and respected. Craig wished he had known her.

The news was out that she had died, and everyone seemed to have a story about her. Every shared remembrance was about a good woman. Not one who was continually soft-spoken and gentle, but the kind of mentor who would lay it out flat — call it as she saw it — and create change with the sheer force of her will.

She had lived many years — a full life.

Still, was it possible that she had been murdered?

"Sir, there's water over here, and coffee is that line, there."

An older fellow in the food line pointed out directions for Craig. "Are you all right?" the man asked.

"Just thinking about Sister Teresa," Craig said softly.

The man made the sign of the cross over his chest. "Amen. Those in need flocked to her, son. She'll be dearly missed. Every now and then, I see someone come in here with a look on their face like they've just been hit in the head — they didn't know until they got here that she's gone. Like the girl there . . . or those two that just came in."

Craig turned casually. He was careful not to twitch or move a wrong muscle.

The one was tiny and blonde.

The other was taller with flaming red hair.

It was, of course, possible that neither woman was one of Kieran's new friends. But, as they walked in and searched out those working the soup line, they seemed to be full of confusion and dismay. He saw someone come to talk to them — a man with ill-kept facial hair and worn, dirty clothing. The two women listened to him; Craig saw tears spring to their eyes.

Then they looked at the serving line — and they seemed to be afraid.

The redhead gave the man with whom she'd been speaking a big hug, and then she linked arms with the tiny blonde.

They turned and went back out the way they'd come in.

Craig set down his bowl and stepped out of the line, hurrying after the young women.

Kieran truly worked for the nicest people in the world. They were, in fact, so nice, that she almost felt she worked with magnanimous puppets that might have been created at a Jim Henson fabrication facility.

Dr. Fuller was good-looking, had a beautiful wife, played tennis, attended PTA meetings — and worked with hardened criminals.

Dr. Miro was a small woman, single, energetic as a flash of lightning, and enthusiastic about learning history and gleaning any knowledge that came her way. She, too, worked with hardened criminals, sometimes the worst of the worst: serial killers, psychopaths, ruthless and remorseless.

But as bosses, they were just great to work for.

"Listen, you know that in a time like this you are certainly allowed to take whatever time you feel you need to take," Dr. Miro told her firmly.

"A baby! Thrust into your arms!" Dr. Fuller exclaimed.

"And a woman, stabbed in the back right on the street in front of you!" Dr. Miro added.

"We've been watching the news, of course," Dr. Fuller said. "Since your beau is working on the case, you're surely up to your neck in it all, as well."

Kieran bit her lip to hide a smile. She hadn't heard a boyfriend or significant other referred to as a *beau* in a very long time.

"I know — you two are wonderful. I so appreciate it. But I had one important appointment on my calendar — Besa Goga. Her court date is coming up and I need to speak with her again. She's had a tough life, and I still don't believe she's really grasped the fact that she can't bite people — that she will wind up in the court system again and again," Kieran said.

Dr. Fuller looked at his watch. "She's due now?"

"Any minute," Kieran told him.

"Okay, well, you know that we're here for you," Dr. Miro said.

"Thank you. I'll finish here with Besa today, and then meet up with Craig," Kieran assured them.

They left her; a moment later, Besa was at her door.

Besa Goga had once been a victim, similar to the women they were seeking. She'd been a teenager when she arrived in New York City on a ship, Eastern European by birth — according to her, she wasn't even sure which country she was from, it had all been part of the USSR when she had left, and the language that she spoke was Russian.

Her parents had been political activists and had been "disappeared" by the regime.

Her aunt, whom she'd never seen or heard from again, had put her on the ship bound for America, in order to protect her.

She'd been semi-adopted by one of the workers on the ship. She'd been vulnerable. He, in turn, had put her to work.

By her sixteenth birthday, she'd been pimped out to hundreds of men. She'd learned to deceive and steal — and she'd gotten hooked on the drugs she'd been dealing.

Caught stealing, she'd been brought into family court, and there, a kindly judge had seen to it that she'd received a second chance.

She used it, getting a job cleaning bathrooms in office buildings and putting herself through school at the same time. She'd become a dental assistant, applied for and been granted American citizenship, and married another immigrant, Jose Sanchez, from Madrid.

The two didn't have children.

They did have a nice home in Queens.

Two cats in the yard . . . Kieran thought, the sound of the song in her head.

But Besa had a temper. She had gotten in trouble once for beating the man from the water company over the head with a loaf of bread.

This time, she'd bitten the cable man because he'd told her that the problem with the cable was her fault — she'd spilled something in the cable box.

Despite the fact that her sessions with Kieran had been court ordered, she'd been extremely forthcoming and honest.

Apparently, the cable man had deserved biting. He'd accused her of stupidity.

Besa now had iron-gray hair that she wore in a severe bun at the nape of her neck. She had gray eyes, too, and a face with broad handsome cheekbones and a generous mouth. She was fit — not skinny, but wiry — and she loved jogging, she had once told Kieran. Jogging used up all the "angry" that she was feeling; it made her happy.

Kieran told her that was very good.

"So!" Besa said. "I am good, yes?"

Kieran laughed softly. "Please, Besa, have a seat. Let's chat for a few minutes."

"We've chatted. I like you. I like chatting with you. But life must go on. I am a busy woman."

"Yes, I know. Work and jogging. Here's the thing — I have to file a report. You know that. And I have to be convinced that you understand that you can't bite anyone because you're mad at the cable company."

Besa took a seat across from Kieran's desk

and smiled at her. "I do understand that. Perfectly. I will wind up arrested. I could do time for that — in prison," she said, her eyes widening. "So I will not bite anyone. I promise that I will not bite anyone."

"The next time you think that a cable man is being nasty to you . . . ?"

"I will not bite him!" Besa swore. "I will scratch the blood out of him instead!" she announced.

"Besa —"

"Kidding! Just kidding. There, you see, that's the point. I understand now. I have to control my temper. We have worked on this anger management. Breathe! I will breathe. I will walk away. I will not resort to violence of any kind."

Kieran was supposed to be good at reading people.

She wasn't sure she believed Besa.

She leaned forward. "You're joking, yes, of course. Very funny. Except, Besa, it isn't funny. Because if you do such a thing again, you might wind up in a mental ward or doing some time. Please, do you understand?"

Besa nodded. "Oh, Kieran. Yes, honestly. I knew it then. He just made me so mad. And he was swinging his arm around and around — and I just bit it. I know . . . I do know that I mustn't do those things. I just . . .

well, you know . . . I do have problems. I dream that I can go back and . . . and hurt the people who hurt me."

"I know that your past was horrible, Besa. But you can't become horrible because of that. You broke out of the horror — so many people wind up dead, Besa."

"Like the woman on the street."

Of course, everyone in the city had heard about the murder.

"We don't know much about that yet, Besa. But . . . yes, it seems she was probably an immigrant, and maybe she was about to blow the whistle on someone abusing others."

"Terrible, terrible," Besa said. "And I heard there was a baby, too. What about that baby?"

"The baby is with Child Services. It's being looked after."

"The woman — did she suffer?"

"Yes, of course. But, she died. In that, I suppose, death does end all suffering. Besa, we have to work on you. You've made incredible strides — you've worked hard. You were helped by the system. You put yourself through school. You married a good man."

"Jose is a good man. A very good man," Besa said.

"So there you go. Keep it all good. Don't throw away your hard work."

"I will not bite anyone again," she said.

"Good."

"Should I shoot them?"

Kieran glared at her, and Besa started to laugh again. "Oh, I am so sorry. You should see your face. I am joking. I am just joking. I know. I swear I know. I cannot bite people. I will not bite people. I will not scratch or shoot them, either."

"Right. That's what I need to hear. What I need to believe."

"You don't believe me?"

"You're doing a lot of joking."

"I'm sorry. Really sorry. It's just that . . . I work just part-time now, you know, yes? Jose and I . . . we have free time! We shop, we sit in the yard. It's not a big yard, but it is a yard. It is good. I will not bite the cable man again."

"What does Jose say?" Kieran asked.

Besa smiled. "He is a grateful man. He married a passionate woman."

"Yes, passionate," Kieran agreed. "Watch that passion."

"I will try to direct it in a better way. Jose is an even happier man when I direct my passion toward him, yes, you think, right?"

"I'm sure," Kieran murmured. She realized that her cell phone was sitting on the desk by her computer.

She was staring at it.

She was waiting for Craig to call her. She wasn't giving Besa the attention she should have been giving her. While her heart bled for the woman — considering all that she had suffered — she was never sure about her.

"You do understand the way the system works. What you did is considered violent, and it was an assault. And every time you wind up back in a courtroom, your record pops up. You have some strikes against you."

"Yes, yes. If I do bite the cable man again, don't get caught," Besa said.

Kieran looked at her.

"Joking, joking!" Besa said.

"I hope so," Kieran said seriously. Kieran did believe that Besa probably would bite the cable man again — and do it happily — if she wasn't afraid that she'd get caught and pay a price.

"You have no sense of humor," Besa told her. She wrinkled her nose. "So much for you being Irish. I am not seeing the smile and the charm."

"I'm not feeling them at this moment, Besa. And my background is Irish. I'm American."

Besa sighed. "Please, please, smile. I will not bite again."

"Just as long as you really understand your actions — and the consequences," Kieran said.

Besa nodded very seriously. "I do! I do!" she promised. She leaned forward, looking intently at Kieran.

"I get to read your report?"

"Yes. You get to read my report."

"After the next session? And then the judge decides if I'm . . . cured. Or, okay, or . . ."

"He'll make a final decision on sentencing. You assaulted a man, but thankfully, he will heal and no irreparable harm was done. I'm sure he'll give you a few months' probation."

Soon after, Besa left.

Writing up the report was not easy. Kieran didn't wish any ill on the woman. Still, she couldn't lie. She had to recommend further counseling if Besa was going to stay out of trouble.

Kieran wasn't focusing on her paperwork. All she wanted to do was leave, and find out if Craig was able to find Riley and Tanya.

Concentrate! she commanded herself.

But she couldn't. She figured she had

done a good enough chunk of work and would wrap up later. And so she was out the door, headed back downtown.

Manhattan has been compared to a concrete jungle, and not without good cause.

Buildings — skyscrapers, giant buildings, modern man's homage to the gods of the clouds — covered so much space that it was impossible sometimes to find a single patch of green.

Downtown Manhattan had the rare distinction of being the oldest general area, and therefore, the few remaining buildings that dated back to the early settlement of the island were interspersed with those that had been built throughout the ensuing centuries and decades into the days when a hundred floors in a building was barely impressive.

There were scattered patches of park and oddly shaped alleys here and there, some leading to dead ends, some cutting through to other avenues or streets.

Craig went after the women; they moved quickly down the street, nervously looking around as they did so. Craig weaved in and out of the crowd, keeping his distance so they wouldn't recognize that he was tailing them. They slid past a 1920s office block that offered a sliver of an alley between buildings. They moved past it, and then quickly doubled back into the alley.

Just as they did so, a man hurried past Craig. He was wearing a black sweatshirt with a hood. His hands were shoved into his pockets and his head was ducked low. The way he walked, there was little way that anyone could see his face.

By the determined direction of his stride, Craig was certain the man was following Riley and Tanya.

Craig quickened his pace, falling into step behind the hooded man, though hanging back a bit.

The man hurried toward the alley and slipped into it.

Craig ran once he had moved out of sight, following him into the narrow space. Coming along the thin path between the two buildings, he heard a muffled scream, and then another. Craig drew his gun from the holster hidden under his coat.

Craig burst into a small open space filled with scraggly weeds trying to take hold in rocky ground. The tiny blonde woman — Tanya — had been shoved to the ground, and the woman with the flaming red hair was in the arms of the man in the hoodie — and he was wielding a knife. He had Riley crushed to him by the waist and the knife held high overhead — ready to be plunged into her chest.

He was young, dark-haired, and lean with a wiry build. He looked at Craig with menacing brown eyes that seemed to hint of drugs or, at the least, a burnt-out life.

"FBI! Drop it. I will shoot," Craig told him, raising his Glock.

Riley, caught in the man's deadly grip, let out a terrified gasp.

Tanya, on the ground, sobbed.

The man brought the knife to Riley's throat. He wasn't going to stop. Die or not himself, he wasn't going to let Riley live.

It wasn't an easy shot.

Riley was whimpering and gasping and trying to escape.

But this man *would* kill her.

"Last warning! Drop the knife!" Craig shouted. He adjusted his aim.

The man's arm started to move.

Craig fired. A good, clean shot. He took him right in the middle of the forehead.

The knife dropped. The man in the hoodie released his hold on Riley. He fell to the ground, and Riley stumbled forward before slumping to her knees in a fit of tears. Tanya rushed over to her, sinking to Riley's side to hold her. She lifted an arm toward Craig, tears streaming down her face, gasping out something in broken Russian.

Craig started walking toward the two women. He felt something whizz by his head and then explode against the wall.

"There!" Riley screamed, jumping to her feet.

"No, down!" Craig warned.

He raced to her position, throwing himself down on the two women, and then rolled with his Glock in position.

The shots had come from the street; whoever had fired them had already moved on.

Craig lifted to an elbow to rise and turned to look into the dark, dead eyes of the knife wielder he had shot.

He could hear sirens on the street; people had heard. The incident had been called in. NYPD would be flooding the area soon.

He pushed himself up.

Riley and Tanya were doing the same.

They were terrified; they were going to bolt and run again.

He leapt up, capturing Riley in a gentle but firm hold.

"No!" he said firmly. "No. The police are coming now. We will protect you. Out there — the shooter will find you. You will die. Stay here!"

She went limp in his arms. Tanya just stood there, shaking and quivering like a frightened terrier. He pulled out his phone. The police were coming, but he needed Mike and Egan.

He didn't get to dial. A call from Kieran was coming in. He answered.

"Can't talk now," he told her. "Meet me at the FBI offices. I've just met a couple of your friends."

Craig had shot and killed a man. That meant handing over his weapon and going through the proper steps needed to justify a "good" kill.

Kieran knew that Craig hated being forced to kill anyone — even when he was certain that the person was guilty of truly heinous crimes. However, he wouldn't hesitate if an innocent victim was in immediate danger from that person.

He wouldn't beat himself up; he'd done what he'd had to do.

But it would bother him.

She knew that now he would have to complete all the paperwork necessary and undergo the questioning that went along with it, as well. And that was all right. Law enforcement should be questioned under such circumstances, or else no one would be safe. But it meant that Craig wasn't there when Kieran arrived at the FBI offices — at least not where she was led.

Director Egan had brought Kieran to a conference room at the downtown NYC offices of the FBI, along with Mike Dalton and the two terrified women, Riley McDonnough and Tanya Petrofskya.

Egan was a bright man — he'd never pushed away a cop or an agent of any kind or a civilian when they might help with a situation.

Kieran realized that she really did admire Richard Egan — she was also aware that he was the kind of leader that others aspired to be.

She was glad he was Craig's boss.

When she first arrived, both Riley and Tanya greeted her as if she was a long-lost relative, throwing themselves at her, sweeping her into teary hugs, and speaking quickly with gratitude. The words were in Russian and English but, in Riley's case, with a brogue so heavy that Kieran couldn't catch everything said.

She tried to assure the two women.

She saw the bandage on Riley's neck that covered the red line where the dead man had nearly brought her down with him.

As to him, he was dead, shot in the center

of his forehead. His body had gone to the morgue. The two women had recognized him; he'd been known as Paco. He worked with — or for — the man who called himself the King. They were all aware that within the King's realm, absolute obedience was expected at all times. There was no lesser punishment; those who stepped out of line received a death sentence — so Paco would have known his fate, either way.

"We're working on the identity of Paco right now," Egan told Kieran. She nodded.

Riley was going on and on.

All kinds of people — many that they might not recognize — worked for the King. Many were immigrants. Some were not. There was also a Queen. She was scarier than the King. Riley had actually seen the Queen. Tanya had not.

Listening, Kieran thought that the enterprise worked in many ways. The King — and his Queen, and upper echelon, she imagined — collected people. Immigrants from everywhere, most of them terrified that they would be sent back and perhaps face some worse kind of retribution.

"That man, Paco, had to know that Craig would be forced to shoot him when he threatened Riley with a knife," Kieran said.

"And there's only one thing that would

cause a man to behave that way. Assuming he wasn't suicidal and wanted to commit suicide by cop," Egan said. "And that would be a fear of something worse than death. I believe that has to mean that these people are able to threaten the children or families of these people. Or that they promise a death far worse than a bullet to the brain if anyone gives them up."

"I just know that people wind up dead," Riley said. "Those who try to escape." She glanced over at Tanya, fear in her eyes again. "They wind up dead!" she whispered.

Egan reached over and put his hand on hers. "Miss McDonnough, I promise you, we will keep you safe. Yes, this criminal element is organized and serious. But, so are we — we're even better, because we have all kinds of resources and excellent people on hand. You two will be granted citizenship, and then you'll enter into our US Marshals witness protection program. You're going to be safe — and with your help, we will crack this ring."

"Is it possible?" Riley murmured, tears in her eyes.

Tanya said something; Kieran turned with surprise when her words received a response from a masculine voice speaking in Russian.

"Ah, Special Agent Wolff. Welcome, and

thank you!" Richard Egan said.

Wolff was probably about thirty. Like most of the young men and women Kieran had met in the FBI offices, he appeared — even fully clad in his navy blue suit — to be exceptionally fit. There was, however, something a bit different about him. His dark hair was long and shaggy. He had facial hair. She had to wonder if he worked undercover, and was not usually in the office, wearing a suit.

Wolff smiled very nicely, a smile that reached all the way to his bright blue eyes. There was something gentle in his look, and whatever he had said had touched Tanya; she started to cry and to speak swiftly again.

He walked over to Tanya and hunkered down, assuring her.

Kieran looked at Riley.

Riley shrugged.

"I learned a lot of the language, but that's way too fast for me," she said.

"It's all right. She's going to be fine," Special Agent Wolff said. "She's sorry that she hasn't learned English. She knows *please* and *thank you* and little things, but she says she is so grateful to be here, and she should speak English."

"Oh, she will if she wants — she just needs time to learn," Kieran said, smiling as she looked at Tanya.

Wolff apparently translated her words. Tanya sniffed and tried to smile. Her mouth seemed to contort for a moment, and then she managed to say, "Thank you. So much . . . thank you."

"It's what we do," Egan assured her. He leaned forward and was about to speak when Craig walked into the room. Riley stood, staring at him.

"My turn," she whispered. "Thank you."

"You're all right? Not cut too badly?" Craig asked her.

Riley shook her head. "Aye, well and good, a wee bit of a scratch. I'll be fine. Thanks to you."

Craig smiled at her. "It's what we do," he said, causing everyone in the room to let out a nervous laugh. He frowned, confused by the reaction. Egan waved a hand in the air. "Never mind. All is well. But here's the thing. We really need to speak with these ladies. A safe house is being set up as we speak. The US Marshals office has already started working, too. For now — and we won't keep you long, I promise — we're all going to talk. We'll get some coffee, sodas, whatever in here, and we'll talk."

Craig apparently knew Agent Wolff; they shook hands and took seats.

And then the agents asked questions.

Kieran coaxed the young women when she could; she wasn't always sure just what the FBI agents wanted to draw out, but she did know how to gently twist a question and cajole an answer.

In her mind, they didn't get very far.

Paco was one of the King's men. They believed that he had been Venezuelan — Riley was pretty sure that the Queen had referred to him as such, saying something nasty about South Americans at the same time. Paco had ignored her, apparently ready to take anything she had to say in order to keep in the good graces of the King. Paco had been a watcher, like a bouncer. When men — johns — came in, or when women were sent out on tricks, Paco looked after them. Sometimes he was on guard at night.

Kieran pressed the women to describe where they were held at night.

"It was . . . almost like a college dormitory," Riley said. "Except, of course, girls don't lie in their beds crying all the time at a college," she added softly. "When a girl was pregnant — very pregnant, about to give birth — she was moved. To another floor, or another place, or . . . I'm not even sure."

Tanya must have understood the topic of the conversation. She started speaking quickly, looking at Riley, and then at Agent Wolff.

He listened, nodding his head, and then he translated. "They loved the murdered woman, Alexandra Callas, so much because she looked after them. The mother of the baby stuffed into Kieran's arms — Yulia — was close with Alexandra. Alexandra didn't work outside of the place where the women were kept anymore, though she once had. Apparently, she'd never been considered beautiful, and so she had been made to clean for people and do other such things. Then it was discovered that she was good with the girls — she really loved them. And so, when they were going to have the babies, Alexandra was taken with them, as well," Wolff explained.

"She was especially close with Yulia," Mike said.

"Go figure. I never knew how well my partner spoke Russian," Craig said.

"Hey, I don't really speak it — and it never came up," Mike said. "You wouldn't want me translating — I know every fifth word. I could really mess something up."

Craig laughed, giving Tanya a very gentle smile and reaching across the table to take her hand. "My Russian *sucks.* Big-time," he told her. "Your English — as poor as you think it is — is way better. And you will learn."

"I will learn," Tanya repeated, and smiled.

"So Paco was more or less an enforcer — an escort and a guard?" Craig asked.

"And a murderer!" Riley said.

"You know this for a fact?"

"I know that he was excellent at throwing knives and at stabbing things," Riley said. "He used to practice in a space by our beds. He would prove how good he was — he would practice throwing on a board, and he had a mannequin that he would stab. He would smile all the while. We didn't know that Alexandra had fled with the baby. You see, Yulia knew that they would take her baby. She said she even knew who was the father, that the father wanted the baby, too. They usually waited until the babies were three months old before having the mothers give them up. That way, people knew that they were getting a healthy baby. You see, years back, they let the women use too many drugs, and the babies were born with serious defects and . . ." She paused, wincing, and then apologized. "I'm sorry. I was a lucky one. I figured out Tanya wanted to escape and determined to go with her. We pretended that we were drugged out — and we were drugged, but we managed to avoid the worst of it. We got out, not knowing where we were, stumbling into a dark alley and hiding, and then moving again by night. But, you see, as I said, Alexandra was someone I came to love. She cared so much for all of us — and for those wee babes. Some were so sick they died, so they said. I wonder if some weren't helped along a bit. If . . . if they weren't perfect. Usually, you see, the children born . . . they're quite beautiful. Desirable to those who may not have been able to find such a child through the customary channels. Not even to say that they were bad people, just people who . . . well, you see, though, if there was a problem, then those people would go for lawyers, perhaps."

They all fell silent for a minute, the horror of what might have gone on too much to really assimilate.

"The thing is," Egan said quietly, "they must be stopped. With the two of you now helping us, we can make it happen."

"How?" Riley whispered. She crossed herself. "My God, they managed to kill a nun."

"We don't know that yet," Egan reminded her gently.

Kieran suddenly heard herself speaking, passionately. "Riley, Tanya, you don't realize it yet, but you do know so much. Maybe enough to bring them down. We'll do sessions, and I'll lead you through everything that you might possibly remember. We'll . . ."

She broke off; she wasn't the boss of any of this. Here, it was Egan.

At her office, it was Drs. Fuller and Miro. But she was going on and on as if she did control things.

But she had to do whatever she could. *They might have murdered helpless infants, for God's sake!*

"Yes," Egan said. "You'll be amazed at the things that will come back to you. And you'll be amazed by what might help — sounds and smells, overheard snippets of conversation. We'll find them — we will."

Tanya said something.

Wolff translated. "She says they'll be on the move. They may not know exactly how he died, but they'll learn soon enough that Paco is dead. And when they do, they'll move everything — and everyone."

"And it's worse," Riley whispered.

"What do you mean?" Craig asked her.

"I'm just so afraid that if they begin to feel cornered . . ."

"What?" Kieran asked.

"They'll kill her," Riley said softly. "They'll kill Yulia, and that way, she can never escape and come for her baby, and they'll hide again and disappear forever!"

CHAPTER TEN

"She died of a heart attack, that much is perfectly clear," Dr. Andrews said.

"So natural causes. She died because she was old and her body gave out?" Mike asked.

"I didn't say that," Andrews told them. "I said she definitely died of a heart attack."

"There's a *but* in there," Craig said to Mike.

"Exactly — and here it is," Andrews said. "I don't know what brought about such a massive heart attack. She might have been terrified, she might have been threatened . . . I just can't say. She might have even been given a tiny dose of some kind of drug to bring on a heart attack. At her age, it wouldn't take much. Do they know if anyone was anywhere near her or not? Yes, she was old. Yes, the body faces wear and tear and yes, it can give out. Yet she wasn't overweight, she hadn't been doing anything more extreme or stressful than she did every day . . . I don't know if I'm helping you out or making matters worse."

"She was dearly loved," Craig said, looking at the body on the gurney. There would always be something empty and tragic about seeing the dead at autopsy. What had been physical remained, and yet there was really nothing of humanity left in a corpse. A corpse was simply sad; it was a memory of a loss.

"I will get her fixed up just as quickly as possible. She's to be taken care of by the folks at Murphy and Sons — they remain members of the church and take care of all the nuns and clergy. I believe the funeral is planned for Saturday. They have asked me to release the body by Friday, if at all possible, and I have agreed. That amount of time allows for my tests and for the official announcement of her death and for her extended family and friends to get here. She was loved. Her funeral, I understand, will be quite an event. A life well lived," he said softly.

Craig thought that even Andrews — who spent his life working with the dead — had feelings about the degradation suffered after death, as well. But Andrews was a passionate man. He was fighting for humanity —

this was his way of doing it, and as an ME, he seemed to do a damned good job of speaking for the dead.

A hell of a way to start the morning, though. He and Kieran hadn't left the office until the wee hours of the morning.

She hadn't even wanted to go then.

But the Marshals office was involved now, and they were good at protecting people. There was a solid understanding between the agencies and the cops at the moment. Human life — civilian life — needed to be protected. Especially when it came to innocents like Riley and Tanya. They were also witnesses; they were needed. Hopefully, they could help.

"She will be granted all honors. She's going to be interred in the crypt at the church. That is high regard, indeed," Dr. Andrews said.

It was Tuesday. Four days until the funeral. And at that event, they would need to have eyes everywhere. If Sister Teresa had indeed been murdered, her killer might attend. If the trafficking network had such broad reach, they might want to see for themselves who came to say goodbye to the woman.

But there were days between now and then. And since everything to do with the gang who had been working well beneath the notice of the city for years now had suddenly been brought to the surface, anything could happen in a number of days.

They needed to move — and quickly. It was frustrating when finding a direction in which to go was like finding a needle in a stack of needles.

"And now . . . to the next," Andrews said.

He moved down a gurney and pulled back the sheet. Like Sister Teresa, this corpse had already received an autopsy. The rapid pace the ME's office was working at was almost unheard of, but with so many law enforcement agencies involved and the city on edge — involve a baby or a dog and the masses always went wild — Andrews had worked through the night.

"Any ID on the man yet?" the doctor asked.

"All we have is Paco," Craig said.

"Well, Paco's prints are in the system," Andrews said. "Our system. Problem is, we have his prints in connection with a number of unsolved crimes. Files have been prepared and emailed to you. We don't have a full name for Paco. Oh, and he never went to the dentist. Horrible teeth. Don't see how he stood it . . . As you can see, and as you know, death was from a bullet directly into the brain. You had pretty amazing aim there,

Special Agent Frasier."

Craig stood silent. He hated killing — but he hated seeing a victim die more. He tried to imagine just what the King was capable of that would make henchmen choose death over arrest.

"I'm glad they cleared you right away — and that all the media got was 'potential victims of stabbing attack saved by a member of law enforcement,' " Andrews said.

"Yep. They could have held him up, kept him on the sidelines, taken his weapon," Mike said, adding pleasantly with wide eyes. "And I might have had some new jackass kid to work with!"

"I'm relieved, too," Craig said. "Thankfully, our people — all our people, law enforcement of every kind who arrived at the scene — were really good. I understand the media and I'm all for freedom of the press, except when too much information can get someone killed," Craig said.

Mike made something that was almost a snorting sound. "Some of those reporters just don't care — they'll say or write anything to sell papers or get page views or whatever. If we hadn't gotten those women out of there fast and their pictures had appeared in the papers . . . it might have been impossible to keep them safe."

"Anyway, your Paco was about six feet even, two hundred pounds. Dark eyes, dark hair, possible ethnicity Middle Eastern or Hispanic, maybe Eastern European. Other than his teeth, he seemed to be in good health, and I'm estimating his age at somewhere between forty and forty-five. I'm having the stomach contents analyzed, but I'm thinking — I'm pretty good with colors and smells — he consumed some borscht not too too long before death. You'll have more when I have more."

"If they were calling the man Paco," Mike said, "it's possible he is from a Spanish or Central or South American background. But his stomach contents suggest borscht."

"Yes, which actually makes sense," Craig said. "We've figured that this ring is exploiting people of all nationalities."

"I think you're right — this doesn't focus on any particular group of immigrants. It targets them all," Andrews agreed.

Craig listened for a few moments longer while Andrews waxed on in medical terms Craig wished he understood; Mike excused himself to report the ME's findings to their counterparts with the NYPD and US Marshals Service. A message from Egan alerted them to the fact that Riley McDonnough and Tanya Petrofskya had been taken to a

244

safe house.

Then they were able to leave the morgue.

Craig found himself thinking about the two women.

Riley had nearly died.

But she hadn't.

The two young women had told them so much about the operation. They appeared so fresh, sweet, young and lovely. And honest.

It was a crazy idea, but what if they weren't? What if they had used the soup kitchen near Finnegan's for some kind of meeting ground? Despite the fact that the police had managed to keep most of what had happened out of the news, maybe the info was out that Kieran Finnegan had been given the baby, that she had a friend — almost a sister-in-law — who helped out at the soup kitchen.

"What are you thinking?"

"That I'm nuts."

"Why?"

"I'm suspicious of Riley and Tanya. That's nuts, right?"

"An Irish immigrant who speaks Russian? Maybe not. And yet . . ."

"Yeah?"

"You just stopped that bastard from slicing her neck."

"Maybe he thought everyone would be better off if she were dead."

"True — but it's a total shot in the dark. Still, we can get them checked out."

"Yep. We'll call Marty and get him looking up whatever records he can find, though most illegal immigrants don't leave much of a paper trail. We can try with the Irish authorities."

"Everyone living leaves some kind of a trail," Mike said. "Beyond that, we watch Riley. And Tanya. We make sure they have no way of contacting the outside world. I'm sure that's happening already. Suspicious or not, you can't protect someone who is corresponding with other people — no matter who they are."

"Good point. I'll voice these concerns to Egan."

"And keep a good eye on Kieran," Mike added.

"That goes without saying."

Craig had left Kieran at the FBI offices, so she would now be at the safe house. It was, Craig thought, one of the best in the city — situated in the heart of Manhattan and right next to a police station. There was a back entrance through a Chinese laundry; the laundry was actually owned by the Bureau. Riley and Tanya seemed to feel secure and as if they had made the right move — perhaps the only move that would have kept them alive. Craig knew — as did Egan — that they were more comfortable with Kieran around, not to mention that Kieran's job was to talk and counsel and coax a person's true thoughts and feelings to the fore.

At least, that's what he saw her job as being . . .

He'd heard Declan tease Kieran, telling her that although he hadn't been through the same training she'd received, some nights when he was behind the bar, his job wasn't much different from hers. Certainly, her hours behind the bar at Finnegan's had prepared her when it came to sitting back and listening to tall tales.

She was very good at her job, he knew. Because she honestly liked and cared about people.

Which, for some reason, made it all the scarier when he was worried about her. Maybe she wasn't as naturally suspicious as he was.

When they arrived at the safe house, they discovered that Egan had come with Riley and Tanya and several members of the police force. McBride, Kendall and David Beard's new partner, Detective Randy

Holmes, were there, along with Jacob Wolff and a few other men and women from the NYC offices of the FBI.

David Beard, Holmes explained quietly, was out on the street. They were trying to cover as much ground and gather as much information as possible.

"And we're having Wolff interpret for Tanya. He's on the case, deeply involved, and safe enough with his undercover persona here."

"I can vouch for Wolff," Craig agreed.

Everyone there, no matter what their office or agency, appeared to be somber and determined, even those not investigating, but who had drawn guard duty for a shift.

Egan sat quietly at a table on the far side of the room.

The officers were hovering in the kitchen. From there — over a little open counter — they could observe the living room of the apartment. Kieran was there in a wingback chair. Riley was across from her, reclining on the sofa. Her eyes were closed. She was listening to whatever questions Kieran was asking, frowning now and then, and replying.

Jacob Wolff nodded to Craig and Mike, his expression serious, almost grim.

"She's very good with people, your Miss

Finnegan," he said.

Craig nodded, not at all sure how Kieran would like being called "his" Miss Finnegan. Then again, she would probably just shrug.

"She is very good," he said, aware of the note of pride in his voice.

"Egan thought she should try speaking with both of them separately, and then together," Jacob said. "They might say things alone that they might not say in front of the other, and then again, after, they might build upon what each is saying."

"He probably made a good call," Mike murmured.

"This whole thing is . . . bad. Really bad," Wolff said. He was watching the conversation between the two women as he spoke. "This young lady, Riley . . . Miss Finnegan has coaxed her into remembering the last place she was kept. She says that she could smell fish, and yes, she was certain — she was from a fishing village in Ireland, after all. And then she said that she could hear a whistle. A regular whistle, sounding at about midnight, and then six in the morning, noon, six and then midnight again."

"And you know the whistle?" Craig asked him.

"I do. It sounds every day at the Victory

Shipyards, right on the river."

"I know the area," Craig said. "There's a fish market just down from it, so if she smells fish, and she hears the whistle . . . somewhere between the two?"

Wolff nodded. "I'm envisioning the area," he said.

"You don't need to envision — we can do better than that," Craig assured him. He dialed Marty at the office.

Within minutes, Marty had provided, via email, a detailed map of the area along with lists of building owners and renters and users. Craig was still studying the map when Riley suddenly spoke up.

"Pizza!" she said.

"Pizza?" Kieran asked.

"Italian food," Wolff murmured.

"Oh, aye, indeed. Pizza! I do love Italian food! And I could smell pizza cooking some days, I'm quite certain," Riley said enthusiastically.

Craig looked at his map. He found a pizza restaurant.

"Give me a minute," he said, pulling out his phone. He called Marty back, told him that Riley remembered the scent of pizza, and that he was pretty sure he'd found — on his map, at least — such a restaurant. It was also by a warehouse.

"Let me get on it. I'll call you right back."

"Thanks. I'm going to head over to that area right now," he said to Marty, and hung up. He turned to Wolff. "We may have something," Craig told him. "I should have more information shortly, but for now, I want to take a look around where I think the pizza smell originated. Mike and me, at least."

"And me," Holmes said. Kendall and McBride both nodded; they were coming, too.

"And me. Let's do it," Wolff said.

Craig shook his head. "You can't. You can't jeopardize your cover right now," he said quietly.

Wolff winced. "Yeah. You're right. Let me know?"

"The second we have anything," Mike assured him.

Craig turned, aware that Kieran had paused midsentence. She'd seen him arrive, and now, of course, she knew that he was rushing out.

Her eyes met his for a moment. He nodded to her, trying to smile, trying to let her know that she had given them a lead.

She tried to smile in return. She gave him a thumbs-up sign.

He hurried out. If they were lucky . . .

They just hadn't been lucky yet on this damned thing.

Riley McDonnough had given them the location.

What exactly did that mean?

Or, did it mean anything at all, other than the fact that she and Tanya had escaped, on the run, terrified, and desperate to help?

He was halfway to his destination when his phone rang; it was Marty again.

"What did you get?" he asked quickly.

"You know how we've been doing extensive searches since we're pretty sure that the King is operating under stolen identities?" Marty asked. "We might have found another dead man doing live business. And he owns a building there — right across from that pizza parlor place by the river."

"Almost there," Craig said.

"I'm Hank LeBlanc. And I work with Madison Smyth. We'll be your friendly US Marshals today."

The man who came over to introduce himself was tall and lean; he also had a personable, almost good-old-boy way about him. The woman at his side was a very pretty brunette with gray eyes and a sophisticated updo for a hairstyle. He was casual; she was all business.

"Hello," she said, shaking Kieran's hand. "We just wanted to come in now and say hello. We're going to be the main protection detail once we get this moving."

"Witness protection," Riley whispered.

"Yes, we'll be talking to you. There are rules if you want to be in the program," Madison said.

"It's not so bad, honestly," Hank LeBlanc said.

"But it is serious," Madison said.

Hank, who had hunkered down to talk to Riley, grimaced. "Madison's a New Yorker. Me, I'm from New Orleans. She's okay. I'm busy teaching her how to make eye contact."

Madison let out a long-suffering sigh. "We're just here to keep abreast of the situation, and to help out if needed. When the police have discerned everything you might know, we come into the picture. But we wanted to meet you."

"She really is nice. Hard to tell, I know. She just has that schoolmarm thing going," LeBlanc said.

Kieran smiled; she glanced up at Madison and saw that the woman had stoically and with amusement decided that she would tolerate her partner. She just stood quietly, patiently listening.

Then she winked at Kieran, and Kieran

smiled, thinking it was a natural little bit that the two of them had going between themselves to try their best to make their charges feel comfortable and safe in their company.

"Tanya is in the bedroom, watching television. She's learning English that way. She's due to come out and chat with me for a few minutes," Kieran said.

Did it matter? she wondered. Craig, Mike and the other cops — except for the undercover guy — had headed out. They knew something; they had a lead on a location. Somewhere by the river, where there was a pizza restaurant and some kind of a bell.

"I'll get Tanya," Egan said easily, rising and heading for the bedroom.

Jacob Wolff, the good-looking young undercover cop, came around from the kitchen, and in a few minutes he was engaged in conversation with the marshals and Riley. Riley seemed somewhat awed by Jacob, who was very kind to her in turn. Then Tanya came out, her hands wrapped around Egan's arm. She still scared very easily, and was frightened of just about everyone. But she, too, seemed more at ease when she saw Jacob Wolff. Understandable, perhaps, since he spoke her language fluently and with the right accent.

"So, Riley, your turn to watch some television and Tanya's turn to speak with Kieran," Egan said.

Kieran looked at Egan. "But . . . Craig and Mike . . ."

"We don't know what they'll find," Egan said. "Let's see what else we can get here, okay?"

She was aware that Egan never counted on anything until it was a done deal. She felt restless herself — anxious. Riley had described a place that the detectives seemed to know. Probably Jacob Wolff was familiar with it; Brooklyn was his stomping ground. Then again, maybe it was something they had all figured out together.

"Are you okay to speak with me?" Kieran asked. Detective Wolff sat down next to her and repeated her words in Russian.

Tanya began to speak.

She was effusive. Wolff smiled and lifted a hand.

"She's just fine with you. You're a wonderful, brave woman. She wishes she could say so herself."

"Please, yes!" Tanya said.

And so Kieran went through the same questions she'd asked Riley.

After a moment, Tanya did have a little more to add. She described the same surroundings. She talked about the young women who did nothing but cry; she talked about the way that language hadn't been a barrier. They had learned to cling to one another. They became friends. They ate well enough — they could only clean houses or entertain gentlemen if they were in good health. And, of course, when they were going to have babies . . . well, they were treated very well.

She frowned and said something very softly to Wolff.

"What is it?" Kieran asked.

"She said that she believes that the babies were all born in the same place — the same place where they were kept. She could swear that she heard babies crying sometimes. But Tanya wanted to come to America so badly because her mother just had another baby, and she wanted to eventually bring her whole family. The other young women thought that she heard babies because she was worried about home."

"How many young women at a time, Tanya? How many were kept in this place?"

Wolff relayed the reply to Kieran. "The numbers varied. Once a girl had a baby, they didn't always see her again."

Kieran tried not to show the shudder that rippled through her.

How many had been killed?

"Ten at a time . . . twenty?" she asked.

Tanya was thoughtful after Wolff translated.

She spoke; Wolff said, "Ten to fifteen."

"Did they ever go out?"

"Sometimes, but rarely. Sometimes, and it was at night, and they were blindfolded before they were put into the back of a car," Wolff translated.

"Did she notice anything when she was out in the car?" Kieran asked.

Wolff translated. Tanya answered in English. "Pizza," she said. "Good . . . so good, the pizza."

Kieran smiled. "We can order pizza. We can order pizza for you right now, I believe?"

She turned and looked at Egan.

"Of course," he said.

He nodded to one of the agents; the man went out to get food.

Kieran thought that he looked at his watch; that he was too pensive.

Did he think that the agents should have called with information by now?

She didn't know; Egan hid his thoughts well. So did Jacob Wolff, at her side.

But as someone went to get Riley McDonnough to come back out and join them, she thought that Wolff slipped — just a bit.

He glanced at his watch.

And he looked anxious.

And naturally, that made her worry, as well.

Craig knew from the moment they reached the building that they were too late.

Looking up at the edifice — a 1930s shell of a building with five floors — he could almost feel the emptiness, and then the enormity of what might have been. It was dull and gray, dingy from years of the pollutants that had spilled into the skies over the city before steps had been taken to slow down the amount of toxins let loose in the air.

There were no windows on the ground floor.

There were windows upstairs; they all appeared to have been blacked out — perhaps covered over with cheap paint.

It was quickly decided; Craig and Mike were going through the front.

Kendall, McBride, Beard and Holmes were heading around back. A slew of officers in uniform had been called, and they'd be arriving momentarily.

"Let's just walk down the street," Craig told Mike. "Check out the entry. It's going to be empty. They've cleaned out. They know that their man Paco is dead — and that he missed killing Riley and Tanya. They've moved on. We don't need a barrage of firepower."

"Situation calls for backup, kid," Mike reminded him.

"And we're waiting. I just want to be at that door in case there is a straggler in there anywhere," Craig said. "These guys must have the ability to move fast. We know it's a pretty major operation. They seem to have the ability to move at the drop of a hat —"

"Easy enough," Mike interrupted, "when you maintain a lot of property that really belongs to dead men."

"Easy enough, but not for forever," Craig said. "And they haven't had much time this go-around."

"They didn't have much time last go-around," Mike reminded him. He sighed softly. "These people . . . they have balls out the kazoo. This Paco guy just about asked you to shoot him. How the hell are they doing it?"

"I'm thinking family," Craig said. "What is a man willing to die for? His children, his wife, his mother. Maybe they have some kind of hold over them. Hell . . . who knows."

"Pizza," Mike said.

"What?"

"You can smell the pizza — big-time."

Mike had barely finished before the sound of an explosion ripped through the air.

To their side, the building seemed to burst into splinters and turn into a roar of fire that sent heat waves streaking up to the sky.

"Down!" Craig shouted, even as the force of the blast pushed them sideways.

He grabbed Mike, and the two of them ran like hell across the street as far as they could.

The world around them burned.

The fire went high and fierce — quickly. In a matter of moments, the shooting flames were gone, and the building was beset with just a few flames here and there.

Car alarms were going off all around.

Craig was on his feet, ready to race for the building.

"Craig!" Mike caught him by the arm.

He swung around. "Mike, what if . . . what if they left someone in there?"

"Oh, God," his partner murmured.

Sirens were blaring. The fire department was near.

Near. Not there yet.

Some windows had been blown out — Craig and Mike were really lucky they weren't injured . . . or dead.

"We gotta go in!" Craig said.

Mike didn't argue. They hurried to the entry; the doors had exploded outward. Glass crunched beneath their feet.

"The basement," he said to Mike. "The basement . . . it's where they kept the women. If someone is in here . . ."

"Jesus." Mike sighed. "We are idiots."

"What if someone is in there who's alive? Seconds can matter!" Craig pulled his shirt up to cover his mouth and nose.

"Then let's go."

Craig rushed in.

Mike plunged after him.

They'd searched the ground level, moving carefully across the smoldering floor, and were doubling back across the building when they saw a firefighter.

"Hey, you guys, we can take it —"

"Yeah, yeah, but we're already in. Follow me, please!" Craig said.

At first, they couldn't find the stairs. Then, Craig saw a charred sign. He tore for the doorway, Mike and the firefighter behind him. Racing down, he entered into a cloud of smoke.

He crouched low.

He saw the remnants of the "dorm" Riley had described. Sheets, feather pillows, half burned, here, there, everywhere, charred and in puffs of white-and-black feathers.

"Smell that?" Mike whispered. "That ain't pizza!" he said.

No.

Only one thing smelled that way.

Burning flesh.

CHAPTER ELEVEN

Kieran was still talking with Tanya and Detective Wolff when word came through that a building in Brooklyn had exploded. They quickly learned that, luckily, no one had been inside. It had gone up before any police officers or agents had entered.

Just hearing what had happened, though, caused ice-cold rivulets of fear — stabbed through with streaks of hot relief — to race through Kieran's body.

She stood.

Her legs wobbled and she sat back down.

She thought about what had happened, and she agreed that she should stay away when Egan made preparations to head over to Brooklyn.

She knew that Wolff couldn't go — he couldn't be seen in the area, lest he chance his undercover position.

She was sure that Craig wouldn't want her at the scene, either.

But Kieran couldn't stay away.

She told the remaining team that she was going to the pub. It wasn't a lie; she would head there right after she went to Brooklyn.

Right after she saw Craig.

Because there was no way in hell she couldn't see him now, couldn't touch him, couldn't make sure for herself that he was absolutely all right.

She allowed Egan to get an officer to drop her off at Finnegan's.

She hopped out, and was about to turn around to quickly head for the subway. But just as the police car pulled away, Danny came walking up.

"Hey! Just finished up a tour. I was going to call you. I was worried. Kind of silly, I guess. I mean, you're not out in Brooklyn often, but with everything going on . . . Did you hear there was a massive explosion? But, thank God, I see you're here, and . . ."

"Craig is there. Come on!" She grabbed her brother by the upper arm of his jacket.

"Hey!" He resisted.

"Come on, Danny, please, before Declan comes out and it turns into a big thing. Please? I need you with me. I have to see Craig. Please, come on!"

Danny let out a breath.

"Yeah, yeah . . . okay. Hurry to the subway . . . speed it up before someone looks out one of the pub windows!" Danny shook his head and blew out a breath. "I sure as hell don't want to explain abetting you in crazy deeds to Declan, either!"

It wasn't really difficult to hide in plain sight — by the time Kieran and Danny arrived at the scene of the explosion in Brooklyn, yellow tape was up, officers were about everywhere, and crowd control was in full effect because there were hundreds — perhaps thousands — of people on the streets. To say that a crowd had formed would be putting it mildly.

That didn't deter Kieran — Craig was somewhere here. She was simply terrified for him; her heart was racing. In pure panic, she started to plow her way through people, determined that she had to get to him.

Danny stopped her, pulling her around, holding her firmly and brooking no argument.

"He's all right. Kieran, don't go off the handle. You can put yourself in danger. You can get yourself killed."

"But, Craig . . ."

"Craig is smart, tough — and more," Danny said.

"No one is tough enough to survive an

explosion!"

"I thought they told you he wasn't in the building. Damn, sis — have some faith in the man."

"I have nothing but faith in him, but how the hell would he know a building was about to explode?"

"He's all right. Believe me."

She inhaled sharply; as they had wedged themselves into the crowd staring at the burnt-out shell of a building, Egan had arrived.

So had the media.

The street was an absolute zoo of people of importance, people wanting to speak to the people of importance, and people just watching the scene of the disaster. As she looked around, she saw that Jacob Wolff had not been able to resist the temptation to find out what was going on, either. He was pressed in the crowd to their left, a look of tortured concern on his face.

He must have somehow felt Kieran's eyes on him because he turned, and he saw her. And since she had taken him unaware, he smiled before turning back.

They were in this together, she determined. They had been told to stay away.

Neither had been able to do so.

An officer spoke over a bullhorn, asking

people to please respect the police line and let the emergency workers do their jobs.

The crowd seemed to shift back a little.

"What the hell?" Danny muttered suddenly as he bumped against Kieran.

"What?" Kieran asked him.

"Someone pushed me."

"It's a crowd, Danny — people push in crowds," she said.

"This girl *shoved.* She seemed scared, worse than you. And it was so weird, I swear she was muttering 'the King is coming.' Don't know where she was from, but someone has to tell her — this is America. We don't have kings and queens."

"What?" Kieran demanded. "Who? Who was it? Where did she go, Danny?"

Someone jostled Kieran. She realized she'd been holding her cell phone.

It went flying.

"Damn," she murmured, diving down to find it. It was impossible, but the damn thing seemed to have cleanly disappeared. She was nearly pushed over as someone walked by her.

"Hey!" she protested. And then, of course, she saw her phone.

Smashed to pieces. She still grabbed it, rising to look around for Danny. He was by her side, reaching for her arm, looking around and shaking his head with disgust. "People!"

"Danny, this woman who was talking about a king. What did she look like? Where is she now? We need to find her."

"She was little, but strong! A blonde woman. She's gone now. We're not going to find her. But . . . Hey! What the bloody hell?"

Danny spun around as he spoke; Kieran saw that someone had grabbed his arm to draw him back from Kieran.

Danny had recently been learning to control his temper. He'd been learning not to behave too rashly. Danny's impulses to help others — especially those he perceived as downtrodden or used or abused — had gotten him into trouble in the past. He was quick to swing a fist.

Kieran gripped his forearm with both hands before he could possibly respond, even as his hand was clenching.

Because the person who had grabbed him was Jacob Wolff.

"I have to get you two out of here," Wolff said.

"Get us out of here? Who the hell are you?" Danny demanded. Jacob was in plainclothes. He looked like any dark-haired slightly scruffy guy on the streets.

"Um . . . a friend," Kieran said. "What is it? What's wrong?" she asked Wolff.

"Come on! Follow me — now!"

Craig was aware that the firefighters were now the only ones who should be in the building.

But he knew that someone was there. Anyone close knew that someone was there. *Dead or alive.*

The thing was — the explosion had been set. The building had been destroyed on purpose.

So if someone had still been in the building, they were either a victim or they knew what had happened, possibly did it . . .

"There!" he said.

A black, smoldering pile lay on the floor. It moved.

Craig raced forward, his heart beating hard.

Was it the baby's mother? Being killed before she could escape, before she could cause trouble? Had she been left behind to die a horrible death as a warning to others?

"Here!" he shouted, knowing that the fire department had EMTs with them, that help would be there in seconds. "Over here!"

He slid down on his knees, lifting a charred blanket.

It wasn't the baby's mother.

It was, however, a human being. A man. His skin was charred so that it was impossible to define the man's race, his age . . . anything about him, other than that he had been at the very wrong end of a fierce explosion.

"Dead?" Mike asked softly, reaching him.

The pile moved slightly. Breath, yes, he saw the man take a breath . . .

Whoever it was . . . *he was still alive*!

"No. Hey, help! Over here!" Craig shouted again.

He had already been heard. Firemen rushed to the victim; as quickly as possible, they secured him onto a backboard and brought him out.

"He is breathing," Craig said. "He's alive."

"Barely," Mike muttered.

Craig looked at the man. He was astonished to see that it seemed one of his eyes opened. He was trying to wet his lips. Trying to speak.

Craig lowered his head and an ear toward the man's mouth, straining to hear his whisper.

"They must think I'm dead, must think I'm dead . . . I am dead. The kids, oh, God, Lily . . ."

"Hey, it's all right," Craig said.

What a stupid thing to say. Nothing was all right. That man was most probably dying.

But, according to his whisper, it seemed he almost needed to be dead.

"Dead, dead. For the kids, Lily . . ."

His voice trailed away. His one half-opened eye closed.

"We've got him," a voice said softly.

An EMT was there. A serious young woman who had a medical bag with her, and a partner who was quickly at her side. They began to rattle off orders and agreements to one another, and her male partner shouted for a stretcher.

A few minutes later, the man was ready for transport.

"Any chance he'll make it?" Craig asked the young female EMT.

"Yeah — he's still breathing. I always say there's a chance — as long as you're still breathing. If there is the hint of a pulse, even, there's a chance," she said. "His is not a good chance. But we don't give up until . . . well, we don't give up. You riding with him?"

"Yeah, thanks!" Craig said. He turned to Mike.

"Meet you at the hospital," Mike said.

"Find Kieran first, please," Craig said. "This group, they're always a step ahead of us. Make sure she's okay, huh? Bring her with you."

"You got it. She was at the safe house, right? With Egan?" Mike asked.

"Yes!"

"I'm on it!" Mike promised.

Craig crawled into the ambulance, keeping the best distance he could in the small space from the EMTs working to save the man's life.

He was still breathing in the horrible scent of burning human flesh . . .

He took a deep breath, anyway. Patience. He was praying hard that they could save this man's life — even though the man didn't particularly seem to want to be alive.

That was it, of course. He'd said, *They must think I'm dead.*

That was the threat.

If he lived, if he talked, they'd kill his wife and kids.

" 'Come with me!' " Danny whispered to Kieran. "He sounds like the friggin' Terminator. I mean, he could have added, 'If you want to live.' "

Kieran turned quickly to stare at her brother as they headed through the crowd in the direction of Jacob Wolff.

"Danny, he may mean just that! There's

someone in that crowd. Come on . . . we have to move, move fast!"

"Holy . . . whatever," Danny muttered.

They moved down one alley and then another.

They were not in a good section of Brooklyn. Trash lay about; a stench rose from the street. The buildings around them appeared to be covered in the soot of decades, or perhaps a century; the whole area had a miasma about it, as if not just the trash and grime of time lay upon it, but as if poverty and hard labor and heartbreak and misery remained, as well.

"Where's he taking us?" Danny demanded.

"I don't know."

"How do you know we should be following him? Who the hell is he? Is this whole thing entirely crazy? He could be taking us down dark alleys to slit our throats —"

"He's an undercover agent, Danny," she whispered back.

"Here!"

Jacob Wolff suddenly stopped, hurriedly used a key in a lock, and pushed open a nondescript door.

He ushered them in and closed and locked the door behind them.

The place was as nondescript as the door.

273

Sparse furnishings, somewhat dark and dingy; it offered something of a living room/ dining room area, a kitchen. There was no desk to be seen, no computer and absolutely nothing that might indicate anything about an owner or a resident.

"Safe house, hideout safe house, really. No one stays here, but it gets you out of the immediate action," Jacob explained.

"Yeah, the immediate action," Danny agreed. He looked at Kieran. He cleared his throat. "Okay, so . . . you're an undercover cop."

"I won't be much longer. This thing is bursting into the open. I'll be seen through soon enough — I've been hanging around the places where the worst of the worst hang out too often," Wolff muttered. He looked at Kieran. She was afraid it might be an accusing look.

"If this blows open, you'll need a break — a real life for a while, anyway," she told him.

He didn't argue with that.

"But . . . what the hell are we doing here? What was going on? Why did you drag us here?" Danny asked.

"The King and Queen are out there somewhere," Jacob said.

Danny looked at Kieran as if she had really dragged him into a madhouse.

"King and Queen. Hey, buddy, sorry — this is America!"

There was a nice ring to his words — very patriotic — Kieran thought.

"They're criminals, Danny, who go by those monikers so that no one knows their real names or even pseudonyms they might use. And to make those working more or less bow down before them," Kieran explained.

"You should have let them come at me. Come on. What New York Irish kid hasn't had a few boxing lessons?" Danny demanded.

"I'm not sure you understand this neighborhood, or these people. For the most part, they've gone to the dark side, some just to survive. They don't fight fair, Mr. Finnegan," Wolff said. "They slip through a crowd with knives, guns, needles . . . you name it. They kill without blinking, without anyone ever knowing who they are."

Danny looked at Kieran. "The woman on the street . . . by your office. She was killed by the King or the Queen?"

"Or someone ordered by them to kill," Kieran said.

"But they don't just kill random people in a crowd," Danny said.

Wolff appeared uncomfortable. He looked

at Kieran, and then shrugged.

She was glad that he didn't assume Danny to be ignorant of what went on around him.

Danny groaned. "I get it. Kieran. They know who Kieran is — they know her association with the case. God, that's horrible. Okay, so — the King and Queen must be caught." He looked at his sister, his lips pressed tightly together until he opened his mouth to speak. "Or you can't ever just walk down a street!"

He didn't wait for a reply from her. He turned to Wolff. "What were they doing out there — the King and the Queen? And who pushed by me — someone terrified of them? And on top of everything else, I've been trying to make her act like a normal human being, so can you find out if Craig is all right? She'll run out in the street like a pawn ready for a sacrifice to a king or a queen if she doesn't find out about him soon."

Danny sounded hard — but calm. And reasonable.

Wolff nodded slowly. "Someone who must have been running from them pushed by you. I saw her, too. I have to get back out on the street — I have to try to find her. My assumption is that our new friends — Riley and Tanya — have proven that escape is possible, so someone else is trying to run.

We were too close to their operation — at the warehouse that just exploded — and they had to move. Maybe someone slipped out in the confusion. I'll make a call and find out about Craig. Uh . . . make yourselves at home. There's water in the refrigerator, maybe some juice or sodas. I'll get someone here to get you safely out as soon as possible."

"We're trapped here?" Danny asked flatly.

"For now."

"Just find out about Craig, please," Kieran urged. "I don't know what he's doing. I assume that he's okay but really busy, but my phone was smashed in the crowd. I can't call him."

Danny pointed a finger at her. "You owe me one. Damn it, you will be careful. You will stay alive! You owe me one."

"Oh, Daniel Finnegan, you have your nerve!" Kieran told him. "After the messes you've gotten me into, not to mention . . ."

She let her voice trail off. Wolff was almost smiling as he watched the two of them.

To Kieran's surprise, he shrugged and told Danny, "Hey, I have a sister, too. It's never easy."

Her mouth opened in astonishment. But she didn't speak. Wolff had already turned away.

And Danny was grinning.

"Yep, sisters. Every guy understands the trauma," he assured her.

Craig had to fight to control himself not to pace or crawl the very walls in his efforts to remain patient.

Their victim was in critical shape. *Critical* was surely an understatement for the condition. It was going to be some time — saving a human life came before any other need in a hospital. Craig might well be desperate to hear the man speak again, but he was going to have to wait.

And nothing could drag him away from the hospital right now.

This man could hold the elusive key to the entire operation.

Craig had just been ushered to a private waiting room when he was joined by Detectives Holmes and Beard. They hurried in, looking at him expectantly and hopefully.

"They said we can wait. Pray, hope, whatever, but his chances aren't good. He suffered extensive burns," Beard said, looking at Craig as if he might just give him something a little more optimistic.

"He's alive right now," Craig said.

"So he could make it," Holmes put in determinedly.

"We'll go on that hope," Craig told them.

Before he could get any further, Lance Kendall came hurrying in. Like Holmes and Beard before him, he stared at Craig hopefully. "Anything? Anything?"

"Something, anyway — he did speak," Craig said.

"What? He spoke? Really. *He spoke?* Then he told you . . . ?" Kendall asked.

"Lord, help us all! Did we get another name?" Beard asked.

"No. I'm sorry. I should have used the words *murmured fairly incoherently,*" Craig said. "He didn't give me a name. But he did give me an understanding. He wasn't terrified of dying — he was ready to die. He was terrified of someone knowing that he *didn't* die. Whoever the hell he was working for — or under. These people — the King and Queen and the crew beneath them — must be threatening the loved ones of anyone who falls under their power. Now, I don't know how far their terror extends. I don't know if they can strike at loved ones only in the States or also back in their homelands — I don't pretend to know how this group manages their reign of terror. Our victim believes that if these people discover that he's not dead, someone else — someone he loves — is in danger. I was about to call my supervising director. I want to put a statement out saying that one man was found dead in the rubble. He has to be protected. He may live. He may come to. But if we're to get any kind of cooperation from him, we're going to have to help him and his family. I believe that helping him means getting the info out there that he was found dead."

"And then we pray he doesn't die — that he *can* tell us something," Holmes said. He swore suddenly, pacing across the room. "He has to live."

"Yeah," David Beard agreed glumly. He looked at Craig. "God, there has to be an end to this. If we lose him . . . another five years, and God knows how many lives may be lost, as well."

Craig's phone was buzzing. He excused himself to answer it.

Mike was on the other end. "Craig, Egan is at the scene of the explosion. Apparently, they took Kieran to Finnegan's."

"Okay, so . . . can you get her and bring her here?"

"I'm going to go to Finnegan's right now," Mike said.

There was something strange in his tone that alerted Craig to trouble.

"You're going there now? Because you've

spoken to her — and she knows you're coming to get her?"

Mike was silent a minute. "She's not answering her phone. I'm going there because I know she was let out there by one of our people." He went quiet again.

"Mike?"

"Okay, well, apparently, she isn't there. But one of the waitresses thinks that she saw her with one of her brothers, so she isn't alone. And I'm going to find her."

"Which brother?"

"Danny."

"Great," Craig said, not entirely honestly.

Kieran was missing.

And so, Craig realized, there *was* something that could drag him away from the hospital.

"I'll meet you at Finnegan's," Craig said. His heart was pounding; his mouth was dry.

On the one hand, he was ready to throttle her.

Why the hell wasn't she safely at the family pub, surrounded by her brothers and a dozen people who were like family?

And on the other hand . . .

He couldn't even begin to imagine losing her.

"Hey, partner, she probably just ran out of battery or something in her phone," Mike said. "You stay there. I'll find her."

"Kendall, Beard *and* Holmes are here. And our fellow isn't going to be able to talk for hours — maybe days — if ever. I'll meet you at Finnegan's," Craig said flatly.

"Craig, I . . . We'll find her."

"Craig is fine," Wolff told Kieran. "I've just reached Director Egan, who's going to help get you safely out of here, and he assured me that Craig's all right. He saw him leave with someone who was injured, but Craig was just fine. Okay?"

Kieran let out a long breath, relief flooding through her. "Thank you," she told him.

"Of course. But you need to remain here until his people are able to come for you," Wolff told them.

"How will we know when his people come?" Danny asked. "You know, neither of us is armed if the wrong person comes here."

"The wrong person won't come here," Wolff assured him. "Egan will send someone you know. You don't open the door until you hear that the agents are here for you. You all right with that?"

"Yes, of course," Kieran said.

"No. You drag us here, and then leave us," Danny said.

"He got us out of a dangerous situation, Danny. And now he has to go back to work," Kieran said. "We're fine," she assured Wolff. "I know Egan. He'll have people here for us right away."

"Hey, I watch television! I've seen all the cop shows. You don't leave witnesses alone," Danny said.

"Danny!"

"If anything happens to you . . ." Danny said, looking at her. "Well, for one, everyone will blame me."

"None of this was your fault. I made you come with me," Kieran said. "And nothing is going to happen to us." She turned from her brother to the undercover cop who had brought them to safety. "We're fine, Jacob. Absolutely. Danny — do you want someone else to die?"

"Of course not." Danny frowned, staring at her.

"I have to see who I can find," Wolff said softly. "Obviously there is at least one person out there trying to escape in the midst of all this. Possibly more than one if you heard her talking to someone."

"Go on. Get out there," Danny said.

Wolff smiled. "I'm going out the back. Come and I'll show you the latch and you can reset it."

"Of course," Danny said. He followed Wolff. Kieran followed Danny — there was no way that she wasn't going to see exactly what was going on.

They went through a little hall. It ended at a wall with a box in front of it. Wolff moved the box; there was a small door. He slid a bolt and she saw that the small door led out into a smoky, rat-infested alley that couldn't have been more than four feet wide. But Wolff headed out into the narrow space.

"Close it and throw the bolt," Wolff told them.

Danny did so. "Done!" he shouted.

They didn't hear more from Wolff. After a moment, Kieran turned and headed into the living area of the little place.

"What are you doing?" Danny asked her.

"Turning on the TV."

"That's it? You're just turning on the TV?" Danny asked.

"Yeah. You have a better idea?"

"I don't like this. I don't like it one bit."

"Yes, but . . ."

"I get it. I get it, Kieran. I just don't have to like it. You hang with scary people."

"You like Craig."

"I love him, like a brother, and I figure he will be my brother-in-law one day. But . . ."

"Craig didn't make this happen, Danny. The woman came and shoved that baby into *my* arms."

"Yeah, I know. I shouldn't have let you talk me into this this afternoon," he said. "I should have said, hell, no, if you're trying to connive with me, something is not right."

"We're in some kind of a safe house, or a crash house, or . . . whatever. I know this guy — Jacob Wolff. He's an amazing man. We're good," Kieran said. She turned the television on, thinking that she'd click around until she found the news about the explosion.

She didn't have to flick channels at all.

A newsman stood among the smoke and flames, the sound of sirens, of shouts, of people on the street, speaking loudly into his microphone.

"No one knows as yet what caused the explosion, though we're assuming — with the amount of law enforcement officials hovering around — that arson is suspected. We're looking into ownership of the building, though here's what's good — it appeared to have been deserted. Sorry to say that one man has been discovered in the building, dead, killed by the blast, but no further details are forthcoming at this moment. Now, if you'll look behind me, you

285

can see that the New York Fire Department is still struggling to control all the flames . . ."

"One man dead," Danny murmured. He looked at his sister. "So someone was killed in the explosion. But it wasn't Craig. You know that."

Kieran nodded. She could see that Egan was there, on the street in the background. She assumed that he was speaking with other high-ranking officials or officers.

"Craig is there somewhere working, you know," Danny said.

"Yes, of course."

"So you shouldn't really be bothering him. In fact, honestly, and not to be a mean brother or anything, but we probably never should have come out here."

"Maybe not," Kieran agreed. And then she felt like an idiot. "You have your phone!"

"Of course I have my phone. If you hadn't had yours out in that insane crowd, you wouldn't have dropped it and it wouldn't be smashed mush right now."

"Not the point. Can you please call Craig for me?" she asked.

"Sure. Or here — you can call him."

"Why the hell didn't you say that before?"

"You never said anything."

"My phone was smashed."

"Yeah? So you should have thought to ask me."

And, of course, she should have.

"Give it to me now."

"Here." He handed her his phone. She found Craig's number on it quickly and hit the speed dial for him.

Craig answered. "Danny? Danny, is Kieran with you? Where the hell is she?"

She inhaled deeply. He was going to be angry.

"Craig, it's me."

"Why in God's name aren't you answering your phone? Where are you?"

She didn't want to tell him her phone had been stomped on in a crowd — he'd know where she'd been. But she did have to tell him where she was, and then, of course, he'd know where she'd been, anyway.

"I broke my phone," she said simply. "I'm safe, and I'm with Danny. I . . . we came to Brooklyn. I was worried about you. We ran into Jacob Wolff in the crowd. He thought we should come with him. We're in some kind of a hideaway or safe house or whatever you all call it. I'm not sure I know how to give you the address for this place —"

"I know where it is. Kieran, what the hell were you doing at the scene of the explosion? Mike was trying to find you for me. I was crazed here, not knowing . . . Damn it — these people are ruthless when it comes to killing!"

"Yes, and I was worried about you. I'm sorry!" she said. "Anyway, we're fine. And you didn't let me know what was going on — I didn't know that you were okay. Seriously, Craig . . ." Her voice trailed. Danny was looking at her, shaking his head.

Craig was trained; she was not. Craig carried a gun; she did not.

She let out a breath. "Look, I apologize, but we're safe. Wolff said that Egan was going to send someone for me —"

"I'll talk to Egan. Hold tight. I'll come and get you myself."

"Okay. We'll be here," she said lamely. Then words rushed from her. "I'm sorry. I saw the news. I know that a man was killed. I know that we're getting information too late. I know that they even killed a nun. I'm . . . so sorry."

"You've got to be careful," he warned softly. "Anyway, hang tight. Mike and I will be there."

"Sounds good," she murmured. She wondered if she should add an "I love you."

People were listening; this was a professional situation.

Danny was staring at her.

288

She was pretty sure that Craig was with Mike.

"Sounds good," she repeated, and she clicked the end button and handed the phone to Danny.

"They're coming."

"What should we do until then?"

"There's always the TV."

"And the news is just great," Danny said drily.

"I'm sure we can find something else."

"I don't think they have a bunch of the premium channels being piped in here," Danny said, playing with the remote control.

He paused as another anchor went on and on about the explosion. This man connected it — somehow — to the murder that had taken place in Manhattan the Friday before.

"Strange happenings, even for this city," the man was saying. "Last week, a Jane Doe murdered in broad daylight. This week, a building going up in a massive mystery explosion, and another man — unidentified — dead. Melinda," he went on, talking to the anchorwoman in the studio, "I'm going to say that police have their hands full with this. And, of course, we're reminded of that poor woman found bleeding to death in Brooklyn five years ago. This is a city of dreams turned into a nightmare for many!"

"I thought the police were being very closemouthed about the things they learned to protect the women who are in danger," Danny muttered.

"They aren't giving out any information, Danny. I guess reporters are going to know what has happened in the past and they'll be able to look up anything that was ever told in a police press conference. They're bound to speculate."

"Everyone is speculating." Danny stared at the television and then turned to her. "Kieran, if they did kill Sister Teresa, they will stop at nothing."

A chill seemed to catch in her heart and streak through her veins. She was about to reassure him, to remind him that Craig and Mike were coming. Before she could speak, she heard a thud against the front door.

Her heart nearly leapt from her throat.

Danny did leap from the sofa where he had been sitting.

They stared at one another for a long second, and then ran on tiptoes together to the door.

There was a tiny peephole. Kieran found it first and looked out.

She could see nothing. Only darkness. Shaking her head, she moved away from the door.

Danny had to see for himself. He pressed his face to the door, one eye to the peephole. He kept changing his position. He shook his head, and then beckoned her away from the door.

"The bolts on it are good and strong," he said in a whisper. "No one is coming in that way without a battering ram. And as for the back entrance . . . no. We're fine. We need to sit tight. If someone knows that anyone is in here, they'll be listening. We need to be quiet."

"The television," Kieran said.

"It's been on — can't turn it off now. That would clearly show that someone is in here."

"But —"

"Trust me. I was one hell of a punk, even if I thought I was a crusader for truth, justice, the American way and little kids who were picked on," he said, grinning. "Me being one of them, of course."

She tried a weak smile for her brother. "The door is good and solid," she said.

They looked at each other; there was nothing more to do.

Kieran tiptoed back to the door, followed by her brother. They both looked out the little peephole again. There was nothing but darkness.

"Guess the city can't afford lights for these

poor alleys, huh?" Danny asked.

"Maybe it's just the way that the lights are set up," Kieran said. "They're on the main streets, so they don't quite glow down the alleyways . . ."

Danny grunted.

Then they heard the sound of something thunderous slamming against the door.

Kieran jumped way back from the door.

Danny hesitated, and then looked out.

Kieran waited, barely daring to breathe.

"Well?" she whispered.

"Nothing," he told her. "Whoever it is," he whispered, "they might be figuring out the fact that the door is solid and the bolts are steel."

"What about the back?" she whispered urgently. "We never checked!"

"No, we didn't," Danny said.

"Let's go," Kieran mouthed.

She led the way; Danny hurried after her down the small hallway. She hadn't put the box back after Wolff had left. They had, at least, latched the bolt.

They had barely reached it when they heard a sound.

This time, it wasn't someone pounding on the door. It was as though someone were trying to test it as quietly as possible. Kieran looked at Danny. His eyes widened. She

292

wasn't imagining it.

She reached out and tested the bolt. It was strongly in place. Whoever was trying the door could twist and twist at the knob — it wouldn't change the fact that steel was holding the door closed.

She wasn't sure it helped any, but she started to shove the box back in front of it. Danny helped. The door was bolted, and now there was a second layer between them and whoever was out there.

Danny beckoned Kieran back in. "Call Craig," he said, barely moving his mouth and making sound. "If he can get here while this is going on, first off, he can save our asses! Secondly, he might catch someone who has something to do with all this."

Kieran started to accept the phone from Danny. As she did so, they heard a strange scratching sound at the front door.

Then, to her surprise, she heard a voice. It was a male voice, deep and rich, but sounded as if the speaker was putting on a deliberately scary tone.

"We know you're in there . . . we're going to get you! We'll huff and we'll puff and . . . eventually, we'll get to you. It will be so, so bad. You can, however, open the door and make it easy, and if it's easy for me, it will be so much easier for you!"

Danny and Kieran stared at each other; they shook their heads simultaneously, almost reading one another's minds.

No. This guy meant to kill them — meant to kill whoever he found. There was no way in hell they were going to make it easy.

Another voice sounded, but softly. The speaker was a female — and she wasn't trying to be heard. She was nearly whispering, and it was impossible to make out her words.

The male voice came to them again, strong and loud. "I'm not going to give you any second chances. You're dying tonight one way or another!"

Kieran stared at Danny.

"What the hell do we do?" she whispered.

He shrugged. "I guess we can pray?"

CHAPTER TWELVE

Randy Holmes didn't mind sitting at the hospital; he seemed to be a good cop, ready to do what was needed. He was a patient man, a team player.

He'd wait forever, if that's what was asked of him.

David Beard was more restless; he was ready to be out chasing whatever slim leads they had — he'd been trying for five years to catch a killer.

When Craig hurried out to the street to meet up with Mike, the cops were standing in front of the hospital entry, still discussing their plans.

Lance Kendall was stoic. "McBride is on the street. I'm here. That's how we're working it," he said with a shrug. "I know that Miss Finnegan is deeply involved in all this. Go see that she's safe. Nothing will happen here that you don't get wind of immediately. You're on my speed dial — I swear it."

Kendall tried to smile. He wasn't very good at it, but his lips did move a little. He did clearly want to get along with his fellow NYPD colleagues, the Bureau men and whoever else he wound up working with.

Craig knew it was ego to ever think he was the only officer or agent capable of solving his cases — most cases were solved by the hard work of a number of people.

And he did have to get to Kieran.

He was watching Mike's car come around the corner down the block when he heard his phone ring.

The call was from Danny Finnegan's number. "Kieran? I'm here. What's going on?"

She didn't reply. He could hear noise in the background.

"Kieran? What is it? You all right?"

But he couldn't hear *her.*

He could hear, though — as if from a great distance, or as if coming from a cave — another speaker. The sound was faint.

He quickly fell silent himself, listening. Straining to hear.

He could make out a cold, detached, controlled voice.

"I've got a razor-sharp blade with your name on it. My knife can be quick or slow. But it is going to hurt, and you're going to die. I mean, will you care how it happened once you are dead? Dead is dead. But I'll know. And I care that it hurts."

Craig didn't call Kieran's name again; he just held his phone in a death grip as he continued to listen.

Where the hell was Mike?

There!

Mike pulled up in front, and Craig hopped into the passenger's seat of the car, phone glued to his ear as he waved out an arm, indicating that his partner should drive.

Mike understood instantly, but he frowned. "What's going on?" he asked.

Craig covered the microphone on the phone. "I don't know. It sounds like there is someone at the door of Wolff's safe house. Get there, Mike — get there as fast as you can," he said.

Then, through the phone, Craig heard Danny whispering urgently. "Kieran, trust me — there's a woman there, too. Listen. She told him to go around back and shoot the damned door. Kieran, they'll get through. There's only one bolt on that door. If they shoot . . ."

"Maybe we should let him come around — and we bolt out the front the second it happens. They won't expect that. They . . ." She sounded scared, but Craig was grateful to hear her voice.

"You're crazy! Don't you think that whispering bitch out front has a gun, too?" Danny demanded.

"Have you got a better idea? I'm fresh out!" Kieran's voice said in a heated whisper that came through the phone line with an eerie, fatalistic sound.

Mike was tearing through the streets at reckless speed, but he glanced from the road ahead of him to Craig. "What's happening?" he demanded. "It's going to be all right. It's not far, Craig — not far at all," Mike said as he took a corner with tires squealing in protest. "I'd call for backup, but I swear we'll make it before anyone else could."

Craig heard Kieran shouting.

"You despicable *creatures*!" Kieran raved loudly and angrily, her voice carrying clearly out of the phone's speaker. "You listen to me, you homicidal maniacs. Do your best! Huff and puff away. Police and FBI agents are hurrying here at this moment. Hell! And Homeland Security and the US Marshals office — they're all involved. And you're the one who is going to be dead. Dead, dead, dead. And it's not going to matter how you got that way, right? It's not going to matter! But you will be the dead ones!"

"I think she's pissed," Mike murmured.

"Get there, Mike, for the love of God . . ."

"I'll pull into the alley. The place is shot anyway — they'll need a new safe house. Sorry! I'm there, I'm there . . ."

"That's it, right? Turn the corner. We're there!"

Mike jerked the car around the corner and came to a jarring halt.

There it was. The door to Jacob Wolff's safe house.

Craig leapt out of the passenger's seat and started running down the alley.

There was a furious, hard slam against the front door again.

And then nothing.

Danny gripped Kieran, pulling her close.

"You either really pissed them off or . . . well, pissing off people like that isn't exactly a good thing. He was making one good point. Dead might be dead, but getting there . . . I mean, a bullet to the brain might be a lot easier than that maniac's knife. Not that we're going to die. Nope! We're going to be just fine . . ." Danny said.

They heard footsteps, running.

Something slammed against the door again.

Kieran's breath went out in a whoosh.

But then she heard her name.

Her name . . .

In Craig's voice.

"Here, here! We're in here, we're fine, all fine!" she cried.

"Careful!" Danny warned.

"It's me! It's Craig!"

Kieran didn't need more; she unbolted the lock and threw the door open.

Craig stood there. She nearly knocked him over, throwing herself into his arms. He held her tightly for a moment. She felt the way his entire body was trembling.

He loved her. He really loved her. She'd known it, and yet, tonight, she felt it. More than ever, felt it even in the way that he touched her.

He pulled away. "What the hell were you doing? Egan had sent you to Finnegan's!"

"I told you I was worried."

"She really was," Danny said.

Craig looked at Danny and reached out a hand, drawing him in. For a moment, Kieran feared that Craig would be angry with her brother.

"Thank God you were with her!" Craig muttered.

Apparently, he wasn't angry with Danny. As much as Craig and her brothers treated her as an equal . . .

When it came to danger, she was always

going to be a girl!

"A building exploded, Craig. A building I thought that you had walked into!" Kieran said, making her own voice hard and stern. "As to being safe . . . Your buddy, Jacob, had us lock ourselves in here. To be safe. But, Craig, there were people here. Trying to get in. Threatening us! I guess you didn't see them, but I swear I'm telling the truth. They would have gotten in in just another few minutes. All they had to do was shoot the bolt. I don't know why they didn't . . ."

"I heard them," Craig said. "I heard them talking, Kieran — through Danny's phone."

"Oh! So I did call you."

"You did. And I heard you and —"

They heard footsteps. It was frightening — in a good way — to see how quickly Craig pulled his gun and turned.

He just as quickly holstered his gun behind his back as they saw that it was Mike.

Mike was panting.

He leaned over, resting his hands on his knees, still breathing heavily as he tried to talk.

"Ran . . . down the alley . . . they might have disappeared into thin air. Or into a window. I thought I saw movement. I ran, I gave chase . . . Nothing. Not even a wisp disappearing. Hell, aliens might have ab-

301

ducted them. They're just gone."

"They know the neighborhood. They — whoever they may be — must have had eyes on Jacob Wolff. Jacob kept a good cover. But maybe someone either followed us the other day when we were with him after the restaurant, or someone followed him tonight when he was with Kieran and Danny. They had someone here."

"It wasn't just a few disposable lackeys," Kieran said suddenly. "It was *them*. As in the King and Queen, Craig. I . . . I mean, he was so comfortable with himself, with threatening me, and he had no accent whatsoever. Middle American, I guess. TV American accent, if there is such a thing. And the woman . . . I don't think that English was her first language."

"How can you know? We couldn't hear her!" Danny said.

"We heard her a little. And I don't think that she was American. And if I'm right, and if everything I've learned from Riley and Tanya is true . . . their *King* is American. And his *Queen* is from somewhere else. And we know they were out there today — others were trying to escape them, Craig. A woman shoved by Danny, telling someone that the King was in the crowd. Then we ran into Wolff, and he brought us here.

Craig! You need experts — people who can check the doors, who can look for footprints — oh! Maybe one of them touched the door. Maybe there are fingerprints. Maybe there's . . . something!"

"Hey, the place is totally compromised, anyway," Mike said, looking at Craig.

Craig stared at Kieran, nodding.

"Where is your phone?" he asked her.

"In my purse. It was crushed. I didn't lose it."

"That's good," he said quietly, drawing out his own. He stepped aside and she could hear him talking rapidly. When he came back, he told them all, "Crime scene teams will be here soon. Every officer in the area has been warned to watch out for the King and the Queen, and they've all been briefed on the situation."

"No one knows what they look like," Kieran said.

"Yeah. That makes it hard. But we'll be on the lookout for anything unusual. Egan wants me to get everyone safely home for some rest."

"I hope he's including me in that," Mike said. "I'm really tired."

"Yeah, Mike, I have a car near Kieran's — you can drop us, and then keep the car we had today. That work for you?"

"Yep, fine. But . . ." Mike paused, glancing at Kieran. "What about the — the hospital?"

"Hospital?" Kieran asked anxiously. "Craig, who . . . ?"

"We don't know. The man who was reported to be dead is actually alive, but barely hanging on."

"Yep, clinging to life," Mike said. "He's burned to pieces. More than half-dead."

Craig told Danny and Kieran, "That's not information anyone but law enforcement has. It's important that this gang — the heads of it, King and Queen, whatever royalty or lackeys — don't get wind of the fact that he isn't dead already. I think he wanted to die — that would have been a guarantee that he'd paid for whatever he'd done wrong, and his family wouldn't have to pay the price. Never saw a man so afraid of *living.* We don't have to go back to the hospital tonight. He's in a medically induced coma. He won't be speaking to anyone until tomorrow — and even that's unlikely. Detectives Kendall and Holmes will be staying, watching over him. And, I do have an idea for tomorrow, bright and early, but as for now . . ."

"Home," Mike said happily. "Danny, I don't know where you live —"

"He's coming to my place," Kieran said.

"I am?" Danny asked. "Hey, come on, you can't boss me around anymore, Kieran. Love you, sis, but honest to God —"

"Danny, please. I was scared to death," Kieran said.

"But now Craig is with you."

"I was scared to death for you as well as me!" Kieran told him. "Humor me. Please, let me get some sleep tonight."

Danny looked at Craig.

Craig shrugged.

"I don't care what we do — let's get home for tonight," Craig said.

Kieran didn't argue. His arm was around her as they headed for the car. As they did so, a van belonging to the crime scene unit came driving in.

Craig urged Kieran forward, letting Mike get her into the car while he went to speak to the head of the unit. Then he joined them in the car.

It was a quiet ride back to Manhattan.

Halfway there, Kieran turned to Craig next to her in the back seat of the Bureau's sedan.

"What is your idea for tomorrow?"

"Riley and Tanya."

"What about them?"

"I want to see if they can identify our

mystery man. Our man in the hospital. He's in a bad way, Kieran. Really bad. He may not make it. I'm not sure his mother could recognize him. We've still got to try."

"Of course," Kieran murmured. "That does sound like a plan. But what if they do have eyes everywhere? What if we're seen going to the hospital? Won't that lead the killers right to a man they really want to be dead?"

"Nope. You won't recognize Riley or Tanya. Or me, for that matter," Craig promised.

Kieran groaned inwardly. Craig was a master of makeup and disguise. He was experienced at undercover operations.

But it scared her. She wanted to know what fail-safes were in place.

Then it occurred to Kieran that if Craig was occupied at the hospital with the survivor and Riley and Tanya, she just might have the opportunity to try to see the baby.

With that thought in mind, she murmured something about the fact that while they were still scared, Tanya and Riley were wonderfully ready to help the police and the Bureau at any time.

It took about thirty minutes to reach Kieran's street in the St. Mark's area of Manhattan. When Mike parked the car,

Danny looked at her with his eyebrows raised — probably hoping that she was going to tell him just to go home. But when she didn't budge, he seemed to give up and he got out of the car along with her and Craig. They bid Mike goodnight; he and Craig would talk in the morning.

In the sushi restaurant, someone was warbling out a frightening rendition of Bon Jovi's "Livin' on a Prayer."

"Last time, I think it was a lady auditioning for *The Lion King,*" Danny said. "Feast or famine entertainment-wise here, huh?"

"You can't hear it upstairs," Kieran said.

"You can't hear it? You've lived here too long."

"Danny, I haven't even been here three years," Kieran protested. "Come on, please, be nice. I'll make grilled cheese. We'll all go to bed."

"Or to couch," Danny muttered.

Kieran let out a sigh of frustration. "To couch, whatever!"

"Shower," Craig said. "I smell like a burning building. I think I even smell like . . ." His voice trailed, but they were both staring at him. "Burning flesh," he said quietly.

"Yes, you need a shower!" Kieran told him. "And your clothing needs to be sterilized!"

Inside, he headed straight for her room and the en suite shower. She wanted to follow him.

She wanted to make sure Danny was okay, too.

"Hey, you made me come here!" Danny told her. "What? Am I putting a bit of a snag in your romantic expectations for the evening? Wait, you've been living together a long time."

"Someone could have followed us. You shouldn't be on your own tonight," Kieran said firmly.

"Well, I'm here. And I'm fine. Go and talk and cuddle . . . or whatever. I don't want to know. I'll get the grilled cheese started."

Kieran nodded, biting her lower lip. Then she hurried into the bedroom, shedding her clothing to join Craig in the shower — and wondering if she had created an awkward situation.

Still, she slipped beneath the cascading water and wrapped her arms around Craig, pressing herself against his back. He stood very still for a long moment. Warmth and steam rose around them while the water beat down.

Suddenly he spun around, sliding his arms around her waist and pulling her close.

"Marry me," he said.

She looked at him, startled. It wasn't something that they hadn't talked about before — they just hadn't been in any hurry. They were young; they were career oriented. They were happy as things were.

"I . . . Where did that come from so suddenly?" she asked.

"We've lived together for almost two years," he reminded her. "Your place mostly, sometimes my place . . ."

"We do need to pick one place to live," she murmured.

"Yes, and . . . well, I always thought that eventually we'd get married."

"We really should," she said. She smiled, feeling a surge of joy. "We'll need an Irish priest. You know my family."

"An Irish priest," he agreed.

He pulled her close. She felt the naked flesh of his chest against her cheek and felt the hard pounding of his heart. He kissed her and ran his fingers down her spine, and then back up again, and with the touch she was pressed closer to his body, closing her eyes, caught for a minute in nothing but sensation.

Maybe they were done talking . . .

"I was truly frightened today," he told her. "Mike couldn't find you. And your phone . . ."

They weren't.

"It broke. I'm so sorry."

"Things happen. You shouldn't have to be sorry. I was just beyond scared. And I thought about life . . . our lives. And I think we should get married."

"I think that we should get married, but . . ."

Because it's right, because we're ready . . . not because of fear . . .

She never said the words. His phone started to ring. He moved back, pulled the curtain aside, and stepped out of the tub.

She heard him speaking curtly to someone. It was mainly a lot of "Oh?"

"Yes." And "No."

"Craig?" she asked.

She realized that he'd hung up and stepped out of the bathroom. When she emerged, wrapped in one of their large fluffy bath towels and headed into the bedroom, she found that he was almost dressed.

"You're going out now?" she asked.

"I have to."

"So . . . what's up? Where are you going? I should probably be with you, you know."

She waited for the argument from him.

It didn't come.

"We're going out now — all of us," he said. "You, me and Danny."

"Oh? Where?"

"We're meeting up with Detectives Beard, Holmes and Kendall — and Riley and Tanya," he added softly. "Their new keepers — the US Marshals Madison Smyth and Hank LeBlanc — will be following, watching out for whatever is going on. We'll fix up at the safe house."

"Oh. Well, good. I do help with Riley and Tanya and —"

"And I'm not leaving you here alone."

"I'd be with Danny."

"I love your brother, Kieran. He's an amazing man — fiercely loyal, almost to a dangerous point. And in a fair fight, I'd back him against a bigger guy because he's a smart fighter, too. But your brother is not a killer. And he's not even licensed to have a firearm. It's not a good time for anyone to be alone, so . . . he'll hang with us. It will be great."

She had to smile. "For now."

"For now. We are going to get these guys — the whole racket, men, women, whoever they may be. We are going to get them. I swear it."

Kieran nodded. "I'll be dressed in five. But . . . I am a bit confused. Why now? Why not in the morning?"

Craig let out a breath. "Our man . . . the

man we found who survived the explosion. He may not make it. One of the doctors has suggested that if we want someone to identify him, now — despite his condition — would be a better time than if . . . than if he does die."

"I see," Kieran murmured. She was sorry — at least she thought that she was sorry. If the man in the hospital had caused misery to anyone — to the captive immigrant women or their babies — she wasn't sure if the pain he was surely suffering now was enough to make up for what he'd done to others.

But maybe he was a victim himself.

"I'm ready in a minute," she assured him. She hurried to her dresser and tossed out undergarments and then headed for the closet where she quickly grabbed an easy pullover knit dress. When it was over her head, she spun back to look at him.

"Craig."

"Yes?"

"What about Sister Teresa? She wound up forgotten today."

"Not forgotten, I promise."

"Then?"

"She died of a heart attack. There is still lab work being processed. And that takes time, even when the guys at the top of the heap are ordering faster-than-a-speeding-bullet results. Kieran, I know she became special to you in just a short time, but . . . she was nearly a hundred. We should all be so blessed."

"I know."

"If she was murdered — if she was hastened toward death in any way — we will find justice for her, along with the others," Craig vowed.

"Thank you."

"Of course. Now, I guess we have to go let Danny know that he's still in a hot spot. Well, he does want to be NYC's top tourist guide. We give him more stories all the time. We're really doing him a favor."

Kieran laughed. "If he's prepared the grilled cheese sandwiches, I'm going to suggest we eat them as we run. Let's get going."

There was no way to treat a man in the condition of the one who'd survived the explosion and fire other than at the finest burn center in the city. He was fighting for his life with the help of some of the best doctors in the world, Craig was certain.

But he couldn't be taken out and hidden anywhere else.

And that made trying to identify him extremely difficult.

While a press conference had clearly stated that the one man found in the building had been deceased, they couldn't count on it remaining secret that a survivor had been taken to a hospital. The burn unit might be under watch.

So while any number of police officers might easily go in and out of the wards — often enough, criminals in the custody of protective services were in the hospital, or an officer might be there on personal business — the motley crew of agents and witnesses couldn't be seen.

When Craig, Kieran and Danny arrived at the safe house, Riley's beautiful red hair was covered in a short black wig; Tanya had become a brunette. They were dressed in generic jeans and nondescript T-shirts.

Madison Smyth and Hank LeBlanc were in similar apparel, and a policewoman was waiting to see that Kieran was duly wigged and given a few appearance-changing bolsters.

It turned out she was going to be fitted with butt padding. Craig couldn't help but be amused by her horror at the situation.

"Actually," he whispered to her, "it's kind of hot."

She glared at him evilly. "What? My derriere is not big enough as it is?"

"It's perfect — sorry! You just have to look kind of different than usual — that's what they're going for," he told her.

"Great. And you get 'surfer dude.'"

"I've been just about everything at some point."

Egan had made the arrangements; Craig discovered that it had been Riley's idea, and that it had been Kieran's discussions with Riley and Tanya that had led to it.

The operation, as they had known, was a big one. Set up just like a monarchy. There was a king and a queen. There was a royal court that consisted of their hired guns, killers, people as bad as they were. Then there were slaves.

Alexandra Callas had been a slave. She had watched over captives; she had been forced to do so, and then her concern for her friends had held her as much prisoner as any outside threat.

This man might have been in the same position. But Craig believed that it was most likely he had followed orders because his family had been threatened. Why he had been set up to be killed, Craig wasn't sure. Maybe they believe that he'd betrayed them somehow, that something he had done had led to the possible discovery of the warehouse, and thus he'd needed his punishment.

If his family was in the States somewhere, the FBI might be able to help them.

With Riley and Tanya helping them, they hoped to find out.

Craig was to arrive with Tanya and Kieran on his arms; they would be loaded with gifts for a new baby, and appear to be heading to the maternity ward.

Mike, Danny and Riley would be together, friends with cards and gifts for a friend in the orthopedic section — one of the city's football players who had suffered an ankle injury.

The US Marshals and other detectives and uniformed officers would follow up, with Smyth and LeBlanc lead on protection. Lance Kendall and Randy Holmes had remained at the hospital since their man had gone in; Larry McBride would be among those on the team watching for any attackers — and watching for anyone who might be watching.

The police backup team were good at their jobs; they held their distance, staying unnoticed as the first little group arrived.

Even as Craig handed over the false IDs they'd been assigned for the night, he heard the voice of Randy Holmes through his two-way radio earpiece. "Your nine o'clock, Frasier. TV news is on in front of him — and he's got a paper. May just be a reader — may not be, you know?"

Craig surreptitiously looked around. The man seemed to be watching them.

Kieran must have sensed something. "A boy! I'm so happy for them, you, Sissy?" she asked Tanya. "I think we'll have a baby, too, one of these days. If your brother ever decides that we can afford one! Oh, can anyone ever really afford a child? I think not!"

The man looked back down at his paper.

"Might be something, might not," Craig murmured back to Holmes and everyone else on the communication system.

"We'll be watching," Holmes promised.

Craig could see Mike, Danny and Riley as they took their turn and stepped up to offer their IDs and received hospital visitor stickers, as well. Danny took a cue from his sister.

"I love the guy — you know, we went to high school together. And he's still a good guy. But, you know, what an idiot, getting hurt that way! Don't you think so, love?" He gave Riley a squeeze.

"Hey, he's been playing good," Mike said.

"Yeah, but will he now?"

The man with the paper looked out the door, ignoring their group.

"Good call!" Craig said softly to Holmes.

"Thanks. I'm on him. I'll be watching."

Soon, they were all gathered in the small room on the burn floor where Lance Kendall had been holding vigil since their victim had gone in. David Beard had joined him a while ago, and an officer in uniform was keeping guard on the floor, as well.

They assured Craig that they were fine, had covered one another for coffee, naps, food and whatever was needed.

Craig thanked them both for sticking it out.

Beard shook his head. "It's a chance," he said hopefully. "And I'd have given a limb to have caught the bastards five years ago."

"We'll get them," Craig said.

Still, he couldn't help but wonder if they'd catch them all. It was a massive operation. He said as much to Kieran in a low voice.

"Maybe it's like . . . like myth and legend as far as werewolves go," Kieran said.

"Huh?" He turned to stare at her, not sure whether or not she was just trying to ease the terrible tension that seemed to be affecting everyone there.

"If you get the werewolf — or vampire, maybe? — that started it all, the others just fall," Kieran said. "What I mean is . . . the King and Queen are managing it all. Catch them, and you've cut off the head of the operation. The whole thing may then tumble down."

He nodded, almost smiling.

"Yeah, I hope so."

One of the man's doctors arrived and explained that the room had to be kept as a "clean" room, as germ-free as they could make it, and while they were welcome to look at the patient as long as they liked, they had to stay outside the room, looking through a glass window.

Craig led Riley and Tanya forward to see the man.

He lay on his back, a small sheet covering his genitals while the rest of his body was treated. Health-care workers were helping him on a twenty-four-hour basis, administering to his flesh with strips covered in painkillers and medication. At Craig's side, Tanya let out a gasp and began to sob softly.

It was horrible; the man looked something like a steak that had fallen off a grill before being fully cooked.

"Aye, lass, aye," Riley murmured, slipping an arm around Tanya and pulling her close. She looked at Craig over Tanya's head.

"We know him, that we do," she said softly. "Oh, Lord, aye, we know the man."

CHAPTER THIRTEEN

Riley appeared to be very distressed. Tears sprang into her eyes.

"Are you okay?" Kieran asked her.

"Riley?" Danny asked softly. He had definitely decided that he was fond of the two immigrant women, and he seemed to feel a special affinity with Riley — but then, they owned an *Irish* pub, so maybe he was feeling that he should defend a young Irish woman.

But he had been just as courteous toward Tanya.

Actually, Kieran was quite proud of her brother. Danny could be quick to get into a bit of trouble when defending others, but, at least, he tended to want to defend those who were in grave difficulty — he didn't want to get into frays for the hell of it.

Riley looked at Danny with a soft gleam in her eye and she smiled.

"I'm okay," Riley said.

"Did — that man — did he hurt you?" Kieran demanded indignantly.

"Oh, no, no! Nothing like that," Riley said. "No, that's just it. He never hurt us. Looking at him . . . Oh, it's so sad! And he's *not* a bad man. He's not a bad man at all."

Tanya, at Riley's side, shook her head. "No. Not bad man," she agreed.

"What's his name?" Kieran asked.

"Jimmy," Riley said.

"Just — Jimmy?" Craig pressed gently.

"Jimmy," Tanya said.

Mike walked over and spoke softly to Craig, who then excused himself from the girls. Kieran realized that Mike Dalton had been on the phone with someone and that he was explaining the conversation to Craig. She wanted to hear for herself what was going on.

"Excuse me," she said, smiling. She looked at Danny, who seemed to believe that he was no part of an investigation. He nodded to her gravely and slipped between the two young women to set a protective arm around their shoulders. "I've got this," he said to Kieran, adding softly to the young women, "We'll move away a bit. You know him. There's no need for you to stare at the poor man. You must realize, he's not suffering now. The doctors here are brilliant.

They're giving him pain medication. If he can be saved, they will save him."

"Hey," Kieran murmured as she approached Craig and Mike. Craig glanced at her. To her relief, neither man acted as if she shouldn't be involved at every level.

"Detective McBride — yes, *our* McBride," he assured her, "had a troop of officers out in the street after the explosion. They're searching for anyone who saw and remembered anything. Trucks, moving vans and — hope against hope — license plates. We've gotten a few things from the officers and agents on the street. McBride called to assure me that all information is being shared."

"With an operation that size," Kieran said, "someone had to have seen something."

"Yes. Anything that McBride gets, he'll tell us. Anyone who might have even the smallest lead, he'll let us know. You know McBride, he's an A-1 detective, Kieran. Obviously, we're all praying for the burn victim here — on many levels and on different levels, I imagine," Craig said. "But you don't move an operation that size and that quickly without making a mistake — without giving yourself away — somehow, or somewhere along the line. We'll get on it."

"Riley and Tanya definitely know this guy.

You want to talk to them more here?" Kieran asked.

"We should get out of here," Mike murmured. "May have been nothing back down in the lobby, but our friends, the US Marshals, are good at spotting people in a crowd who might be trouble."

"And these people are relentless," Kieran spoke, then looked at Craig and winced. "We're protected, and I feel safe. But this organization has no problem sending in suicide assassins. We definitely shouldn't spend more time here than necessary when there is a hospital full of people we don't want winding up as collateral damage."

Craig walked over to the other little group.

"Come on," Craig said quietly to Tanya, Riley and Danny, indicating the elevators. "We'll get you back to safety. And then we'll talk."

Kieran hung back as Craig urged the women toward Mike. One of the doctors was still by the window, arms crossed over his chest as he looked at the victim and all the administrations being performed.

"Does he have much of a chance?" she asked softly.

"You know, he seems to have a good heart. A strong heart, strong lungs. If the poor fellow wasn't half-dead, he'd be darned

324

healthy. That's in his favor. He's in his early thirties. That's in his favor. He has a chance. Slim, but, yes, he has a chance."

"Thank you, doctor," Kieran said. She looked toward the elevator.

They were waiting for her.

She hurried over to join them, lest she cause any delay when she had pushed to leave as quickly as possible.

The investigation was still in the dark — they didn't have one damned solid lead when it came to finding the power behind the operation, but Craig still felt as if they were moving forward. Riley and Tanya knew the burn victim. And they just might know something that would identify him, and every time they had anything new, it was a lead that could be followed.

If there had been any danger or any strange or unexpected event down in the lobby or beyond, they would have been notified. Craig knew that. Still, it was important to him that he follow protocol and announce the fact that they'd shortly be taking the elevators to the ground floor — his earpiece also was a two-way wireless microphone sensitive enough for them to hear him.

The people at the top of the human trafficking organization did seem to have eyes everywhere. Craig thought it was for the best that Egan had determined that they all go in disguise — if they were seen coming or going, it appeared that they were friends of a downed football player and the doting relatives of a couple who had just given birth.

The hospital security guards had kept an eye out, as had others.

Entry to the burn unit was controlled; they had been in a private room.

Every precaution had been taken.

Now it was important that they get out and make sure that Tanya and Riley were safe.

He spoke softly but clearly.

"We're about to come down. Detective Holmes, anything?"

"He's still sitting here. The man with the paper. I don't like it. I'm going to create a diversion. Hold up a few more minutes if you can," Holmes told him.

"Careful, Holmes." It was Egan who was speaking, listening in on anything that occurred throughout the evening. "I don't like it, either."

"I'm moving over by the restroom door, Holmes," another voice said. It was Hank LeBlanc. Craig could easily recognize the soft Louisiana cadence to his voice. "Watching — ready."

A moment later, something pinged in Craig's ear and he heard an angry man yelping and yelling — and a bunch of apologies.

"Come out, three by three," Egan said.

Three by three. Just as they had gone in. The one group, softly chatting about a newborn baby. The other group shaking their heads — just how had such an injury occurred? So sad — oh, yes, funny — if it weren't so sad.

"Go on down," Craig told Mike.

Mike headed out. Craig took the time to thank Kendall and Beard again, and the doctors looking out for their patient.

Then he led Kieran and Tanya into the elevator and took them down.

The man who had been reading the paper was still busy mopping up his lap. Holmes and LeBlanc were fighting over the man, calling each other idiots. Madison Smyth was helping the fellow dab at his clothing and the coffee that was all over him.

"Seriously, we're so sorry — we can get your clothing cleaned," Madison was offering. "Oh, oh my! Are you burned? We're in a hospital. A little help over here," she said.

"No, no, I'm fine —"

The man tried to rise. He wasn't going to

be able to do so — Madison was standing over him. "My husband is just an idiot, and I don't know how to apologize enough. I mean, he's like an accident waiting to happen, and I am so, so sorry."

By then, they were out of the hospital.

Around the corner, they were quickly ushered into official cars, and soon they were back in the safe house by the Chinese laundry.

It took about twenty minutes of confusion for all the little costume parts and hairpieces to be disassembled and returned to the proper officers for future use. He grinned at Kieran when she headed with Riley and Tanya into the bedroom to discard her wig and padding and oversize pants.

She arched a brow, glared at him and sighed, shaking her head. Then she wiggled her artificially generous bottom at him.

He laughed softly. She didn't really care, he knew.

Kieran would try what worked, no matter what — unless it was illegal or immoral.

Hmm. Depending on the law, she might go with the illegal.

Never the immoral.

The thought made him smile.

In the security of the safe house, changed back to normal, they were able to sit down at last and talk about the man, Jimmy, who was in the burn unit at the hospital, fighting for his life.

Egan had arrived, along with Jacob. The US Marshals had not returned yet. They, like Detective Holmes, were still behind, most probably getting together a full dossier on the man who had been — in their minds — suspiciously reading the paper.

Or they were watching him, determining if he had anything to do with the King or Queen — or any of their court.

"I'm not sure we ever know *real* names," Riley said. "Maybe because they don't really matter — we're nothing but a numbers game, really. Bottom line. The man in the hospital — we knew him as Jimmy. I don't know where he came from. He speaks English fine."

"The man," Tanya said, "never hurt . . . Never hurt anyone."

"But . . . that's a big guy in good condition — or, he was in good condition before he was burned nearly to death," Craig said. "It doesn't appear that he was used as any kind of a slave, or that he might have been bought in any kind of a trafficking situation."

Tanya tried to speak — and seemed to jumble her words. She threw her hands into the air. "I'm so sorry. America! I will speak English."

"It's all right. We need to hear what you have to say," Craig said. "Tell Detective Wolff or Riley, and they'll translate."

Tanya began to talk, swiftly and passionately.

"She cared about him," Craig whispered to Mike.

"I'm only getting every third word," Mike said. "But, yes . . . they had a long talk one day. He was always kind. He apologized that he could not let them go."

Craig nodded, and then waited.

At last, Wolff turned to them.

"His name is Jimmy. They don't know his last name. Jimmy got caught up in their drug ring," Wolff said.

"And so sweet!" Riley put in. "He told me that he was really just a good old boy from Alabama."

Jacob Wolff nodded and then began again. "At first, they sold him some pills. Then they got him hooked on heroin, and told him he could work for them to pay off his bill. He was just going to go to the cops, but they threatened his wife. Her name is Lily, and she lives in the Bronx. She must be going crazy now — she never knew about Jimmy's drug use, and never knew that he was involved with horrible criminals, and that he kept working for them to keep her safe."

"He has three little girls," Riley said, barely whispering. "Mary, Susie and Katie. I believe they're six, nine and eleven now — or ages close to that. I'm not sure. He's showed me photos of them . . . lovely children," she added with a whisper.

Craig felt Kieran looking at him.

They had to do something, and quickly. There were more children involved . . .

Of course, it seemed the immigrants that this group had been taking in were often hardly more than children themselves . . .

"He's a good guy. He tried to help us many times," Riley said. She gasped in a breath suddenly, turning to them, her eyes very wide. "Oh, my God. This happened to Jimmy because of us! Because of Tanya and me."

"Why do you say that? Was Jimmy supposed to be guarding you when you disappeared?" Craig asked.

Riley shook her head. "No, no . . . he was with us right before. He knew about the laundry truck coming and he 'mentioned it' within our hearing. Someone must have said something about it, and they must have believed that Jimmy was responsible for everything going wrong now!"

"You must help!" Tanya said.

"This is a decent guy — he couldn't hurt people even when he was threatened," Riley said. "I think they knew that about him and used him in a way that . . . worked for them. For a while, at least. And, yes, he would have readily died to keep his family safe."

Craig rose and hunkered down before Riley. "What did Jimmy do when he wasn't working off his drug debt to the King and Queen?"

"I . . ." Riley frowned fiercely, thinking.

Tanya started to speak in English, then turned to Jacob Wolff.

"She believes that he was a teacher. He mentioned children that *weren't* his, and how proud of them he was at times. And he was often working with papers and folders," Wolff told them.

"Then we'll know soon enough," Craig said, rising. "Egan can get word out to the schools. We need to know what teachers don't show for work tomorrow morning."

"For now . . . Hell, it's 1:00 a.m.," Mike said. "And it's been one hell of a long day!"

It had been. And now there was little they could do until morning came.

Egan was standing at the edge of the group. "We may be far off Broadway at the moment," he said. "But, I'm feeling a bit of a Broadway tune playing in my head. 'Tomorrow! Tomorrow, it's only a day away.' Let's wrap up. Everyone get some sleep. Have some faith in our counterparts around the city. There are many shifts of cops and agents, all doing their best to keep the city safe, even though we all know it is one hell of a challenge most of the time. I don't want to call Smyth or LeBlanc directly and possibly cause them difficulty at the moment, or to feel obliged to give away their position. But I did call my fellow supervising officer over at the US Marshals office to find out what's going on with them. I can tell by the way Kieran is looking at me that she doesn't intend to leave here until we know."

"No, sir," Kieran said.

"It is best if they're back," Craig agreed. "Did they discover anything?"

Egan nodded. "Yes and no. They followed the man with the newspaper home from the hospital. We have our people checking out the address — and everything that's on record about the man. They called in reinforcements to watch him for any movement through the night. So they'll be back here momentarily," Egan told them.

"They're excellent marshals," Craig said to Kieran. "They're on to something that was worth following up, but they're going to be safe and they'll be here soon."

"Everyone else, go home," Egan said. "Miss McDonnough, Miss Petrofskya, you two get some sleep. We have a small host of agents and officers just outside to keep guard."

"I've got to get back out on the street," Jacob said.

"No," Egan told him.

"Pardon?" Wolff said. "Sir, not to disrespect your position, but I don't work for —"

"I've spoken with your supervisor. Your entire setup has been compromised. It's likely that you're under suspicion. It's time for someone else to go in."

"But —"

"Detective Wolff, speak with your people, please. I truly have no authority over you," Egan said. "But I do assume you are an invaluable asset as an officer, and preserving your life seems to make excellent sense to me."

Wolff nodded grimly. "Yes, sir. I am quite fond of living."

He glanced around the room, nodded a grim good-night to all, and then started out. He turned, looking at Egan. "Sir, I worked that area a long time. You will keep me informed?"

"Absolutely," Egan promised.

Craig nodded, too.

He was pretty sure that Wolff wouldn't let it all go; too many people had died over a long period of time. The King and Queen had created an empire, and they had been ruling — and killing — far too long.

Craig knew, too, that he wouldn't have been able to just leave it all behind, either, were he in Wolff's position.

Wolff almost smiled as he looked at Craig; maybe they had read one another's minds. "Thanks for all your help, Jacob," Craig told him.

"Watching you guys in action," Danny interrupted enthusiastically, "was all very cool. This is an amazing group of people."

"We're so blessed!" Riley whispered.

Was that true? Was she feeling blessed? Craig wondered. There hadn't been a thing — not a single thing — to suggest that Riley McDonnough was anything other than exactly what she appeared to be.

Craig looked at Kieran. "We'll go just as soon as the marshals get here," he said.

"Of course," she agreed. But she was frowning, staring at him as though she was wondering what was going on in his mind.

He forced himself to smile. He didn't

want her — or anyone other than his partner and coworkers — to know about his suspicions at the moment.

She smiled back after a moment.

And then she suggested that she make tea — a great comfort for both the Irish and the Russian people, warm and delicious, and a wee bit more gentle than coffee as they waited.

Everyone agreed.

"So you like big butts and you cannot lie?" Kieran asked Craig.

They were lying together in their own bed. They should have been sleeping. However, it was impossible to turn off the adrenaline that had been sweeping through all of them that night by simply lying down. It had been easy, however, to fall into one another's arms, to remember what was good in life, what was precious, and what always needed to be appreciated, lest it should be lost.

"I like perfect butts," he told her, "like yours."

"Ah, suddenly perfect," she said.

"Frankly, I'm a toe man."

"A toe man?"

"Indeed. And you have the most gorgeous toes I've ever seen."

"Really? So you love the toes to make up

for the butt?"

"Perfect butt . . . perfect toes . . ."

"Perfect lines," she said with a laugh.

"Perfect toes," he repeated, shifting around in bed. He proceeded to plant light, teasing kisses on her toes.

And then on the arch of her foot.

Her ankles . . . calves . . . thighs . . .

A moment later, she was both laughing and writhing, and then her laughter faded. He was on top of her and in her. They rocked together, and she felt lightning exploding all around her.

She lay in his arms. She smiled.

The world could be so ugly, so horrible. And they each fought what was ugly and horrible, in their own way . . . It was simply a part of who they were.

And there was this. Heaven in his arms.

And the faith and knowledge that the world could be beautiful, too.

CHAPTER FOURTEEN

Craig liked large status-and-info boards.

There was one at the end of the conference room where they had all gathered, a task force meeting that would — from this initial sharing of what information they had — spread forth, with the police bringing info to their precincts, the FBI briefing all the NYC and environs agents, and the US Marshals sharing with any pertinent marshals and personnel, as well.

It started here.

They had the picture of Alexandra Callas, one of "Paco," one of "Jimmy," one of the girl who had bled to death in an alley five years earlier, and even one of Sister Teresa.

To the right, they had pictures of Riley McDonnough and Tanya Petrofskya.

The room was filled with those closest to the case: Richard Egan, Mike and Craig for the FBI; David Beard and Randy Holmes specifically for Brooklyn PD; and Larry

McBride, Lance Kendall and Jacob Wolff for Major Case.

They were creating a baseline for what they knew, what they believed, and where certain clues might bring them. They were preparing to make sure that every officer in every agency in the city knew what they were up against — and just how long the King and Queen and their retinue had been active, turning the Great American Dream into dust.

"A summation here," Craig said to the others. "Our part of the case began last Friday when this woman, Alexandra Callas, ran into the offices of Drs. Fuller and Miro, found Kieran Finnegan and thrust a baby into her arms. Kieran chased her out into the street — where someone had been following her — only to discover Ms. Callas dying, a knife in her back. Since then, we learned about this poor young woman who bled to death on the streets, just after childbirth. Her child was never found. We suspect a human trafficking ring that also deals in black market adoptions. Then, through Sister Teresa — born Teresa Maria Barilla ninety-six years ago — and the soup kitchen, Riley McDonnough and Tanya Petrofskya found Kieran, as well. Sister Teresa was found deceased at her convent.

Cause of death hasn't been proven conclusively yet. She was one fine feisty lady, so I understand. After that, the young women came to the soup kitchen again. I was there that day, as we all know, and followed them out — and shot and killed the man we know as Paco, as he was threatening Riley. We then brought them in for questioning, and shortly after rushed to the warehouse the young women described for us, only too late. The trafficking operation had made it out completely just minutes before we arrived. It was set with explosives, with the man we know as Jimmy inside, left to die, as punishment for his infraction of the rules, and possibly causing them to have to lift up stakes and move their operation. What we've gathered as well is that the organization likens itself to a monarchy — with the two heads actually calling themselves the King and the Queen. Apparently, they have a royal court as well — those who are trusted. And then, they have perhaps *dozens* of worker bees, drones or pawns in their little realm of use and abuse. We are left with several objectives, including, of course, keeping our witnesses — Tanya and Riley — safe, finding and also keeping safe the family of the man Jimmy, while we pray that he lives. Jacob Wolff's assignment has been compromised and he can no longer safely work his undercover gig. He is — as we all know and appreciate — still attached to this case. There are two aspects possibly moving in our favor right now; Jimmy — if he survives — and witnesses who might have seen something at the warehouse. It's almost impossible to make that kind of a move without people noticing. We've had officers on the street, and we have a list of people to be reinterviewed, to see if they can help in any way. We've also got a sketch artist working with Riley and Tanya. They're going to do their best to get us images of the King and the Queen. Of course, Tanya says she never saw the Queen, so we'll have to depend on Riley. Oh, and they both argue over what the King really looks like — our guy may change hats, use disguises at times . . . I don't know."

"So we hit the streets again," Randy Holmes said. "With a vengeance!"

"And we hope we get a hit from the sketches the women are able to give us. I doubt that these people show the same face to their captives as they do to the world," Craig said. "And still, there might be something caught in a sketch that gives someone out there an inkling of who we're looking for."

"What if these two never show their faces?" Jacob Wolff asked him. "That's why I considered my cover so important. We've had higher-ups in the Brighton Beach crime world before who never traveled out of their realm. The only people who ever saw them were sunk deep into their worlds. Hell, they never had to go to the drug or grocery store — or even a doctor — because everything came to them."

"There is always hiding in plain sight," David Beard said. "They might be leading double lives — and if so, sketches will definitely help us."

"They went somewhere," Craig said. "They were holding a warehouse owned by a dead man. They have a large operation — they are keeping several immigrants prisoner at any given time. Part of the plan is prostitution, and part of the plan is that the prostitution leads to pregnancy and baby sales. That means they had to move a lot of people. They're down three now — Alexandra Callas, Paco — the man I shot, and Jimmy — the man in the hospital. But they had to get a lot of things out of there before the explosion. Someone out there saw something. And we're going to find who saw what and catch these guys."

"Thing is," Wolff said, "we're going to

have to be very careful. They will kill everyone if they're cornered. Every hostage they
have."

The room fell silent.

Because it was most probably true; they
were going to have to proceed with extreme
care against extreme killers.

"So Kendall and I will report to Major
Crimes. We're expecting reports from our
people on the streets. We'll inform you
about anyone we're re-questioning," Mc-
Bride said.

"And we'll get on it from Brooklyn,"
Beard said.

Craig's, Mike's and Egan's cells went off
at the same time.

"Medical examiner," Egan said.

"Andrews," Craig said, answering his
phone.

"I've got you all, right?" Andrews asked
over Craig's cell.

"Egan, Mike and I are here — and we're
in the middle of a task force meeting, so
this is perfect," Craig said. "I'm going to
put you on speakerphone. What do you have
for us?"

"Succinylcholine," Andrews said.

There was silence. They all looked at one
another; Wolff arched a brow.

Egan was the one to speak.

"Thanks, doctor, but simple language for those of us without medical degrees," he said.

"It's a drug. It was in Sister Teresa's system. We can't actually find a needle mark, so we're not sure how it was administered — hard to say exactly when or how. We'll keep looking. It causes the same symptoms of a heart attack. It was easy — she was an old woman. It didn't take much. Even in autopsy, it appeared she had a heart attack, but due to the circumstances, we did a lot more testing, and . . . well, I found traces of succinylcholine."

"How did someone get close enough to her to do such a thing?" Craig asked.

"Easy enough, I assume," Andrews said. "She was a nun. Nuns — even cool, smart-mouthed nuns, as I've heard her described — are out to serve God, and therefore, to serve His people. She might have been hit while handing out food, while walking down the street . . . someone needed just a moment to get close enough to hit her with a needle. And she might have said, 'Ouch!' and thought that she'd been bitten by some bug or even that she passed by some kind of sharp corner too closely. But, as far as the toxicology report goes, I'd say we have something. So, yes, your nun was helped into the grave."

"Damn it," Mike said, shaking his head.

"Let's pray that there is a hell, and that they rot there," Randy Holmes muttered. "And if not . . . well, we have some great prisons where we can hope they rot — if they last long enough." He looked at the others. "Hey, I happen to know that even convicted men have a hierarchy. People who hurt kids and — I'm sure — nun killers have a very, very bad time."

A police escort saw that Kieran reached the offices of Fuller and Miro without incident. They drove her to her office, and brought her right into the building. Ralph Miller was on duty at the front desk, as usual. His eyes widened.

"Kieran, hey!" He looked at the cops.

"Hi, Ralph," she said, and told him, "Meet my new friends, Officer Abel Harding and his partner, Officer June Chopra."

"Um, hi," Ralph said, and frowned. "I think you still have to sign in," he told the police officers.

"Hi, back at ya — and not a problem," Chopra assured him. She smiled. Kieran already liked her very much. June Chopra had been an NYC police officer for two decades. Her parents were from India, but she had a broad Brooklyn accent herself. She was in her thirties, but had premature gray hair that came in taut curls cut close to her head and huge, beautiful dark eyes. Harding was twice her size, a big man, most probably about the same age, with a blond crew cut and bright hazel eyes. They were both fine — personable, and easy. Though she liked them both, she wasn't really comfortable with uniformed officers following her everywhere she went.

The alternative — being on her own with someone trying to kill her — wasn't so great, either. As soon as she was certain that Craig had finished with his meeting and was back out in the field, she intended to call Egan.

She really wanted to see the baby.

Upstairs, the two police officers made themselves comfortable in the waiting room.

Kieran went into her office and looked through the files of clients with whom she was currently working.

Declan was right: being a bartender was often like being a therapist. A lot of what she did was simply listen when people needed to talk. Most of the time, people knew what was right and what was wrong. Sometimes, they needed right and wrong reinforced. Sometimes, they knew what they had to do, but didn't want to do it.

The hardest cases often involved abuse — the problem being that often people couldn't admit that they were being abused, or that the abuse was escalating — and that they were in danger. It was often incredibly difficult to show a spouse — even beaten within an inch of life — that love didn't always conquer all, and death could be the final blow.

She looked at her calendar and knew that her day was open. She needed to wrap up the report on Besa Goga, but she had a good beginning on it and she could finish it later. She was free to try to see the baby — just to make sure that she was okay.

Kieran realized that she had learned the mother's name — Yulia Decebel — but she didn't know the baby's name. She made a mental note to ask Riley if she or Tanya knew. The baby was certainly old enough to have been given a name, even if she didn't have a proper birth certificate.

Kieran glanced at her watch; she could probably call Egan now, but then again, she might need to wait a few minutes.

She read over the beginning of her report on Besa Goga, and then she paused.

Besa Goga. The woman had come to the country only to be met with very hard times. In Kieran's last conversation with her, she'd asked about the murdered woman, asked if she had suffered. Was that because . . . she had wanted her to suffer?

And the baby — she had specifically asked about the baby. Had she been *too* interested?

Could she be . . . the Queen?

No. Besa liked to laugh too much. She liked to joke — and she had bitten a cable guy, for God's sake!

But, surely . . . Even criminal kingpins had cable!

She had come from Eastern Europe. She had never really known her parents. She hadn't had it easy; she'd been taken and used and abused and . . .

Learned where to go from there?

No . . . she had a husband, and a home in the city.

Unless Besa's husband, Jose Sanchez, was the King?

No — the King was American. They had been told that several times. And Jose had a very strong Hispanic accent when speaking English.

Could he fake that kind of accent?

Kieran hesitated and then picked up her phone. Jose worked for a trading company. His contact information was in Besa's file.

She put through a call and didn't ask to speak with him, but with the personnel office. She didn't exactly lie; she fudged a bit. She said that she was with the courts, just verifying that Jose was employed by the company and that he was a good employee.

A Miss Bertram there assured her that Jose had been working for the company for years and other than a bout with the flu two years back, he had nearly perfect attendance. He was a favorite employee, never late, always helping out when a little extra time or assistance was needed.

In fact, Miss Bertram raved about Jose; he was one of their finest, most dependable employees.

Kieran hung up, frustrated, but also relieved. A moment later, her cell phone rang. She'd had her smashed one repaired overnight at a little shop down the street from her apartment.

In the office, she usually used the landline. Her cell phone ringing indicated that it was a personal call.

Mary Kathleen was on the line. "Sorry to bother you at work," she said to Kieran.

"Not a bother at all. What can I do for you?" Kieran asked her.

Mary Kathleen was quiet for a minute. Then she asked, "Um . . . Sister Teresa.

Have you found out anything new?"

"No, I'm sorry. I can ask Craig later, but I haven't heard anything more."

"Ah," Mary Kathleen murmured. Then she added, "I may be a terrible person."

That surprised Kieran. "Mary Kathleen, I'm almost positive you aren't a terrible person. But why would you say so?"

"I must have a suspicious nature."

"In NYC, that's not always a bad thing. Tell me. What's going on?"

"Okay. It's probably silly, but — it's Riley. I'm curious about Riley. I was taken by her, of course, and I want the best for her . . ."

"But?"

Kieran could hear the rush of air that left Mary Kathleen. "I can't help but be curious. Ireland is not — at this moment — a war-torn nation, thankfully. Leaving Ireland isn't a desperate act, as it may be from other countries."

"You're suspicious of Riley?"

"I can't help but wonder."

"She and Tanya have given us so much information. Every lead we've gotten."

"But just what have we gotten?" Mary Kathleen asked. "Always, there are clues, but it seems you've been a step behind."

"I'm afraid that's the case in many instances. The law has to work . . . lawfully.

Crooks don't care about laws, life or limb, or anything but their own goals."

"Right. Like I said, I feel terrible for thinking it. And I don't understand why it bothers me. I don't know. Perhaps I'm upset because of Sister Teresa. I was wondering how a young Irish woman of *today* came to be in her situation. I'm just talking to myself, maybe, using you as a sounding board. Still . . ."

"It's true, Mary Kathleen. You may be right to be suspicious. It is something to think about. The Republic of Ireland isn't having any troubles at the moment. Why would she be desperate?" Kieran mused.

"Who knows what kind of situation she left, so this is probably absolutely crazy. I started worrying, and I felt that I had to talk to you. Please see that you're careful. If I were to have brought anything horrible into your life, I'd feel so bloody rotten. You're Declan's only sister . . . my only hope for a sister! And then there's Finnegan's. If I put the pub into any danger, I'd be so horrified. These people might have murdered a nun! And — Irish or not — anyone who has had anything to do with this should definitely face the worst possible punishment!"

Kieran smiled. Mary Kathleen was a very

modern woman — independent, fiery, passionate. She was still also a product of her upbringing: she was a church girl, through and through.

And Kieran recognized she herself was horrified, too. So afraid, so knotted up inside, furious and heartsick over the very idea that Sister Teresa might have been a victim of foul play. Because no matter what her background or religion, Sister Teresa had truly been one kick-ass and admirable woman.

"Mary Kathleen, I'm sure everything will be all right," Kieran said. "Trust me — Riley has been watched from the get-go. She's with federal marshals right now. There are always police around her."

"I know. And I keep telling myself that. But I'm so afraid that I want to like her and believe in her because she's Irish, but . . . Kieran, why does she speak Russian?"

Kieran didn't really have a satisfactory answer for that. "She's been helping Tanya out. We know that," she said.

"Right. I guess it was easier for her to learn Russian than it was for Tanya to get a grasp of English."

"Some people are just good with languages, naturally able to pick them up easily. Like Kevin — he didn't take anything in school, but he's decent in Spanish, French and Creole, and has a good ear for accents."

"Aye," Mary Kathleen agreed. "Again, I pray that I am way off the mark."

"I understand how you're feeling, absolutely. It's always important to bounce these ideas off someone. Thank you," Kieran told her. "I'll make sure — discreetly — that all the officers and agents involved are aware of your concern."

"Thank you, Kieran. And take care of yourself, right?"

"I promise I will be very careful."

After they said goodbye, Kieran thought about it all for a minute. It seemed a stretch. Riley had sought out Kieran; she had been surrounded by law enforcement and was helping them. She couldn't be the head of anything criminal.

But she hadn't been with them when Sister Teresa had died.

She had been with them when the building had exploded — with Jimmy in it.

She took a deep breath and tried Craig's number. She hadn't wanted to talk to him quite yet.

She'd wanted to see the baby first.

For a moment, she hoped that he wouldn't answer.

But he did. "Everything's all right with

you?" he asked.

"Fine. But I just had an interesting conversation with Mary Kathleen."

She told him about their speculations; he promised to look into anything he could find that involved Riley McDonnough. "Witness protection was already checking into Riley, but not with any real focus. I'll see that we ask the right questions."

"It would be crazy if she were in on it, right?" she asked hopefully.

"This whole thing is crazy," Craig said, "so what's something that's a little crazier?" She heard him take a breath. There was something that he didn't want to tell her.

"What's happening there?" she asked him.

"Dr. Andrews, the medical examiner, called. Sister Teresa was struck with a poison. Apparently, just a little. But, at her age, it was enough."

Kieran was silent. Something inside her felt dark and empty. Logically, it shouldn't have felt quite as bad as some of the other events that had taken place recently. Sister Teresa had led a long life, and in that life, she had actually *lived* — she had gotten out in the world and made a difference. But knowing for certain that someone had taken her sooner than her natural time . . . It hurt.

"Kieran, I'm sorry. I think we were all

hoping it was simply her time. But here's the thing — we know Riley and Tanya were followed. The traffickers knew the two were at the soup kitchen, and they knew Sister Teresa was helping. It's really frightening, just how they manage to see so very much."

"Could that mean that Mary Kathleen isn't so far off the mark? That Riley isn't such an innocent — that she's a criminal herself, leading us down a very wrong path and reporting every movement made by the police and the FBI?"

"I don't know how she'd be getting through to members of the gang — she hasn't had a cell phone. We don't keep landlines in any of the safe houses. She's been with someone all the time." He was quiet for a minute and then said softly, "We have seen some strange things, but I don't want to believe that she is a killer."

"Have you suspected her of being involved?"

"She has been around it all."

Frowning, Kieran pulled the phone away from her ear and stared at it — as if she could somehow see Craig through the phone.

If Craig had already thought of this — if Mary Kathleen had thought it — why hadn't she?

"You do think she's innocent, right?"

"I do. Mostly."

"It's that she speaks Russian that makes you pause, isn't it?"

"It's a total wild card. I'm an agent . . . we're naturally a little suspicious of everyone. And Russian as a second language is an unusual choice for an immigrant. I mean, if you want to go into politics, or become an interpreter, or travel extensively in the Soviet Union, yes. Or if you wind up with Russian-speaking in-laws. In Riley's case, she's apparently spent time with a lot of Russian-speaking people."

"So . . ."

"So these are all things we bear in mind. But, then again, Kieran, she may be exactly as she presents herself — a victim. Don't fear. We are watching. We are weighing everything that both girls say." He hesitated. "And . . ."

"And?"

"You will never be alone with them, so there shouldn't be any cause for concern."

She smiled. Poor Craig. He didn't want to change her. And he couldn't blame her for finding herself in what could be a dangerous position in this case. He had to support her, had to allow her to do the work she loved — and manage not to get macho on her while protecting her all at the same time.

"Love you," she murmured.

"Yep. You, too. Hold on to that police protection, you hear? Don't go anywhere alone."

"They're charming. I like Officers Chopra and Harding very much."

"Great. All right, I've got to get working. I'm checking into the man we know as Jimmy. We've got it narrowed down to about five people. Do you know how many teachers there are in the tristate area with the name James or Jimmy?"

"A lot, I can only imagine."

"Yeah. But I think we're getting close — we need to find and protect his family."

"Call me if you need me — or if you learn anything that I should know. If it gets late and I don't hear from you, I'll take my charming bodyguards to Finnegan's. Almost everyone likes a good slice of shepherd's pie."

"Take care. See you later."

She hung up, a slight curve on her lips. She really loved him so much. But he wasn't much for using terms of endearment on a phone.

For a minute, she drummed her fingers on the desk.

She wasn't sure why she didn't want to

tell Craig that she really wanted to see the baby.

There was nothing wrong with it.

She was omitting. That wasn't lying. And she wasn't going to do anything that wasn't safe. She was going to call Craig's boss — entirely safe!

Why not just tell Craig?

Because she was afraid that he would think she was getting too personally involved.

Maybe she was — just a little bit. She couldn't forget holding the infant girl and thinking that it would be the most horrible thing in the world if the mother had been killed, if she would never get to cuddle her sweet child, smell her sweet baby flesh, love her and watch her grow.

It wasn't that she wanted her own child. She really wasn't ready for a baby herself.

She just wanted the best for Yulia Decebel's baby. That meant the FBI had to find Yulia.

Still feeling guilty, she called Egan. She asked him about visiting the baby, escorted by the police officers assigned to keep watch over her.

Egan thought it was fine. He wasn't surprised by her call, she realized. He seemed to think it was natural that she should want to check up on the baby.

"Of course, you must see for yourself that the baby is doing well. I'm still praying we find her mother alive," Egan said.

She really liked and admired Egan. He was in such a high position, but was still a man who admitted to praying, managing both authority and humanity very well.

"Me, too," she said. She thanked him, but before she hung up, she voiced Mary Kathleen's concerns. Craig would have also passed on her comments, but since she happened to be talking to Egan, she found herself needing to tell him about the conversation, too.

"Interesting," he said. "I'll give the marshals a call and make sure that both women are behaving. No contact outside the safe house."

Kieran thanked him.

He must have gotten right on the phone again after they hung up. She was still tidying papers when the officers came in for her.

"I've been told we're paying a visit to Child Services," Abel Harding said.

"Checking on a babe," June Chopra echoed, nodding sagely.

"Do you mind?" Kieran asked.

"Of course not! Serve and protect, ma'am, that's what we do!" Harding told her.

"And I, for one, would love to see this little one," June Chopra said.

Ten minutes later, Kieran let Jake out in reception know that she was leaving with Officers Chopra and Harding.

She waved to Ralph Miller at his security post by the building's entrance, and Ralph returned her wave. "You going to be back at the office today?" he asked Kieran.

"Maybe and maybe no, Ralph. Don't worry."

"Ah, seeing your companions, I know you'll be fine."

She agreed and headed toward the door.

"Hey," he called softly.

She paused and turned back; it was touching the way the officers instantly followed suit.

"Anything new?" Ralph asked her anxiously. "The poor mom of that baby . . . did they find anything yet?"

Kieran shook her head. "Not that I know about."

"Hope you find her," Ralph said. "I truly do."

She nodded. "Thanks, Ralph."

Kieran pushed through the front doors and headed out to go visit the abandoned baby girl that she couldn't stop thinking about.

CHAPTER FIFTEEN

"James Bryan Baron!" Craig said. "We have to get to his family."

Marty had provided Craig with a list of teachers who had not shown up for work. Since the area they were looking at was fairly massive, it had been a good-sized list. And while they weren't completely certain that their burn victim's name was really Jimmy, there was a possibility that it was. And it was all they'd had to go on.

James Bryan Baron was in his late thirties. He was married with children. His wife's name was Lillian; his daughters were Mary, ten; Susan, eight; and Katie, just five years old.

Craig stood, nearly knocking his computer from his desk.

Mike, sitting across from him, jumped to his feet, as well.

"Okay, you think we've got our guy? We have to make a call, Craig. We can't get out there faster than the local cops can. They may already be alerted — it's more than possible that his wife reported him missing."

"I'm headed to Egan's office. He has to get the captain there to make sure that this is handled as discreetly as possible. There are kids involved, an innocent woman —"

"They'll take care of it," Mike said quietly. "Yes — let's get Egan."

Egan was quickly on the phone to the captain of the precinct; as of now, James Bryan Baron had not been reported missing.

They would have a plainclothes detective out to the house as quickly as possible; they would be expecting Special Agents Frasier and Dalton at the precinct, ready to take the family into protective custody.

"The girls might be at school — they probably are at school," Craig said. "Unless someone's already got to them."

"As far as anyone knows, the man they meant to kill in that explosion *is* dead," Egan reminded Craig.

"But remember, there was a man at the hospital last night, watching. Maybe someone from the gang waiting to see who came and who went. I know that the marshals were checking up on it and didn't discover anything. The thing is, their henchmen may appear to be nobody on the surface. And whether or not James was willing to die in order to save his family, they may still be after the wife and kids. Tying up loose ends," Craig said.

"Trust me — we were top-notch on this. It did appear that James Baron died. No one could have seen our cops and agents come or go," Egan said. "But, yes, this group may want to tie up loose ends. So as we speak, the cops are heading out to the victim's home. Everything will be done to protect them. I suggest you two —"

"Already moving, sir. Already moving," Craig said.

"I'll keep in touch, let you know how the local men are progressing," Egan called after them.

Down by the car, it was tacitly determined that Craig would drive. He and Mike didn't try to talk; they had been partners too long for any need to fill the air with chatter. Craig knew Mike — they were both thinking that this group was ruthless and that there were children's lives at stake. They were nearing the bridge — moving at a decent clip despite New York traffic — when they received the first call from Egan.

"No one is answering at the home address," Egan said.

"What about the girls?" Mike asked anxiously.

"They didn't report to school today," Egan said.

"The uniforms have gone into the house?" Mike asked.

"They're there now — they've just gone in. I'll keep you abreast."

Craig glanced over at Mike. The police would be *in* the house long before they could get there.

Neither one of them wanted to imagine what might be found: a woman, three children, dead. Shot, left in their rooms. The little ones killed gently, maybe, pillows over their heads before bullets were sent into their brains. Maybe not. Maybe all had been stabbed, gathered together, tied and strangled . . .

There was no pretty picture.

It was just a few minutes before Egan was back with them.

"Nothing," Egan said. "No one was found in the house."

"What? And they know that the girls weren't at school?"

"The locals are trying every avenue. The neighbors are being questioned. Cops are going door-to-door. You'll be there in thirty minutes or so —"

"We'll be there in fifteen," Craig vowed grimly.

Chopra and Harding had a patrol car just down the street. Harding offered to get the car; Kieran assured him she'd walk dead center between the two officers and that she could reach it on foot just fine — no one had to drive to retrieve her, or worry about who stayed with her while the other went for the car.

They got in, buckled up and pulled out into traffic. Chopra said with a bit of obvious excitement, "Off to see the babe."

"I feel like we should be singing, though, huh?" Harding asked. " 'The babe. What babe?' I mean . . . didn't you ever see *Labyrinth*?"

"I did indeed. And in that, my Lord! Bowie as the goblin king . . . you could have taken me anytime!" Chopra said. She made a face at Kieran. "Sadly, I haven't seen anyone at Child Services who remotely looks like David Bowie."

"Hey! You have a husband," Harding reminded her.

"I do. And I adore the man. But Bowie as the goblin king . . . well, he was always my secret love. So sad. I can still dream, but he's passed on to that great gilded studio in the sky." She paused to sigh.

"A brilliant talent lost," Kieran said.

Chopra smiled and nodded and turned to Harding. "See? She appreciates the beauty of the goblin king. Anyway, there may be no goblin king, but to the best of my knowledge, Sandy Cleveland is there and will be waiting for us so that you might have a visit with the wee one, Kieran."

"She's no goblin king," Harding said. "Even I agree on that."

"But she is a very nice woman," Kieran said, "and I'm sure she's taking wonderful care of the baby."

Ten minutes later, they were at Child Services.

While the city did the best it could — and many fine people worked for and with the children — it was almost impossible for Kieran not to feel her heart sink painfully low into her chest. Children were such a precious gift, and here were so many who were abandoned, who had been taken from abusive homes, who lived without the love that should have been a birthright.

Kieran was considered an "official" visitor as she arrived with the cops; that meant that she didn't sit in an office vestibule, away from all the action. Instead, she walked along halls with glass windows where social workers looked over children of different ages; toddlers playing with well-used toys, five-year-olds listening to a story, preteens watching a DVD. One room offered a slightly older group, busy at computers, flirting with one another, laughing, teasing . . .

Some bore looks of confusion and hopelessness. Some had already been toughened by the system; their faces were hard and cold. They were nearly ready to head out into the world, aware that it was a tough place and that their defenses must be up at all times.

Sandy Cleveland's office was a small room that attached to a larger one that looked almost like a hospital delivery room — except that it was filled with little cribs instead of tiny newborn bassinets. Two aides were in with the babies; Kieran estimated that there were twelve little ones in the nursery.

It appeared that those working with the children were good at their jobs; they were gentle and loving with the babies. Kieran wondered if it could begin to compensate for the love little ones should get from their parents. Naturally, she didn't know what had brought the infants here, to be cared for by strangers — maybe their parents were just getting back on their feet. Maybe they had lost both of them in tragic accidents.

"So sad," Kieran murmured.

"The hospital is worse. Trust me. In our line, a lot of the witnesses we wind up protecting can testify against crime lords because they've been in their clutches — and often have used all kinds of drugs. The babies born to mothers on crack or with fetal alcohol syndrome," June Chopra said. "Thing is, most people looking to adopt want a perfect little child. There are only a brave few who'll take on a child who may have medical problems as they get older. Family members tend to disappear when it comes to taking in a little relative who is blind or deaf or facing a situation like juvenile diabetes . . . Sad, yes. So sad. And yet, there are thousands of people waiting to adopt, but to adopt perfect little babes."

Like the little girl thrust into her own arms, Kieran thought.

Sandy Cleveland waved to them from within the infant room. They could see her through the glass, picking up one of the little bundles.

Baby Jane Doe, received into the system Friday last, when Alexandra Callas had passed her over to Kieran, and then been stabbed to death in the street.

A moment later, Sandy was out with them, handing the child to Kieran. "Miss Frasier, how nice to see you. June, great to see you, too. And you, too, Abel," she added to Officer Harding.

Kieran glanced at the officers.

"We've been here before — a few times. The innocent — little ones — are often the collateral damage in the world of crime," Harding said.

"June and Abel helped wrest a baby from a dad trying to toss her off the balcony," Sandy Cleveland told Kieran. "She got adopted, by the way, despite many difficulties — legal and medical hurdles. See, good things do happen here. Foster families are found, biological families are sometimes reunited. You must know that. Don't you work with parents struggling to get back on their feet?"

"Our office does, yes," Kieran said. "And I'm glad — and surprised — that it worked out so well for the little one you rescued, June. Often — in our experience, anyway — it's the parents who are most abusive who aren't willing to give up their children. The father gave up his rights? And the mom?" Kieran asked.

"The father couldn't get the child over

369

the balcony, so he went over himself," June said. "The baby's mother was long gone," she added softly. "Being a cop is what I always wanted to do. But sometimes, I guess, we come across the kind of stuff that really haunts you."

Her words made them all fall silent for a moment, at a lack of what to say against such a truth.

"I'm so sorry," Kieran murmured at last.

"Anyway," Sandy said, "as you can see here, we have our hands full. Enjoy your time with our little Baby Doe."

"Thank you," Kieran said. "What are you calling her? We do have a last name for her — just not a first."

Sandy glanced at June. "Well, we call her Baby Doe. She's actually Baby Doe Seven."

"Oh," Kieran said. "Well, she is Miss Decebel, from what we understand. And I know that all forms of law enforcement are still working very hard to find her mother."

"And I'm sure they will," Sandy said. "We'll just hope that they find her . . ." Sandy's voice trailed. They all knew the unspoken word. *Alive.*

"There's a little playroom down the hall. You can spend some time with the baby there," Sandy told her.

"Great!"

The playroom contained the kind of flooring — cheap foam squares, easily replaceable — that allowed for little ones to crawl or shimmy about on their own without obstacles that might hurt them. There were all kinds of toys just right for very little ones — a dog that sang "Bingo" when a paw was squeezed, big plastic blocks, mobiles, blankets and more.

Officers June Chopra and Abel Harding were both good with children. Seeing them all together from the outside, it might have been a very strange family reunion.

The baby was still beautiful. She was healthy. And she smiled. She definitely smiled.

"Miss Decebel! You are so beautiful. And we are going to find your mommy for you. I'll bet she is very nice, and lovely, just like you! We will find her!"

Sandy Cleveland looked on like a loving godmother.

Kieran was glad that they had come. She was laughing as Abel Harding sang and made faces for the baby when her phone rang.

It was Craig.

She thought maybe she just wouldn't answer. Which was, of course, ridiculous. She was just worried what he'd think about her continuing to have a relationship with the baby, though — he had never suggested that she not check up on the infant who had been thrust into her arms.

"Hey," she answered.

"You're all right?" he asked, not bothering with hello or any other such greeting.

"Yes, I'm fine. Thank you. My police protection officers are with me," she told him.

"Where are you?"

She winced. "Child Services, at one of their facilities. I spoke with Egan and he said that it was okay to visit. And it is fine, I'm good, I'll be safe — I have a couple of lovely NYPD guards," she said, and then paused for breath. "Where are you?"

"Brooklyn. Looking for our burn victim's family. Mike and I are almost there, but the police haven't been able to find the wife or the children. I don't like this. I don't know how this gang is one step ahead all the time. There was no way anyone should have known that Jimmy was still alive. There's got to be something going on that we're not seeing. These people literally seem to have eyes everywhere. Kieran, please — let the officers get you home safely. Make them stay with you."

"We can go to Finnegan's," Kieran said.

"No."

Kieran cringed inwardly at his tone. Then again, they had met when murderers had been using her family pub as their meeting point.

And, to be honest, did she want to bring any kind of danger back to her family?

"All right. We'll head to my apartment. We'll lock in. We'll watch Netflix. They'll keep their guns out. They'll be armed. We'll all be safe."

"Thank you," he said. "Let me know when you're in, okay?"

"Will do, I promise," she told him.

She hung up. The baby was still cooing at a face Abel had made.

The three adults in the room looked at her.

She glanced at Sandy.

The killers always seemed to be a step ahead. They always knew what was happening, even before it happened, or so it seemed.

Someone close had to be involved.

A king and queen.

A queen.

Besa Goga?

Or . . .

Worse.

Riley McDonnough, the young and lovely Irish woman?

She realized that she was growing suspicious of everyone.

Even Sandy Cleveland!

And so she said simply, "Sandy, thank you so much for this visit. The baby is beautiful, and it did mean so much to me to get to see her. Officers, I believe it's time to go!"

Jimmy's home was nice. It was a modest family home. It had a typical perfect little cookie-cutter New York facsimile of a yard.

Inside, there were three bedrooms, a kitchen, dining room and family room; the three bedrooms were upstairs, one taking up half of the house on a side, and the other two smaller rooms just across a hallway.

The house was beautifully maintained, clean as a whistle. Lillian Baron was obviously an excellent housekeeper. Or possibly James Baron was just as good.

Craig couldn't help but imagine the family once they had reached the house.

There were pictures on the wall. Mom, Dad, three kids. Smiling, huddled together in a park, posing together at a restaurant. There were baby pictures on the wall.

It appeared to have been a very loving home.

How had Lillian Baron not known that her husband had fallen into drug abuse?

Working as he had over the years, Craig was far too familiar with the havoc uppers, downers, cocaine, heroin and alcohol had on the human body and mind.

Had she known . . . had she been a user herself?

The pictures about the house did not show a man or a woman who had been affected by the ravages of such abuse. According to Tanya, Jimmy had gotten a grip on himself, but not in time to save himself from falling into debt with the King and Queen of the crime ring.

So maybe . . . Maybe his wife had known. And if she had known, they had talked. And she would have been warned that if anything happened to him, it was up to her to save the children.

Craig asked the officer in charge if the family owned a car; the man immediately made a call.

Yes, they owned a Volvo.

It wasn't in the garage.

So they were gone. Lillian had known what was going on. She had fled with her children.

Which might have been fine at first . . .

"All points bulletin out on the car — and the missus?" the officer in charge asked.

Craig wondered, *What if there was a cop*

involved? David Beard himself, Randy Holmes. Or what if Jacob Wolff hadn't just been undercover? What if he was crooked?

No.

He liked to think he was a better judge of people than that. But still . . .

Lance Kendall . . . what about him? Or even McBride . . . ?

There was also the matter that he and Mike weren't superheroes — they never had and most probably never would manage to solve this kind of case on their own. They needed their fellow workers — cops, agents, marshals, everyone.

"Hold off just an hour on that," Craig said.

"Time could mean everything," Mike said quietly.

"I know. In many ways," Craig said. He smiled grimly for the officer and Mike.

And as soon as the officer was gone, Craig said, "Sorry — I'm afraid if we do an APB right away, we might seal her fate. Info is getting out somehow. If we tear this place apart ourselves, we may find a clue to where they've gone. I'm going to start in the bedroom. Can you give Marty a call? He can find out about relatives, any other property they might own . . ."

"I'm on it," Mike said.

Craig headed up the stairs and looked

around the neat and charming bedroom where the Baron couple had slept together. Quilted bed cover — handmade, he was certain. Kids' pictures on the walls. Lovely lace doily thingies on the furniture.

A family home . . .

"So where did you go, Mrs. Baron?" he asked softly.

Walking in, he began to search.

Kieran knew that her guests weren't two friends who had just happened to stop at her place to binge-watch the next hit show.

They were cops, on duty, and on guard.

But Harding and Chopra were easy about every move they made.

They were in her apartment, door was locked, and Kieran was pretty sure that a patrol car was cruising by now and then.

She did make coffee and tea. Coffee for Chopra and tea for Harding. And she did turn on the television. But Harding sat in a chair by the door; she knew that he was ready to leap to his feet at any given moment, that he was probably even listening and would be watching no matter who came into the building for any reason. Chopra seemed to be hovering closer to her, ready to use her own body to protect Kieran's life, if need be.

It might have felt excessive, but right now, Kieran was glad of the extra protection. She had heard the level of concern in Craig's voice when he'd told her to go to her apartment.

Kieran had been to the gun range one time with Craig after the diamond heists case when they had met, but she knew that she needed to go back and take it all incredibly seriously — and actually get a permit to carry. She just hated the very idea of it; she wasn't a fan of guns in any form.

Well, neither was she a fan of having a knife in her back, or having someone with a knife in their back fall dead before her.

"Amazing!" Chopra said. "Cable — better stuff on television these days than in the movies!"

"Ah, come on. There are still good movi—" Even as Harding spoke, he leapt up. He must have heard someone on the stairs.

He had.

There was a knock at the door. He looked out the peephole, and then at Kieran.

"Asian guy, young, late twenties," he told her.

She saw that his hand was in place to draw his weapon.

It was the same with Chopra.

"Should be okay — that's Lee Chan. His family owns the karaoke bar and sushi restaurant right beneath my apartment."

Harding stepped back slightly. Kieran saw that Chopra was in position to shoot — if she was threatened in any way once the door opened.

"Lee!" Kieran said as she pulled the door open.

"Kieran, hey," Lee said. He frowned. She realized that he could see June Chopra behind her.

"I'm sorry to disturb you," he said. "But, I had a visit from a young woman who came to karaoke on the night you sang with me."

"You did?" Kieran recalled speaking with the immigration officer. "Esperanza?" she asked.

"She said her name was Esperanza Rodriguez. Yes, exactly! Oh, good, you do remember her, then."

"Yes, of course. She's very nice. What was her message?"

He handed her a card. "She said to call her. One of her fellow officers might have some information that could be useful to you."

"Great. Anything else?"

Lee shook his head. "That was it. Sorry — I was in the middle of sashimi, sushi and a coconut California roll. She was in a hurry. All I did was get that message."

"That's great, thank you, Lee."

"Could it really help you in some way?"

"Maybe."

Lee grinned. "Well, there you go. Come down for karaoke and sushi soon."

"I will," Kieran agreed. "Thank you so much."

He gave her a wave, looking over her shoulder again at June Chopra.

"My friend June," Kieran said, smiling.

"Hello!" Lee said, and waved. "Does she like sushi?" he asked.

June, back against the wall, assured him, "Love sushi."

"We are really good," Lee said.

"Yep, they are!" Kieran said cheerfully. "Thanks again, Lee."

He seemed to be staring past her and into her apartment.

Yes, he was looking at June Chopra.

He couldn't know she was a cop.

Kieran was seriously becoming almost ridiculously distrustful of everyone. She'd lived in the apartment over two years; she'd been above the sushi restaurant all that time. They were good neighbors. Except for an occasional slaughter of Bon Jovi's "Livin' on a Prayer," the restaurant and the people

380

there were peaceful, kind and great.

This situation was getting to her. Even Lee was suddenly suspicious to her!

Kieran smiled tightly and said goodbye to Lee, closing and locking the door behind her.

"Is everything all right?" Chopra asked.

"Anything we should worry about?" Harding asked.

"No, I don't think so," Kieran said. "I've known Lee and his family several years. If they're hiding something, they're doing it incredibly well — though, I must admit, their sushi is so good it would make a great cover."

Neither of the cops smiled.

"He was letting me know someone stopped by to see me. Her name is Esperanza Rodriguez and she's with INS. Immigration and Naturalization Service." The two officers stared at her, politely waiting. Of course, they would know what INS meant. Kieran grimaced and continued. "Esperanza — like everyone in the city and probably beyond — knew about the woman murdered on the street. We chatted, and I asked her to let me know if she heard anything about trafficking babies. I'm going to give her a call."

"Okay," Harding said.

Kieran didn't walk away from the officers. She perched on the edge of the sofa and dialed the number listed on the card.

Esperanza answered with her full name and position in a professional voice.

"Hello, it's Kieran Finnegan. I just saw Lee. He gave me your message, said you asked that I call you."

"Kieran! Great. I was afraid you might have forgotten me and wondered, who in the hell is this woman and why is she bothering me. I think I really have something for you."

"I certainly hadn't forgotten you," Kieran assured her. "Thank you for getting in touch."

"I'm not positive that I have anything that will help, but I was chatting with my co-worker, Alyssa Ryan, and she became very excited. About four months ago, Alyssa had just left the office when she was approached by a young woman who was very visibly pregnant. She was Romanian, and she was trying to find out the right way to legally apply for help. But when Alyssa started asking questions, she suddenly seemed to panic, and she ran off. As she ran, she dropped something. Alyssa picked it up, hoping to get it back to her. It was a prayer card from a church in Brooklyn. Very worn, as if the woman had touched it and held it over and over again. Alyssa asked around to see if anyone knew anything about a pregnant young girl, but . . . well, our social agencies are overburdened, and no one knew who she was talking about or cared to find out. Anyway, if you want to speak with Alyssa, I can set it up for tomorrow."

"That would be wonderful. Thank you. And yes, please, we would love to have that slip of paper."

"We — are you a cop now?"

"No, no . . . our office just works with the cops and the FBI. And I know they'll want it. Thank you so much. Would now be a good time?"

"Oh, I'm sorry — she's gone for the day. I can try to call her for you, if it's that important."

It just might be.

A prayer card. That could lead them to a church. And maybe a priest. And a priest might be someone that the woman talked to . . .

"Will you try for me, please, to reach her now?"

"Of course. I'll call you right back."

Both Harding and Chopra were staring at Kieran, naturally anxious.

"We might have a bit of a clue," she said.

"Maybe nothing, but . . ."

"We check out tons of nothing. That's the only way you ever get to *something*," Harding said.

Kieran nodded; he was so right.

Her phone rang a minute later. It was Esperanza. "I'm so sorry. I can't reach Alyssa. I've left her a message. She has a two-year-old, so sometimes she just doesn't get to her phone."

"Thanks."

Esperanza hesitated. "Normally, I would never do this, but . . . you are a professional. I'm going to give you her number — you can keep trying. I know that she would want to help in any way. She said she had the feeling something was really wrong with that woman."

"Thank you!"

Esperanza gave her Alyssa's information. She lived near Times Square.

When Kieran hung up again, she looked at Harding and Chopra. "It might just be important that we talk to this woman," she murmured.

She was hesitant; she didn't want to cause more of a problem than she was solving by dragging her police escort all over town. She knew that Craig felt best when she was in one place, protected.

If they could just capture these horrible people . . .

Well, not just capture the traffickers. Find Jimmy's family, find Yulia Decebel, find the others who were used and abused and held hostage by them.

"Sorry, guys. Wee bit of a road trip, I think!"

Investigation, most of the time, didn't involve high-speed chases or guns going off.

It was tedious and meticulous searching.

And that could be frustratingly slow, especially when it wasn't even clear what one should be looking for.

It hadn't been that long — though it did feel like hours and hours — that they had searched through James and Lillian Baron's home when Craig finally came upon a small stack of receipts in the bottom of a drawer.

At first the pile appeared to be nothing.

A little toy pony from a local toy shop.

Doughnuts.

Vitamins and shampoo and other sundries.

And then, small and mixed in with the other casual receipts, was a bill for maintenance. It was folded in with the others, but the name on it was spelled wrong — it was written out to James Barow. It was for the yearly maintenance of a cabin in Norwalk, Connecticut.

"Here!" Craig exclaimed.

Mike, digging through drawers on the other side of the bed, looked up at him.

"Connecticut," Craig said. He spoke softly. He truly believed that, most of the time, people in law enforcement were honest and doing their best at a tough job. But there could be bad seeds.

And there could be those who just talked too much sometimes, no malice intended.

"This place . . . you and me. We can be there in thirty minutes. We'll let Egan know. No one else."

"You think that someone working with us could be a leak?" Mike asked him.

"I don't know. I think we shouldn't take any chances." He hesitated. "We know McBride — we've worked with him before. Solid. Lance Kendall . . . broomstick up his backside, but hey, doesn't mean he isn't a top-notch cop. Jacob Wolff had our backs, and helped Kieran and Danny. The marshals — Madison Smith and Hank LeBlanc — are new on this. Can't see how they'd be compromised. Close — working on the inside — we've got David Beard and Randy Holmes. Beard has been around for years. Holmes presents himself as invested in figuring out what's been happening — passionate to all ends. They seem to be great. But . . . someone does always seem to be a step ahead of us. Let's just tell these cops here that we're moving on — ask them to let us know of anything that they find. Then, let's get going on our own."

"Gotcha. Okay, let's do it," Mike said.

"This is a family in danger, Mike."

"Yep, I agree. Like I said — let's do it."

Craig strode out of the room to find the police officer in charge; he didn't tell him where they were going. He wasn't bringing backup.

He hoped to hell that he wasn't making a mistake.

And that ruthless killers weren't already one step ahead.

Officers Harding and Chopra were, Kieran determined, just about the best possible bodyguards one could hope to have. Kieran was completely honest with them and explained what she wanted to do. They understood. June Chopra told her, "Kieran, honey, you're not a prisoner. It's easier, of course, to guard you here — but we know what we're doing. If there is something important for you to do, let's do it."

"You might want to let Agent Frasier

know what's up," Harding said.

"Or we can call our boss," Chopra said.

"It's just a suggestion," Harding said.

"Not to worry. I have no problem calling Craig or Mike or even Egan," Kieran assured him.

But she did have a problem — a technical one. Neither Craig nor Mike answered their phones. She tried Egan. It still always surprised and pleased her that he was so ready to accept her calls. She wasn't one of his agents. She wasn't even a cop. She just sometimes wound up in a situation where she could try to help.

She explained about her connection to the INS worker.

"Any lead is wonderful," Egan said. "I can have some agents or a police officer go by and leave a message for her if she isn't there."

"I'd rather just try. I'm restless. And this is a loose, loose connection. A wild card. Still, a bunch of cops at her door could scare her. I think it's okay if I just go."

"Not alone."

"No, of course not," Kieran assured him. "I've got my protection detail. I don't want to bring a lot of people with me — we're just going to have a casual chat with this woman, and I hope she might have a clue

388

in tracing the baby's mother, Yulia De-cebel."

"Keep in contact with me, then. And if you get something — something physical — please bring it here, to our offices. Good luck."

Harding and Chopra had politely waited for her to finish her conversation.

"A few ground rules when we're moving about," Harding told her. "One of us is slightly ahead of you, one slightly behind, and you listen to every word we say. If we ask you to drop to the ground —"

"I drop," Kieran agreed.

"Slide to cover," Chopra said.

"Whatever you say — it's my wish to obey," she assured them. "Come on, guys, I kind of know this drill."

As soon as they left her building, they had her flanked. Harding was slightly in front of her. Chopra was slightly behind her. They were well trained.

They even understood that she didn't know exactly what they were going to find once they reached the address that Esperanza Rodriguez had given Kieran. They knew that they were going to try to find someone who couldn't be reached by phone. And if they were concerned that something might have happened to Alyssa

Ryan, they didn't show it.

Then again, why should they be concerned?

And that was probably the sane way to see things. It was possible — maybe even likely — that the woman wasn't going to be home. People went out. And while people rarely left their phones at home these days, sometimes it happened. The woman had a two-year-old — that often meant that a phone was forgotten, or hidden even — lest little fingers find every kid's video possible, call someone by accident, or even order an Uber.

Alyssa Ryan lived in a building in Midtown, not far from Times Square. Harding drove fluidly through the streets of the city, unfazed by whatever traffic they encountered. Kieran was aware that both her escorts were taking notice of everyone around them.

Chopra would mention a vehicle; Harding would study it in the rearview mirror. They were obviously talking about cars that might bear suspicious passengers. After consulting each other each time, it appeared that none of them really seemed to offer a threat.

Kieran was anxious to be out of the car when they drew up near the building's entry, but she bit her lip and forced herself to wait until both Chopra and Harding were properly positioned. Outside the door, they noted twenty call boxes and found the one for the Ryan residence. They rang a couple times . . . and no one responded.

Kieran tried dialing Alyssa Ryan's cell phone number again. There was no answer. As Kieran listened to the sound of the unanswered call ringing and ringing, she gazed about the street. She looked down.

There was blood on the concrete.

Little droplets of something dark red and shiny.

They led to the door going into the building.

"Oh, Lord!" she cried.

Chopra and Harding were at her side. Kieran began to pull at the handle and shake the door.

"Kieran, please stand back!" Harding said.

She stepped away. Harding had her by a good hundred pounds. Definitely had much better shoulders.

And he wasn't holding back.

He slammed his shoulder against the door. Again and again.

It gave way with a sharp snap, the lock breaking, and then they were in.

Before the door, there were more spots.

Leading down the hall to the apartments, a trail of blood.

CHAPTER SIXTEEN

Craig was a good driver — a skill honed over the years. He was capable of being a good *fast* driver, as well. He was intent on reaching the address they had discovered on the receipt — hiding in plain sight at the Baron home — as quickly as possible.

Once they were out of the city, the roads were dark.

Darker still as the roads became smaller and narrower, until Craig followed nothing but a trail of dirt up toward a cabin sitting in the midst of a small clearing and surrounded by pines. The trees seemed to hug the little building like a protective cape.

Craig could have sworn he'd seen a light in the cabin through the trees when they first came around on the dirt trail leading to it. But when they reached the rocky dirt driveway in front of the house, it was pitch-black. Only the car's headlamps gave any glow at all, other than a smattering of stars above them. Even the moon had hidden, so it seemed.

Craig looked at Mike. Mike groaned softly, then shrugged. "Let's check it out. At worst? They can arrest us for breaking and entering."

Craig nodded and grinned. Mike had Craig's back anytime — even if he liked to make a show of warning against anything that wasn't completely within legal limits.

"I saw a light," Craig said quietly. "I'm certain of it."

"You think we scared them?"

"Possibly. But that's better than . . ."

"Than?"

"Better than us getting here and them already dead."

Craig opened the car door, leaving the keys hanging in the ignition and the lights on. He walked around to the trunk and drew out two of the flashlights they kept there, tossing one to Mike as he emerged from the car, as well. He aimed the light at the wooden porch steps and then the main door of the cabin. He walked up and tried the door — certain it would be locked, but testing it, anyway.

It didn't budge.

Mike came up behind him, prepared with a little tool he carried that wasn't exactly

FBI issue. In a matter of seconds, he'd jim-
mied the lock open. They slowly swung
open the door and stepped cautiously into
the pitch-black cabin.

Craig threw the glow of his flashlight over
the living room.

There was a needle-hook rug on the floor
between a large fireplace and a worn leather
sofa with matching side chairs. On the rug
was a dollhouse and various figurines. A
copy of a well-loved children's book lay
open beside it. A sippy cup was on a table
by the sofa.

Someone had just been there.

Someone had just run.

"Outside," Mike told Craig.

"Rooms, attic, basement," Craig said.

They both nodded. Mike headed out.

Craig started out quickly moving to the
left — dining room and kitchen — and then
through the living room to the right — two
bedrooms, one with a full-sized bed and the
other with a twin bed and bunk beds.

The cabin was warm. It had heating; it
had water and electric. He was willing to
bet that it had cable, and that all of it was
held and paid under an assumed name.

The place seemed to have what was
needed for day-to-day use — even for three
girls. It had been there for some time, Craig

thought.

Waiting — prepared.

Lily Baron had known that her husband might well wind up in trouble. And he had been honest enough to try to make sure that if sacrificing his own life didn't work, she'd still be safe with their girls.

But Lily clearly also knew that her husband's enemies were many, that they were cunning, and that they wielded great power.

That they might find her.

Maybe they had.

He refused to believe that. Jimmy Baron was in the hospital, most probably dying. Maybe it was just too much to think that his whole family might have been killed, as well.

The rooms were empty.

He found the one ladder to the attic next, pulled it down, and climbed up. It wasn't much of an attic; it was really a crawl space that held a few boxes.

No one was hiding up there. The dust was undisturbed. No one had been there.

As he came down the ladder, he softly called Lily's name. "I'm Special Agent Craig Frasier. I'm with the FBI. You don't need to be afraid of me."

There was no answer. He didn't really expect one.

Only one place was left inside — the basement. He found stairs that led down into what was basically little more than a plastered-over foundation. It was full of barrels and boxes and chests — all manner of storage.

"Lily, please, if you're here, let me help you," he said.

Nothing.

But then he heard a sniffle.

And then a soft cry.

And one little voice that urged another to be quiet.

He didn't realize how hard his heart had been beating until he felt it then; one slam against his chest and it started to slow.

"Lily, please, I'm with the FBI. I'm here to see that you and your children are safe — really safe." He pulled out his wallet and his credentials. "Not sure where you are in here, but I hope you can see these. I don't want the girls to be unduly frightened."

She stood then.

She had been taking refuge behind one of the storage chests.

Lily Baron was a slender woman of medium height. She had pale blond hair, a color echoed in the three little heads that soon appeared near her, one popping out from behind the dressmaker's dummy, and two of them arising from behind trunks.

She would have been very pretty if she didn't wear such a weary look of concern and worry.

"Really, Lily, it's okay. You're safe," he said, and she began to cry.

It was a crime scene. Kieran prayed that she wasn't going to find a dead woman. She knew she shouldn't go rushing through the apartment; she wasn't armed in case there was still a threat, and she might contaminate the scene if she didn't move carefully.

Life was most important.

She prayed Alyssa was alive.

And she had a child . . .

No one in the living room. Chopra and Harding were with her — armed protectors — and she should have let them go first.

Later, she would admit that.

But in the moment, she just rushed through. Ran at full speed through to the back, and there, on the kitchen floor, she found Alyssa Ryan.

Alyssa had huge dark eyes. She looked lost and afraid and completely bewildered as she cradled a bundle in her bloody arms.

"Help!" she whispered.

"Help is here, hold on, hold on . . ."

Kieran reached for the bundle.

Alyssa Ryan's little two-year-old. "I have him, I have him, help is coming!" She could hear June Chopra on her radio; an ambulance was on the way, cops were on the way.

As if she instinctively believed that Kieran was real help, she nodded.

Her eyes closed and she fell still.

Again, with more urgency, Kieran prayed that she wasn't dead.

Craig called Richard Egan to let him know that they had found Lily Baron and her daughters — alive. He didn't intend to tell anyone else, though, and he let Egan know why.

"Slippery slope there, my friend, thinking some kind of law enforcement agent or officer might be involved," Egan said. "Then again, I have nothing against keeping information on a need-to-know basis." He was quiet for a minute. "You're aware that either McBride or Kendall or Beard or his partner, Holmes, have been at the hospital continually. Not the marshals, of course. Their one job —"

"Keep Riley and Tanya safe, yeah," Craig said.

He was standing just inside the front door of the little cabin. Mike had taken the car around back — a precaution — while Craig kept watch on the road. Craig had no desire to see anyone arrive as he and Mike tried to get the Baron family secretly to safety.

"They haven't been alone there, have they?" he asked. "I don't mean alone — obviously, there are doctors and nurses and hospital personnel, but it never occurred to me that our explosion victim might be left alone with . . . with cops," he said, finishing a little lamely.

"You've worked with me a long time," Egan said. There might have been amusement in his voice; there might have been reproach. "Do you really think that I wouldn't be looking out for our interests? I've had an agent in there 24/7. We've been keeping our eye on the cops. Oh, and, I guess, the cops have been keeping an eye on us."

"In what way?"

"Your new friend — or Mike's old friend. Jacob Wolff. It's too dangerous for him to go undercover again. His superiors have agreed, however, that he can pinch-hit with the US Marshals when it comes to watching over Tanya and Riley. Or our man in the hospital."

"What about the fellow who was followed to his apartment? Who was in the waiting room the other night?" Craig asked.

"Ah, him. Hmm. You know, it was odd. The whole building was checked out. We have not been able to find anyone legally in that building who matches the man's description. How he got in — and out again — we don't know. Whoever he was, no one has been able to ascertain — not any of the best research guys from the federal or local agencies," Egan said.

"So he must have been there because he suspected something. Because he was trying to see if the place would crawl with cops."

"Highly likely," Egan said. "Then again, the man, thus far — should we figure out who he is — has not done anything illegal. It isn't against the law to sit in a hospital waiting room." Egan let out something of a frustrated and weary sigh. "With this gang, we need an entire squad room to watch everyone involved all of the time. Anyway, get that woman and her kids here, to safety, ASAP. I'll let the US Marshals office know that we're about to add to their burden." He was quiet for a minute. "A miracle if that man pulls through. If he does, he's going to have to make one hell of a deal with the state's attorney. Don't that really beat all, huh? The man manages to control his personal and physical demons, and then the poor bastard is burned nearly to death.

Good thing is, if he gets a new life, he will live it well."

"I've met his wife and kids. He's got something to live for," Craig said. They ended the call.

All of a sudden, Craig could see lights on the road. He frowned. There wasn't much out this way. Was someone headed here?

His phone rang. It was Mike.

"We're ready here. Mom and kids tucked into the back of the car. Let's go."

Craig hesitated.

What if someone was coming out here to kill the Baron family?

"Craig?"

Didn't matter; there was nothing else he could do right now. He couldn't leave Mike alone to defend the family if something happened in the car.

"On my way."

He hurried through the house. Out back, he quickly slipped into the car. He glanced around. Lily Baron sat white-faced, her oldest and youngest daughters to her left, her middle child to the right. They were only more or less in seat belts, but, at that moment, they had to do a little minor lawbreaking.

He smiled at Lily. He hoped it was a reassuring smile. She tried to smile back. It had to be hard as hell for her.

She needed to hold it together for the kids.

She knew that her husband was lying in the hospital on the verge of death.

He hadn't found out much about her yet, but he admired her. She had known about her husband's fall into addiction; she knew about his struggle out. She also knew the cost they were all paying. And she still loved him.

"We're going to be fine," he assured her.

Mike was driving; Craig tried to settle back. They drove around the house. Whatever car had been on the road, it was gone now. It had most likely just driven on by.

As Mike pulled out from the cabin's trail and onto the bumpy main road, Craig saw lights again. For some reason, he was pretty sure that a car had doubled back.

He wished he was the one driving. He honestly liked and admired his partner tremendously, but maybe it was an unavoidable male-DNA thing. He thought he was a better driver.

He was also on edge, and wanted to be in control.

Was someone out here looking to kill these little innocents? A real message to anyone who stood against the gang and its plans?

He unobtrusively drew his gun from the

holster at the back of his waistband.

The kids hadn't noticed. The bigger ones were singing "The Wheels on the Bus" softly to the smallest one.

But Lily knew. He could see it in her eyes when he glanced at her through the rearview mirror.

"I'm moving, not to worry," Mike assured them.

"Yep, thanks."

And Mike did motor.

He drove so fast and fluidly that Craig thought he'd been paranoid at first; they made it back to the highway without anyone sticking to them like glue or appearing constantly in the rearview mirrors.

He had just begun to relax when he noted a dark SUV keeping pace.

Craig realized that his phone was ringing.

Kieran! They needed to keep in touch. If she was calling . . .

He went to answer his phone.

Too late; it had stopped.

But Mike's phone was ringing now. Mike picked up.

Craig barely heard him speaking; he was watching the SUV running close behind them. Then it pulled up around them on Craig's side of the car.

When he looked out the window, he saw

that something was leaning past the driver.

Taking aim with a pistol at his face.

Alyssa had closed her eyes, but she hadn't passed out. She opened her eyes and reached for Kieran, catching her arm.

"Please, please, watch over the baby . . . please. Don't leave him. Don't leave him until I can take him."

"It's okay, help is coming," Kieran promised.

Alyssa blinked, holding her side.

"Alyssa, an ambulance is coming," Kieran assured her.

"Thank you. I have to talk. Have to tell you . . . in case. They've been watching me!" she said. "Since that girl, Yulia, came to me . . . She was so afraid, and so pregnant. She came up to me out of the office, and we'd spoken for hardly any time when she suddenly ran. And I tried to find out more about her. I had inquiries out there . . . I looked for her . . . and I think the wrong people might have seen me or overheard me, or found out somehow that I was trying to get involved and help her and her baby."

"If you can, tell us what happened," Harding said.

Kieran looked up. Officer Harding was hunkering down. He knew something about emergency medicine; he'd taken a dishcloth and wadded it. He warned her as he pressed it to her, "This will hurt. But, you can't keep bleeding."

"Knife wound . . . side . . ." Alyssa said.

The little boy wriggled in Kieran's arms. She was holding him too closely, she realized. He pushed against her, fighting her hold, wanting his mother.

"Your mommy's there, right there, right with us!" Kieran said, standing the little boy up beside her. "Mommy's there. Mommy is fine!" she said.

She was a liar. But it was a lie the boy needed at that moment. And she prayed that Alyssa Ryan would be fine once help came, once she had time to heal.

"It's okay, baby, it's okay," Alyssa said. She managed to get a hand up again, to run it over her toddler's head.

Tears suddenly filled her eyes. "I should have come forward before. When Esperanza spoke to me . . . I knew I had to talk to someone. I was trying to find Yulia, figure out what was going on, but . . . I should have gone to the police, really pushed it, made someone do something."

And that was all; the EMTs arrived. Kieran wanted to ride in the ambulance, but Alyssa was nearly hysterical, insisting that Kieran look after her son. Kieran would follow the ambulance with Abel Harding and June Chopra so that she could hold onto the boy, whose name was Jerome.

Sirens sounded loud and blaring in the street with Harding driving and staying tight on the ambulance. Naturally by then, Jerome was crying, and Kieran was racking her mind for any nursery rhymes or anything else she could possibly say or sing that might help.

As it happened, June Chopra reached into her purse and produced a toy to hand to the toddler.

"Thomas the Train," June explained. "Hey, I've got a two-year-old nephew," she said.

It worked; Jerome was happy with the train. There was a song about Thomas that June knew and Jerome knew, and soon, the sound of all of them singing or humming joined with the wail of the sirens.

When they reached the hospital, Kieran realized they were right back where they had been.

As soon as they arrived, Alyssa was rushed in for care. There was nothing to do but wait. And in the waiting room, Kieran suddenly grew anxious.

She still hadn't spoken with Craig.

She dialed his number.

There was no answer.

She dialed Mike. And, after a second, he picked up.

"Kieran!" he said. "Hey, yeah, busy night, but going well — ah, never mind! Got to call you back!"

She heard gunshots.

And then . . .

Nothing.

CHAPTER SEVENTEEN

Craig — with his Glock already in his hand — had the jump on the other guy.

The other guy was trying to aim.

Craig just fired out his open window.

The SUV went veering off the highway and onto the embankment.

In the back seat, Lily and the girls screamed. Mike dropped his phone to his lap and gripped the wheel as their sedan careened with the impetus.

"Get down!" Craig ordered Lily and her daughters.

They instantly obeyed.

He had hit the driver of the SUV, Craig was certain.

But that didn't mean that he'd killed him.

A second later, he knew he hadn't as he saw that the SUV was back on the asphalt, maybe five car lengths behind them.

Mike was on the radio, reporting what was happening in a flat, steady voice.

It was one hell of a fast SUV.

But it was never best to be in back — even with a high-powered rifle. Someone shot again, but while the rear windshield of the sedan gave off a crackling sound, it didn't shatter. The sedan was, thankfully, equipped with bulletproof glass. But it had limits. A few more high-velocity bullets, and it would give out.

Craig turned and took aim out his window at the SUV's tires.

His first shot failed.

The SUV was just a few car lengths behind them now.

He shot again.

Missed!

He prayed he didn't cause an accident involving bystanders, but then again, if this guy managed to kill him and Mike, their sedan would soar over the highway and cause just as much potentially lethal danger.

Now, the SUV was almost on top of them again.

He fired again.

He caught a tire. The SUV began to veer off the road . . . and then it flipped and flipped and flipped and careened down the embankment.

Mike muttered an expletive.

Craig was pretty sure he did, too. Yeah,

there were kids in the car. At least they were alive.

The dispatcher's voice crackled over the radio; troopers would be at the scene of the accident within minutes. In the interest of the lives of the passengers in the car, they were to proceed directly to the FBI offices. State police were on the way for an escort, as well.

Mike asked Craig to dial Egan for him, then he took the phone. He rapidly filled Egan in, then fell silent, listening to what their director had to say.

"We're not going to make it!" Lily whispered from the back.

Craig turned to look at her. "Yes we are."

Mike set down his cell. He turned to look at Craig and smiled. "Miss Lily!" he said, glancing quickly to the back. "Not only are we going to make it, but your husband has come out of the coma. They're keeping him sedated, but by tomorrow morning, you'll be able to see him. And he knows that you're just fine!"

Just fine . . .

Craig noted a flash of red light and turned. They'd been joined by state police. A cruiser was at his side. A serious young officer lifted a hand to him in greeting.

Craig returned the salute.

"There's one over here, too," Mike said, indicating his window — and the state police vehicle on the driver's side of the highway.

Lily started to cry quietly.

Craig looked at her. She looked back at him.

Now, her eyes seemed enormous — with wonder instead of fear.

She almost smiled.

"Thank you!" she whispered.

Incredibly, Alyssa Ryan wasn't critical. Her would-be assassin hadn't caused fatal damage. She'd lost some blood, but no major vessels or organs had been breached in any significant way. While she had suffered a great deal of terror, she wasn't fighting for her life. She was all stitched up; all she'd have was a nice scar.

Kieran and her guardian officers had been at the hospital a few hours when they were informed they could see Alyssa.

Director Egan had come to the hospital to check on Jimmy Baron, who was out of his coma, but still sedated against the pain of his condition. Egan had managed to be back almost the second the doctors finished with Alyssa and said that it was all right if she was questioned, but for no more than ten minutes. Just because the injury hadn't been life-threatening didn't mean that it couldn't become life-threatening.

Abel Harding stood outside the door. June Chopra came in, aware that she was excellent with Jerome and that he couldn't crawl over his newly stitched-up mom as they spoke with her.

Alyssa was ready to speak.

"I'd say it was about two or three months ago now," Alyssa said, looking from Egan to Kieran. "I had just left the office. And this lovely girl with sound English but a noted accent came running up to me. She started panting — and, of course, I saw that she was about pregnant enough to pop. She asked me about asylum — political asylum, religious asylum — any kind of asylum. I asked her to come see me in the office and assured her that I would do anything I could, but it was curious. She didn't appear to be homeless or hurting. She seemed healthy — well, and as I said, ready to pop. Since I have Jerome . . ." She paused for a minute, looking across the room at her toddler, still playing with the train and Officer Chopra. "Well, I wanted to know how she was feeling, if the baby's father was American, and, of course, I assured her that her child, born on American soil, was automatically an American citizen. I remember glancing at my watch, thinking I could take her for coffee before picking up Jerome. But she suddenly stood straight up and looked across the street. She went white — whiter than a sheet of new-fallen snow. And she turned and ran away from me, saying that she'd check in with me at the office. I found the prayer card she had dropped, and, at first, I waited. Of course, she never came back. I put out feelers for her, asking my coworkers if they'd seen her and asking around at various social agencies — and in a few Russian coffee houses. I checked at the local women's shelters and several churches. Sadly, I've come to know some of the junkies on the streets, and I even asked them about her. About a week or so later, I thought I was being watched. That went on for a week or so, and then it seemed to stop, and then . . ." She paused and let out a long, soft sigh. "I stopped thinking about it, I guess. Then last Friday night, I heard about the woman who was stabbed in the back on the street. And in the office, Esperanza and I started talking . . . I felt that I needed to mention the young woman. I can't even imagine what it might have been like for her if she was someone's prisoner . . . if her baby was taken." She paused

414

again. "I know how I love my son!" she said in a whisper.

"What happened? Who stabbed you? How did you get away?" Egan asked her softly.

"I picked up Jerome at day care. We started home. I had this feeling I was being followed, and so I went down the street toward the avenue — they were having a fresh market thing, the street was closed . . . I wanted to stay in the crowds. I passed through a group of people, and then suddenly, I felt something in my side. I didn't understand what at first. Then I heard a woman screaming that some guy had a bloody knife, and I remembered that the woman had been killed on Friday in broad daylight in the midst of thousands of other people. There was blood *on me.* I realized that I was the one who had been stabbed. I was going to scream for help, but there were so many people there. I didn't know. I didn't know who would help and who would hurt, and I had Jerome with me. I thought that if I could just reach my house, I could lock myself in and call for help and . . . I was afraid of everyone around me," she ended in a whisper. "I was almost at my own door, I could get to my phone, call for help. I don't think I was behaving rationally. I just . . . I thought I might get home and be safe. If I could just get home . . ." She fell quiet, and then she whispered, "I'm alive! That other woman . . . stabbed in the street . . . is dead." She paused and looked from Kieran to Egan. "I'm so grateful!"

"We're grateful, too!" Kieran told her.

"Thomas!" Jerome suddenly announced, escaping June's playful care and rushing around to the side of his mother's bed. He offered her a beautiful grin. "Thomas!" he said. He showed her the little toy train.

Alyssa reached out for her son.

"Be careful — you don't want to pull out any stitches," Officer Chopra warned, plucking up Jerome and setting him carefully on the bed by his mother.

Alyssa began to cry again. "I'm so grateful!" she said, hugging her little boy. "And afraid. They can strike anywhere . . . you can't stop them. They have so many people, and the people they have become their weapons."

"But we will stop them!"

The announcement came from the doorway to the room. Kieran jumped up, spinning to see that Craig had arrived at the hospital. She let out a little cry of relief and leapt up, rushing over to throw herself into his arms, heedless of where they were or any kind of propriety.

He held her, offered her a quick, concerned smile, and then looked over at Alyssa. "Mrs. Ryan, we can never thank you enough for attempting to be a good citizen and a truly decent human being. We will stop them all. Bit by bit. It's unraveling, and we will get to the bottom of it all, I swear it."

It was nearly three in the morning. While certain cases had them up around the clock at times, Craig knew that he was exhausted and that he wouldn't be much good to anyone if he didn't get sleep.

He felt himself listing as he stood behind Kieran, his hands on her shoulders, as they both looked through the glass window at the burn unit where Jimmy Baron lay. He was sedated and in a deep sleep again, but his status was changing, and he'd soon be able to talk, really talk, to law enforcement.

His wife was in with him. The doctors had told her it was best if the girls didn't see Jimmy yet, and so they were at the safe house, being watched over by the United States Marshals office with NYPD and FBI personnel backing them up at all times.

Craig had been able to speak with Hank LeBlanc — the girls were fine. Both Riley and Tanya seemed delighted to have young company.

"A strange sleepover," Hank told him. "I'm loving it. My partner now has nail polish on her in a dozen shades. Oh, wait. So do I. Anyway, every agency in the city is in on this — nothing is going to happen here."

After the call, Craig wondered what was bothering him. And then he realized that it had been LeBlanc's words: *every agency in the city is in on this.*

Somewhere along the line, someone in the know had to be on the payroll of an organization other than the city, the state or the federal government.

He'd discussed it with his director. Egan was certain that the upper echelon of each office or agency had been informed that they might be looking for someone within their own ranks. It was horrible. It did happen that those sworn to protect lives were ready to take them — or turn a blind eye to murders taking place at their feet.

This operation had to be massive. There seemed to be a slug crawling out of every rock that was overturned. Someone was running it all from a pinnacle — gathering information, seeing that it went out. Someone known as the King, or the Queen, or an odd marriage that allowed for this massive kind of control, killers everywhere, ordered to murder — or die in the attempt.

"If it weren't so tragic, it would be beautiful," Kieran said softly.

He looked at her and she flashed him a glance before looking through the glass again. "Seriously. She's just sitting there, holding his hand. She'll keep doing so. And if what the doctors say is right, he will open his eyes again — he'll look up, and she'll be there!"

"And he'll split this whole thing wide open, I hope," Craig said.

Kieran made a face at him. "Okay, for a moment, I was thinking of the beauty of the human spirit and love and the pact between partners. And you . . ."

"Sorry. I'm thinking of the beauty that will unfold once we catch these bastards," he said, and grimaced.

Kieran shrugged. "That, too," she said.

"Let's go home."

She nodded. "Sounds good. My place? We've been staying there. We have more things there — both of us — right now."

"We should move into mine. I actually have the larger home, you know. Dare I say better or nicer home?"

"Ah, well, you don't live over a karaoke bar. No entertainment, you know. And didn't we just talk about this?"

"We did. And marriage."

"Absolutely," she said softly.

"A real plan," he told her.

She smiled. "A real plan. And you do have the best apartment. We do need to go there, even though we will miss the entertainment."

"Do I need to ask Declan's blessing?"

"He'll want to know what the hell you've been waiting for."

"I'll have to tell him his sister is slow to say yes."

"Yes."

They both smiled. He kissed her. Tenderly, for the moment.

"Seriously, for tonight, what about my wonderful guardians, Chopra and Harding? Do they get a day off tomorrow or what? And Jerome — thankfully, Alyssa wasn't that badly injured, but she can't watch a toddler from a hospital bed, and she's alone. I believe her husband is on his way home, but he was in Germany, so . . ."

"Brakes on!" Craig told her. "Egan has taken care of everything. Through the Bureau, he's keeping everything internal. You might have noticed we're alone here. He made sure that everyone was sent away, other than two of his most trusted field agents, before we came in with Lily Baron.

Someone knew we had her. Someone found out about their safe cabin in the woods and tried to kill her and the girls — even on the way here."

"Yes! What the hell happened? I heard what I thought were gunshots!"

"Yeah, but, honestly, no big deal. It was barely an attack," he lied. *People shooting on the interstate really couldn't be described as "barely an attack."* But it was late at night, and they were both exhausted.

"Honestly, short-lived, over quickly. I can tell you more later. Harding and Chopra have already been let off for the night. I had my friend Marty in tech go through their dossiers with a very fine-tooth comb. They're the good guys, or guy and girl, whatever." He hesitated. "I have Marty looking at everyone we know who has been close on this case, though — McBride and Kendall, Beard and Holmes, Jacob Wolff, and even Madison Smyth and Hank Le-Blanc, our marshals. Something is funny — I don't know what or how. But, from now on, we're keeping some of this strictly in-house."

"What if it is an agent?" Kieran asked quietly.

"I don't believe it can be. The only agents constantly on the case have been me and

421

Mike. From the US Marshals office, we have just Madison Smyth and Hank Le-Blanc. As far as NYPD, there have been a number of officers involved, and a number of them have been involved pretty closely."

"I can't believe it. I don't want to believe it."

"Neither do I. But, anyway, we have to go home. Have to. I'm about to keel over."

She nodded. "Me, too."

"Yeah, I heard about you, just running into a crime scene."

"Don't start . . . I didn't mean to do anything dangerous. I didn't ask for any of this to happen. I certainly didn't plan to have a baby thrust into my arms. Twice! They're both adorable, by the way."

"Jimmy and Lily Baron have beautiful children, too."

"So while this group has killed nearly half a dozen people that we know about, we can say that five little ones are alive?"

"Yes. Sometimes, you have to take pleasure in those things," he said. With his hand on her shoulder, he steered her around.

Mike was out at the desk with Egan, a nurse, and a doctor.

"Sir," Kieran said, and Craig hid a smile, aware that she was still going to assure herself that it was all right for them to leave, that the survivors — Jimmy Baron and Alyssa Ryan — were going to still be survivors when morning came. "I do realize that a tremendous burden seems to have fallen on your office because of . . ." She lost a beat, not wanting to say aloud that they had suspicions regarding the local police. "Because of the situation," she finished. "But —"

"Actually, it's all good," Egan told them. "I have a room here. First time I've asked for a room at a hospital." He offered them a humorless grin. "I'm here, Mike will stay, and I have two of our people coming on in five minutes. We'll be good here. You two go sleep. There's a patrol car downstairs — the officer will drop you off."

Craig was glad of the drop-off; even with a company car, parking at night could be a bitch — it was New York City. But, when he wasn't on duty, he didn't usually care. Hell, it might be New York City, but he was a New Yorker.

Tonight, though, he wasn't leaving Kieran anywhere to go park himself. Nor did he want her walking with him down streets that would be almost empty now.

He'd never seen the patrol officer who drove them before, so he sat in the back with one arm around Kieran and the other ready to go for his gun.

Even the karaoke bar was quiet as they headed up to Kieran's apartment.

Once inside, he started for the bathroom, telling her he was going to hop in for a quick shower. He probably could have just keeled over, but the ugliness of the day — the car chase, the glass exploding, bullets flying . . .

He needed the shower. And, of course, he knew that Kieran would follow him.

Some of her clothing was dotted with Alyssa Ryan's blood.

But she didn't follow him, and he walked out five minutes later in a towel to find her sitting on the bed, staring at the news. She looked at him, frowning intently. "My God! You didn't tell me that some guy shot at you, point-blank, from his vehicle, that you had an insanely dangerous car chase on the highway, and that you sent the car flying over the embankment!"

He sat down by her, picking up the remote, turning up the volume for a minute. "I didn't know his name, and I didn't know what happened after the SUV went over the embankment. There will be an inquiry, but at the time it happened, Mike and I had Lily Baron and her little girls in the car. We were told to get them into safety. Highway patrol went down to deal with the vehicle and the man driving. What else are they saying?"

Kieran looked at him, shaking her head, smiling slightly, and then sighing. "The driver's neck was broken. They found a bunch of guns in the vehicle. According to the news, no one knows exactly what happened."

"Egan is good at spin," Craig said simply.

He started to draw her to him, but she leapt up, shaking her head, and headed into the bathroom. He waited a second, and then heard the shower, and rose.

In the bathroom, he dropped the towel and joined her.

"Not clean enough, eh?" she asked as he stepped in behind her.

"Not close enough," he told her, his hands forming over the soap, and then over her body. He loved to watch the way water played over the ivory smoothness of her back, sliding down sleek and pure, and somehow in an exceptionally sensual way.

She turned in to his arms. That was even better, breasts and curves fit against him, steam rising around them, flesh so hot and damp. He cupped his hand around her jaw and kissed her lips as the water fell around them.

He'd been about to fall over with fatigue.

He was suddenly excruciatingly awake and aware and on fire.

They kissed . . . they touched . . . and they spoke against one another's lips. She laughed as he lifted her over the rim of the shower, as they tried to share a towel, as they just backed into the room again . . . half dry and half wet, and still steaming from the heat of the shower.

They were both suddenly and keenly awake and aware: passionate, alive and vital. Moving together, kissing, touching, here, there, one aggressive, and then the other, and then him rising above her, stretching her arms over her head, meeting her eyes and thrusting into her at last, in love with the way she looked back at him, smiling.

After, as he held her in his arms, content and at peace, he was out. Just out. And it wasn't until his inner clock felt the sun rise that he realized that he was dealing with the odd sensation that he needed more time.

That he had his finger on something.

It was right there, like whispers on the tip of his tongue.

But he didn't know what it was.

At his side, Kieran stirred. He hiked up on an elbow to look at her. She smiled.

"It's a workday. Do you have to go in?" he asked her.

"I have one of my last interviews with a client I'm trying to keep out of jail."

"Maybe you could just stay in the FBI offices?"

"Craig, we can't live that way. You know that. And I'm no fool. We both like and trust Harding and Chopra — Abel and June! Marty even vetted them. They're very good."

"Yeah. That's how you wound up racing into an unknown apartment after following a trail of blood."

"And all was well because Harding was two steps behind me. Craig, I am your basic coward. I love living. Key word — *living*. We've been through all of this. I can call one of my brothers, if that will make you happier."

He sighed softly, pulled her to him, and kissed her.

"I know you're only trying to help. You're amazing."

"What's bothering you?"

He hesitated, then shook his head. "Keep in touch with me. Promise."

"I promise," Kieran swore. She wagged a finger at him. "And you!"

"Yeah?"

"No somehow forgetting to tell me about a high-speed car chase and being shot at!"

He rose, ready to head into the bathroom and dress for the day, but he paused and gave her a teasing and cocky smile. "Aw, shucks, that was nothing."

"Yeah, that's what scares the hell out of me. So you — yeah, you! You keep in touch with me, understand?"

"Absolutely. What was that? Keep touching you?"

"No. I said, 'keep in touch!'"

"Keep touching . . ."

He leapt back into the bed. They both laughed, and then their laughter faded . . .

It was okay if they took a little extra time.

"I didn't bite anyone else," Besa Goga said, her attitude indignant. "You're not bad to talk to — you're not a bad person. But, I am here too many times. I have been controlling my temper. I have been pleasant and charming to all those around me."

If the circumstances weren't quite so grim, Kieran would have been amused. The thought of Besa actually being pleasant and charming was a stretch.

Hopefully, this would be their last meeting.

"Besa, you aren't in any trouble. The court had a last session scheduled for you. But, you could also help me, maybe. You could possibly help many people, here in the city. Do you mind?"

"What do you mean?" Besa asked.

"You know about the woman who was murdered. The man who was shot by the FBI. And the building that exploded in Brooklyn." She hesitated and then added, "You may have even heard about the death of a very popular nun in the city. Other people — attacked and killed. All these things were done by a gang that hurts newcomers to this country — from Eastern Europe, Africa — anywhere."

"Yes," Besa said simply.

"Would you help me understand everything about your experience? Very bad things are happening to people. We're trying hard to stop people from being hurt, tortured and killed."

Besa studied Kieran for a long time in silence.

"There is a price, you know," she said at last. She shrugged. "Sometimes, you just have to pay a price."

"A price?" Kieran asked her, frowning. Did Besa think that was the way you became American, no matter what? And the price was being used by others in illegal and immoral and degrading ways?

Besa waved a hand in the air. "A price —

you forget. You all forget because you are born here, yes, and you grow up whining, like little children, always wanting what you don't have. What you do have is everything. You have lights. You have water. So much food. You walk the street and if you say something — words that people don't like — no one shoots you. Not legally, anyway! I came here. My parents disappeared. I barely remember them. Yes, it was bad for a while, but I was a child. I knew no different. Back when I came, it was the same — what was done to me — as what I had left, and there was a promise that it would change. It did. Those people, the ones who were hurt or killed — they were not born here. They were not lucky. That's life. Some of us are born here, some of us are born in places that are a form of hell. Some are rich, some have nothing and will do anything to have something. I understand that. I paid a price. Sometimes, others must pay a price, too."

"But it's wrong, Besa. What happened to you was a crime. It shouldn't happen to others."

"Biting is a crime. I learned that. They made me come to you," she said.

Kieran inhaled deeply, not sure just how deeply she should be offended. She wasn't sure if Besa was trying to be funny and avoid the conversation, or if she was serious.

Besa spoke quickly.

"Kidding, just kidding. I like you, Kieran."

"Besa, no one should pay as you paid. No one should be threatened, or have their loved ones threatened. We need help. The people doing this are very, very bad. We have to stop it from happening. You say there is a price, and yes, there is a price for freedom, and there should be — but that is to come here and work hard for your own dreams and to keep the dream of what a country should be. And the dream of America is *not* to exact an illegal or immoral toll on those who want to try and create their own life here. Bad things happen, yes, even here. The point is that we do our best to stop them from happening. Allowing them to happen would turn us into a place worse than any place that was left behind. Thousands come, Besa. They work. They have families. They don't have to become prostitutes or baby-making machines or drug runners. Anyone forcing such a life on anyone else should be locked away for the safety of all others."

Besa was quiet for a minute, and then said softly, "Do you know how history has always gone? The Nazis, the dictators who have ruled throughout time about the world?

Fear. People living under such regimes weren't bad people — they were *terrified* people. And sometimes others think they should have had some courage — some guts. But, you have a husband, a wife, an ailing mother . . . yourself! You know about guns, or gas chambers, or beheadings and . . ." She stopped speaking and looked at Kieran and shook her head. "Fear. You prove you have endless power. Like . . . oh, yes. Like Alexandra Callas dying in the street. You show that you can kill a woman on a crowded sidewalk in the middle of the day. That you can reach anyone at any time. And when you have done that, you can control a man, say, even when he stands in the middle of a police station."

"Besa, do you know anyone who might know anything about this? Anyone at all?"

"Everyone knows someone — they just don't know it."

"I'm not into playing games right now. No riddles."

Besa shook her head. "I have been lucky for a long time now," she whispered. "My husband and I, we are so lucky. That dream — that real dream — we have found it. We have each other. Okay, so I bit the cable man. Yes, things come back to haunt us. I have what they call *issues*, yes. But we

432

work. We have different languages ourselves, but we both speak English — mostly. It's the language here, right? So we speak it proudly. That is the dream. We hold and love our culture, but we have become Americans!"

She sat straighter as she said the last.

Besa was silent for a moment, then she lowered her head.

"I was helped when I was young," she said quietly. "After the police caught me stealing things to eat, they sent me to juvenile detention. That took me from the man who was abusing me. He happened to be the king of a group at the time — not so powerful or bold as this group. The thing is, he always had someone on the inside. Most police, they are good. Not angels. But good. They want to keep the law. But every once in a while, you find the person who is weak. The one who needs a little money to cover a gambling debt, to pay child support, to manage a drug habit. People who abuse other people have a talent for finding cops or other officers who will turn the other way. Do you understand what I'm saying?"

"Are you saying that you do know something?" Kieran asked her.

"No. Honestly, right now, I don't. But, I will ask my beloved Jose if he has heard anything. What I'm telling you is this — if it seems that there are eyes watching you — eyes everywhere — it is because it is true. Someone close to you, someone supposedly helping, is hurting you. Find them, and maybe, just maybe, you'll have a chance. And if not . . ." She sighed and shrugged. " 'Meet the new boss, same as the old boss,' eh?"

"No," Kieran told her quietly. "You arrest them both — both bosses — and they are the ones who will then pay the price."

"You are so determined."

"Yes, because I believe in the ideal," Kieran told her. "And you never stop reaching for it. That, you see, is part of the dream, as well. No, it is not perfect. But, we keep trying — decade by decade — to make it more so."

"The beautiful ideal!" Besa said, and sounded as if she was somewhat scoffing at the concept. But she looked at Kieran earnestly, then. "I will see what I can find out, yes, because I like you. You are pretty okay. I wouldn't dream of biting you — honestly. Just kidding. I'm not biting anyone again — swear it. Well, unless they bite me first." She grinned and let out a sigh. "So? So do I see you again? I don't mind, really . . . you're okay. But so often?

Please . . . it's too much."

Kieran didn't remind her that she might have gotten jail time for assault.

"Besa, you do need counseling for all you went through. You should see someone — if not me — on a regular basis."

Besa waved a hand in the air. "But now, I must go. Okay?"

Kieran nodded and sat back. "You may go now."

"Thank you. Goodbye." She started out, but then came back, looking at Kieran. "You be careful. You are a good guy, right? You be careful."

"I will be careful," Kieran promised.

Besa nodded solemnly and left Kieran's office.

The one real possibility they had to discover exactly who was pulling the strings on the case lay with Jimmy Baron.

And while his condition was no longer described as a coma, his state of sedation was such that he couldn't really talk much. According to the doctors, if he was pressed, he could go into shock and die.

Lily Baron remained at her husband's side, holding his hand.

Craig stood at the window into Jimmy's room at the hospital.

Mike came to stand by his side, handing him his phone. "It's Marty," Mike said. "He's been digging into records, looking at everyone."

Craig took the phone and nodded. "Hey, Marty," he said. "You have something for me?"

"Yeah . . . no. What I have for you," Marty said, "is that I can't find anything. I swear, I've gone through applications, service records . . . I can't find anything that would suggest that a single cop or agent or anyone in our circle could be dirty."

"What about Holmes? The new guy? Speaking of which — were you ever able to reach Beard's old partner? The one who caught the original case with him?"

He liked Holmes. But some of the world's most heinous serial killers had supposedly been *likeable* people.

"Can't find anything. He was an Eagle Scout, for God's sake."

"Maybe that means he liked to camp and kill creatures."

"Not that I can find."

Craig thought for a minute. It wasn't McBride — they had worked with McBride before. He was solid as hell.

Jacob Wolff? He'd been undercover in the area. He was the closest to what had been going on.

"Jacob Wolff?"

"He went to high school in Manhattan and graduated from Columbia. He has a service record and a Purple Heart. He went into the academy soon after he left the military. He speaks several languages, by the way, not just Russian. Ukrainian, Polish, as well as Albanian, Italian, French and Spanish. He's just about a walking encyclopedia and could have worked just about anywhere."

"Let's hope he's not at the head of this!" Craig murmured.

"Well, whoever is doing this has some kind of internal intelligence," Marty said. "We're running out of possibilities. Lance Kendall has been a cop for nearly twenty-five years and has all kinds of commendations from a number of mayors. You know Larry McBride. I mean, there are others involved. I checked out Kieran's guard squad with a fine-tooth comb, even though they came on later."

"Keep looking. There's got to be something."

"There's something, Craig. But damn if I know what! Maybe I'm looking in the wrong place."

"Maybe I'm making you look too hard.

Take a breath."

"Yeah. Then I'll be back on it!"

Craig hung up. Mike looked at him. "What is it?"

Craig hunched his shoulders and shook his head. "I don't know. I keep getting the feeling that something is right in front of us, and I'm missing it."

"Then we're all missing it."

"It would be damned convenient if Jimmy Baron would come to and just tell us what is going on," Craig said.

"Yeah, now, that would be nice. And, from what they're saying, the guy has a good chance at survival. In another week or so, he could be talking."

"And how much more will happen in a week?" Craig asked. "Alexandra Callas, dead, Sister Teresa, dead, Paco, dead, the guy in the car . . . Alyssa Ryan under attack just because the baby's mother — who is still missing — might have talked to her. And last night . . . Lily and those little girls under attack. We can't wait any longer," he added quietly.

Mike was silent, staring through the glass. "I believe they've gotten Riley and Tanya to finish up with a sketch artist. I guess it took our artist some time because they didn't always agree on what people looked like.

And then Tanya thought one person was the Queen, and Riley was convinced someone else was the Queen . . . anyway, we should have something today."

"Could help."

"And could just be pictures."

"Then the public might help."

Craig nodded.

What the hell was it that he wasn't seeing?

His phone rang. It was US Marshal Hank LeBlanc. "We've got the alert out everywhere. They're gone, Special Agent Frasier. Riley and Tanya. Don't know how the hell it happened, except that they ripped out the ventilation system. A dozen cops and agents and us here, and somehow, they're just gone!"

CHAPTER EIGHTEEN

"Kieran!"

She wasn't sure why Craig sounded as rough as he did; she'd answered her phone on the first ring.

"Yes, I'm here."

"And everything is fine?"

"Yep. Harding and Chopra are in reception. They've got their eyes — and their guns — on anyone who walks in. So . . . what's wrong?"

"I'm at the safe house. We have techs poring over the place, trying like hell to figure out how this was possible. Someone broke into the safe house. Riley and Tanya are gone."

"It's surrounded — that would take an army!"

"We're figuring that whoever is responsible got their hands on the architectural plans, and that they got in and out through the airshafts. They came while the women were supposedly sleeping. It's bugging the hell out of me, though, I got to say. Even with the plans, unless . . ."

"Unless what?"

"Not sure yet. I'm working on an idea."

"What about the kids? Jimmy and Lily Baron's kids."

"Kids are fine. Just the two women are gone."

"Thank God about the children, at least!" she breathed.

"Yes, but I want to get back to the hospital. The key player in all this now is Jimmy Baron — for everyone's sake, we've got to keep him alive. I want to see our situation there firsthand — we'll be doubling up guards and keeping it within the FBI. I'm worried that we're going to find corpses somewhere soon. Kieran, I want you here. Egan and some of our best and brightest are going to be at the hospital. Mike and I have to get out there, find witnesses, find the women —" He paused. "Dead or alive. So I'd like to get you over here. Not sure how and exactly when yet. I'll let you know when I'm on the way or when I have someone coming for you."

"Okay. What about Drs. Fuller and Miro? Are they going to be all right here, Craig?"

"We'll leave them with a few agents on

detail. They weren't targeted the way that you were. We'll make sure that you leave the building with a full escort that is clearly seen. We'll bring Harding and Chopra with us, and leave the doctors covered, as well."

"Okay. I'm ready to go wherever you want me to be." She hesitated. "I just had Besa Goga in here."

"Who?"

"Besa Goga. I know that I've talked to you about her — there was no client privilege since it hit the back burner in the news. She's the one who bit the cable man."

"Oh, yeah, right."

She could tell that he was being polite, but wondering why she was worried about one of her relatively ordinary clients when people seemed to be dropping like flies with a murderer on the loose.

"She was horribly used and abused when she first came to this country, Craig. She said that even then there was a king and a queen, and that it's kind of like the saying, 'meet the new boss, same as the old boss.' She also strongly suggested that some kind of cop or law enforcement officer was involved. We never want to think that, but —"

"We have thought it. You're good with Chopra and Harding. Marty stripped down their credentials, their lives . . . stripped them bare."

"See you soon," she promised him. "Go to work. I have to read a half-dozen character references regarding custody in a divorce case."

"See you soon," Craig said solemnly.

Then he was gone.

She did have reports to read; she had to try to understand people through the written word before meeting with them. This area of what she did was her least favorite. Divorce was always sad — divorce with children involved was worse. Leaving children in a household where everything was a fight was equally as bad.

She needed to concentrate.

There was no way in hell she was going to be able to focus — not right away, not after her last conversation with Craig. People *were* dropping like flies.

That thought scared her.

It suddenly occurred to Kieran that she had first come across the young women because of Mary Kathleen and her work at the soup kitchen.

That could put Mary Kathleen — and Finnegan's and everyone in it — in danger.

She reached for the phone again. Declan, Mary Kathleen, Chef and the cooks would be at Finnegan's.

Declan answered. Then she had to hold it a few inches from her ear; he had apparently called her yesterday. She had not called back. He'd been forced to call Craig to make sure that she was all right, and he'd been ready to call Egan.

She winced, listening to her older brother yell. She apologized and asked anxiously about Mary Kathleen.

A second later, Mary Kathleen was on the phone with her.

Kieran explained what had happened — the best she could, anyway.

"The safe house, you say? That just doesn't sound possible, except with a team of navy SEALs!" Mary Kathleen said.

"It seems they got in through the inner workings of the building. Took the girls and got out in the middle of the night. I guess they were late sleepers, and the officers just discovered them missing about an hour or so ago."

Mary Kathleen was suddenly gone and Declan was back on the phone. "We're fine here, Kieran. This is a pub. Our precinct is still filled with good old Irish cops. And other cops who just love a good old Irish pub. I'm calling Craig. He needs to get his FBI ass over to get *you* — now!"

And suddenly, she was holding a phone connected to empty air. Declan was gone.

She sighed and set the phone down on her desk. Her fault. She should have been paying attention to her family!

As she set the phone down, she realized that the office seemed very quiet.

The office was often quiet.

Not this quiet. People came and went.

She glanced at the calendar on her wall. Well, for one, Dr. Fuller was over at NYU, giving a speech. Dr. Miro had probably gone to lunch. She had told Kieran she was on a "petite person's" diet, and that meant very regular meals. But even if the doctors were both out, Jake, in reception, wouldn't have left without telling her. Although, come to think of it, he might have told Harding and Chopra. While Harding and Chopra were great at reading and occupying themselves, even they had to stretch their legs or use the facilities sometimes.

She didn't know if she would have felt quite so nervous if it hadn't been for Craig's call.

These people had even gotten inside a safe house in order to kidnap Riley and Tanya.

She rose, very quietly and very carefully.

There were two cops with Jake out in reception.

Except that they weren't.

Kieran tiptoed from her office and down the hall, and peeked out, and all around.

And there was no one there; no one at all.

She heard a soft groan. She ran around behind Jake's desk. Jake wasn't there, but Harding was, down on the ground, a streak of blood running from his temple.

She almost screamed; she caught the sound.

Because as she'd run to the desk, she realized she'd passed someone searching around in Dr. Miro's office.

She rose, ready to streak for the door.

Instead, she raced back into the offices, back to the little kitchenette at the far end of the space. Because the front door was opening.

Craig had been through every inch of space at the safe house when they'd initially set it up.

Now he went through it all again.

There was no question that whoever had gotten to the women had used extraordinary measures. The grate was still out of the air-shaft through which the women had been dragged or forced to crawl. The officers, agents and marshals were, to say the least, completely humiliated. They were passionate in their certainty that no way in hell had anyone gotten past them.

Craig was in the midst of his discussions with the US Marshals — Smyth and LeBlanc — when his phone rang. Declan Finnegan was on the other end. He was trying hard not to be governed by anger or fear as he spoke, Craig could tell. He was angry, though. Craig and Kieran had not been keeping in touch with the rest of the family under these circumstances. Yes, it had only been a day or so, but nevertheless. And he was worried sick about his sister at that moment, and to make matters worse, Mary Kathleen wanted to take off to find Riley and Tanya, and Declan was doing just about everything he could to keep her at the pub.

Craig promised him that he'd shortly be with Kieran and that he'd send help to the pub. Declan assured him that the pub would be just fine, that he just had to see to Kieran.

Craig noticed that Egan was watching him as he spoke, and he couldn't help but wonder if his superior wasn't thinking that he allowed his personal life to interfere with his work.

He was wrong.

Egan walked over to him. "Kieran Finnegan is key in this case. Our involvement in a massive pile of ants began with that poor woman, Alexandra Callas, shoving the baby into Kieran's arms. I'd say it all rests with her, and with Jimmy Baron. While they're working here, I'm going to suggest you head back to the hospital, and hang tight next to Baron, with Kieran. I'll be there soon myself."

Craig nodded and looked around.

"I can't figure it," Hank LeBlanc said.

"Not at all," Madison Smyth said, and she flushed, glancing at Craig. "We didn't hear anything — anything at all. You'd have thought . . ."

"We should have been in that bedroom."

"Oh, come on, Hank!" Madison protested. "We can't take a leak with everyone! No one would accept witness protection at all if we literally stared at their every move."

"There were a dozen people here," Craig reminded them. He didn't say that they weren't at fault; someone was at fault, or, at the least, someone would be made to be at fault. That was the way the system worked — someone was going to have to take the fall.

And he knew that every officer and agent there felt responsible, and was frightened.

They had all liked Riley and Tanya.

They could all imagine them dead.

He turned to head out, but something pulled him back. He looked around the living area, the kitchen and the passage out.

He walked into the bedroom and saw where the grating to the shaft lay.

And it hit him.

He walked over to Egan, ready to explain what he feared just might be the truth.

The office had been so quiet; now it seemed to be filled with noise.

She could hear every little whisper of movement, she was so attuned.

And there were people in the office; she wasn't sure who they were at first, but she could hear talking — heated, angry whispers — coming from Dr. Miro's office.

"You said that she was here. You said that she hadn't left the building. You were supposed to be watching her!"

"I was watching her — she didn't leave the building. And I got rid of the one cop and took the other down. I did what I was supposed to do!" The second voice wasn't angry.

The second voice was scared.

Hunched down behind the little Formica work counter, Kieran tried desperately to figure out a way to get back down the hallway to the exit.

But someone had also come in through the office entry.

Who the hell was it?

She hadn't shut the door. She suddenly saw that someone was coming back out into the hallway. She nearly gasped aloud, she was so startled.

Ralph Miller!

He had been downstairs, day after day, watching her, watching the cops, watching all of them, every time they came and left the building. Of course, Alexandra Callas had slipped by him with the baby. Had he let her? How long had he been working for these guys?

Kieran needed her cell phone.

Which she had left on her desk.

"Stop!"

The sudden command came from the reception area. Kieran flattened herself to the floor, trying to see who had arrived.

Jacob Wolff.

She wanted to cry out in warning, to let him know that Ralph wasn't the only one in the offices.

But, too quickly, she heard the sound of a bullet whizzing by.

Ralph was suddenly down on the floor. He let out only a grunt of sound.

Was he dead?

Had Wolff fired? Had someone else fired at Wolff? Whoever was in the office had been the one who had been threatening Ralph Miller, but now she wasn't sure who was in charge.

From her vantage point, she could see down the hall, past the offices — her office, Dr. Miro's office, Dr. Fuller's office and the storage room. She could almost see the front door.

"This place is going to crawl with FBI in about five minutes!" Wolff cried out. "Cops, agents, deputies . . . you name it! Time to get out!"

Was that a warning that the killers were about to get caught?

Or a warning that they needed to get out before they were caught?

"Wolff, stand down. I've got this," a male voice called from Miro's office. And then, as Kieran watched, Detective David Beard stepped into view.

David Beard! Yes, of course, the head cop on the case five years ago.

And all these years, he had been using people.

Abusing them.

And killing them.

"I've got this, Wolff," Beard repeated.

"Where's Kieran?" Wolff asked. "Where

the hell . . . ?"

"They're out. They're all out at lunch. Ralph said that Kieran didn't get by —"

"What do you mean, they're all at lunch?" Wolff demanded. "What about Officers Harding and Chopra? They would have been with Kieran. They did — or they didn't — get out of here with her?"

Why had she left her damned cell on her desk?

David Beard stood in the hallway, staring at Wolff. She had to warn Wolff. Had to let him know that Beard was dirty.

Before she could scream, the office door burst open behind Wolff.

It was Tanya Petrofskya. She threw herself into Wolff's arms, screaming. "Help!"

Kieran heard the explosive sound of a gun going off once again.

And then she saw Wolff fall to the floor, his body protecting that of the young Russian émigré.

Craig was on his way to get Kieran, certain that he knew at least part of what was going on, and more determined than ever that both Jimmy Baron and Kieran had to be protected.

Back at the safe house, he'd pulled Egan aside. "Sir, you know that I've had Marty searching and researching."

"Yes, what?"

"David Beard. He's dirty. We've had a dirty cop on this, and it's Beard."

Egan was silent for a minute. "What makes you so certain? I've talked to Marty, too. His record is clean."

"Elimination. I know who it can't be — and who was around when, and who it could be. Sir, you can keep a clean record and still be dirty. He made a point of never being seen by Tanya and Riley. He was there, involved, when it all started. He's claimed to be doing all kinds of things, but Holmes — his partner — hasn't really known where he is half the time."

"So you think that Beard is dirty — How the hell, without Holmes knowing?"

"Because Holmes is junior in their duo. He does what Beard tells him. Beard must laugh his ass off — Holmes is so passionate."

"And you're sure that Holmes is no part of it?"

"No, but that's my gut feeling on Holmes." He hesitated. "I think that Beard isn't just in on it — I think he's the King." Egan stared at him, and Craig went on, "There's a lot of money in what he's doing. He might well be saving up and ready to fly to an island or country with no extradition agreement with the States."

"How has he left no paper trail?"

"I don't know. Accounts out of the country, for one. Assumed names, business fronts."

Egan swore softly. "There goes the credibility of every cop in the city. All right — we'll get the word out that he has to be found and brought in. Go get Kieran, and I'll meet you at the hospital."

Now Craig was making his way through midday traffic, trying to get to the offices of Fuller and Miro. Craig's phone rang. He thought that it was Egan calling.

It wasn't.

It was Randy Holmes.

Craig listened to him.

He was only a few short blocks away from the doctors' offices.

Traffic was bad.

He pulled the car over, jumped out and started to run.

"Come out, come out, wherever you are!"

It was David Beard, calling to her.

At that moment, Kieran had absolutely no idea if Wolff was still alive. If he was dead, if Tanya was dead . . .

454

And if Tanya had been alone, or if she was with Riley.

Or with whoever it was who had broken them out. Who had removed them from the safe house?

Her mind raced. David Beard. He was here. He'd been using Ralph Miller. Besa had been here. She had warned Kieran about law enforcement. And yes, it had been something that had surely occurred to everyone, because too much was known by the killers that shouldn't have been known. Every time law enforcement took a step closer to what was going on.

Beard had been there from the start.

Was he calling all the shots? Alone?

"Kieran, come out, come out from wherever you are!"

He was out in the hallway then, stepping over the body of Ralph Miller. Kieran stayed where she was, watching as he moved down the hall, opening the door to the storage room, then Dr. Fuller's office.

He was coming closer and closer.

He started into the little kitchenette.

She looked to her side. The trash can was the only thing there.

It was plastic. It would not do much good as a weapon.

It would have to do.

Beard stepped into the kitchen. He was careful, but he was going to come around the little prep island.

In just a few more steps . . . She was ready.

She threw like a girl. Yeah, a damned good-at-throwing girl who had grown up with three brothers. She hit him dead center in the head, and he staggered back and fell.

All she had to do was reach the entrance, get the door open, get out and get help!

She raced down the hallway and reached the reception area. Both Wolff and Tanya were there, on the floor, Wolff still lying in a protective curl around Tanya's body. But, there was blood on his forehead, trickling along his temple. And Tanya wasn't moving . . .

The door to the outer hallway opened.

Riley appeared in the doorway.

"Kieran!" she cried, throwing her arms around her.

There was no getting out of the front door; David Beard fired a warning shot over their heads. They dropped into crouches.

"Come out, come out . . ." he said. "Oh, look, you are out." He stepped by Kieran, dragging Riley into his arms. "Now, you will listen to me, or she'll die first. Nice and slowly. At the moment, I think I just might need you. You are my only ticket out if they've begun to suspect me. That ass of a good-boy partner of mine is getting itchy, and they're saying Jimmy might just make it, and if he does, well . . ."

He set the muzzle of his gun against Riley's head.

He smiled at Kieran.

"Help me!" Riley sobbed softly.

And then they all spun around, because the door opened again.

"Fucking Grand Central Station!" Beard cried out. With his free hand, he reached out for Kieran and dragged her hard against him.

Craig was there. He was ready — he'd known. Somehow, he'd known. He had his Glock out, aimed at Beard.

But Beard moved the muzzle of his gun against Kieran's temple.

"Who do I shoot first?" Beard asked Craig.

Craig couldn't allow so much as a flicker of emotion to show as he stared down Beard.

The man had killed or ordered the deaths of dozens of people, who knew how many more through the years. He had inflicted misery unknown or unsuspected by most sane and decent people.

He would kill without blinking.

"Let Riley go," Kieran said flatly. "You

have me. Let her go."

Let Riley go. Yes, Kieran would say that.

"Ah, yes, good point. No good having two young women squirming around. How valiant, Miss Finnegan. What honor and courage — why, you are the real deal, huh?" Beard said.

He shoved Riley toward Craig. Craig managed to step back and catch her without losing his dead-eye aim on Beard.

Riley.

If he was right about what he'd suspected at the safe house, Riley and Tanya had broken out themselves. One of them might have still been innocent, forced into action by the other. But which one?

Even as he held Riley and Beard held Kieran and they glared at one another, the door burst open again.

"Kieran! Oh!"

It was Besa Goga. She stared at them all, and then stepped back.

"Well . . . the new King!" she said softly, staring at Beard.

Craig backed away.

Could the Queen be this woman? Did he need to have his gun trained on her and David Beard?

He decided to go with logic first.

"Beard, come on, now. Killers like you

458

don't usually want to die yourselves. You can get out of this alive. You shouldn't. But I will let you walk out of here. There's really no other way out — except with you dead. Obviously, if you shoot one of these women, I will shoot and kill you."

Beard smiled.

"I'm not alone, Special Agent Frasier!" he said.

Craig knew. One of the women was on Beard's side. Besa Goga, or Riley McDonnough.

Tanya lay on the floor. Dead? Alive? Knocked out?

Craig was startled when Kieran suddenly spoke softly.

"Beidh tú ag íoc," she said. She repeated the words, staring at Riley. *"Beidh tú ag íoc!"*

Riley stared back at her, tensing against Craig.

Kieran shouted, "It's her! It's not Besa, it's her — it's Riley. She is the Queen!"

Craig thrust Riley back hard — so hard that she slammed into David Beard. At the same time, Besa Goga flew forward, as well.

David Beard screamed. His gun went flying.

Craig stepped forward, shoving Riley farther into the room and stepping over Beard, who had fallen to the floor.

"Don't move," he warned. "Really, don't move. I'd give a whole lot to have a legitimate reason to shoot you."

Kieran retrieved Beard's gun and turned it on Riley McDonnough.

Craig almost smiled, realizing just how hard Beard had really gone down.

There were teeth marks clearly visible on his hand.

Besa Goga had bitten the bastard.

EPILOGUE

Sister Teresa had been interred with all the honor, love and respect due to such a giving and wonderful woman.

The service, delivered beautifully by the archbishop, was over.

Naturally, the mourners had all gathered at Finnegan's.

With the amount of people who had attended the service and then come to the pub, Kieran had spent the first hour running back and forth with each and every one of her siblings and all their employees to keep the beer, wine, whiskey, water, soda, tea, coffee and food all moving at a respectable rate.

Eventually, it all died down, others were able to manage, and Kieran sat with Craig, Mike and Egan, and her brothers and Mary Kathleen, along with a number of the detectives who had joined them throughout the day — Jacob Wolff, Randy Holmes, Abel

Harding and June Chopra.

Jacob still had a bandage on his head — luckily, David Beard's shot had just nicked him.

The shot had knocked him out. Tanya had hit her head on the edge of Jake's desk when they fell together.

Abel Harding was also all right; Ralph Miller had creamed him over the head with a stapler after luring Chopra out on the street with a report that someone with a gun was down there, threatening people who were just walking by.

Ralph Miller had, though, paid the price. He'd been shot straight through the heart. From what they could figure out, Ralph had been a late addition to the crime family; after Alexandra had come to Kieran, they'd threatened his life — and his mother's. It would have been sad if the detectives hadn't discovered Ralph had also been paid off. With money — and with girls.

"Such a terrible thing. They killed so easily. And they used the goodness of a woman like Sister Teresa, and they stole what might have been years more of life from her!" Mary Kathleen said, shaking her head. "And that Riley woman. Oh, she used me. I'll be Declan's wife and an American, but I'll always love Ireland. How could she do that? I'll always want to help people. And now . . ."

"You'll still help people," Declan assured her.

"You won't stop me?" Mary Kathleen asked.

"I'd be afraid to try," he said with a laugh, and she smiled.

They were so perfectly suited, Kieran thought.

"Riley wasn't Irish at all," Craig informed them. "Just like David Beard, Riley was homegrown American. We discovered that she might have had an ancestor on the Mayflower, so go figure. She was an actress. She had that Irish accent down pat. She speaks a number of languages, all to help threaten and manipulate people."

"An actress?" Kevin said. "Ouch. That hurts the profession."

"She was a very good actress, really," Mary Kathleen said.

"She even had Tanya fooled. She escaped with Tanya and used her innocence to find out just what the police were doing, what they knew, and if everyone was suspecting David Beard. She used Tanya to get close to all of us," Kieran said.

"She had me fooled," Jacob Wolff said with disgust. "At the end . . ."

"At the end, she gave herself away. I'd never known Kieran speaks Gaelic!" Craig said, smiling at Kieran across the table.

She laughed softly. "I don't."

"Then . . . ?"

"That happens to be one of the few sentences I do know," Kieran said. She looked over at Declan, who had finally seemed to forgive both her and Craig. Not for the danger they might have been in, or even for the danger they might have caused Mary Kathleen or the pub.

Simply for not staying in closer contact.

"I know it thanks to the pub."

"What was the sentence?" Declan asked her.

"Beidh tú ag íoc," Kieran said.

Declan laughed.

"What does it mean?" Craig demanded.

"You will pay," Declan told him. "We have some old guys who come in here. They argue over the check every time. You will pay! You will pay!"

"When she didn't know the sentence, I knew that Besa was the innocent woman in the room," Kieran said.

"Go figure!" Mike said. "All those languages that Riley knew, but Irish wasn't among them. Guess she figured she wouldn't need it."

"But what will happen with poor Besa now? Didn't you just teach her not to bite?" Mary Kathleen asked.

"I think Besa will be fine," Jacob Wolff assured them.

"There are certainly no charges against her that we know about," Randy Holmes said.

"No. No charges," Egan said. "As to Riley — whose real name is Linda Jones, by the way — and David Beard . . . Federal charges. State charges. They'll never be on the streets again. As to those who were threatened by them, or under them, hopefully, we'll mop up what's left of the operation soon." He paused, grim for a moment. "Beard wants the possible federal death sentence off the table. He's talking like a parrot. A true reign of terror is actually over."

There was a lot to talk about. And the group talked until they were the last ones in the pub. Finally, it was time to head out, to go home.

And have a few days off — the good Drs. Fuller and Miro had told Kieran that she must take some time, and Egan had done the same with Craig and Mike.

They had all agreed.

And they were about to take off for a

lovely Caribbean island.

But Egan had promised them a surprise. The surprise was coming late, but it was coming.

Right when everyone else was gone and Declan was about to lock up, the door opened instead and a beautiful young woman stepped in, accompanied by Tanya and the US Marshals Madison Smyth and Hank LeBlanc.

She was holding a bundle in her arm.

A bundle Kieran knew well.

She let out a squeal of delight.

Then they were all introduced to Yulia Decebel, the mother of the baby. Her English was poor — her language was Romanian — but Jacob Wolff managed just fine translating for them all.

Yulia Decebel had not been killed; she had stayed deep in hiding, barely even coming out of the basement where she had found a refuge to look for food. But the news of the downfall of the King and the Queen had brought her out.

It was an amazing evening.

Despite the fact that the King and the Queen were down, it would take a long time to make sure that the entire operation had really been dismantled.

And so, Tanya, Yulia and the precious babe

would go into Witness Protection.

They were lucky.

They would have each other.

Finally, the night drew to a close.

Kieran and Craig went back to Kieran's apartment; it was where they had been staying, and though they had finally decided they were going to move everything over to Craig's better apartment soon, they just hadn't done it yet.

Karaoke was done for the evening.

But, Kieran thought, heading up the stairs, she did owe Lee a big thank you somewhere along the line. This case had been full of pieces, like puzzle pieces, and every time a missing piece had been found, it had brought them closer to seeing the real picture.

Upstairs, she headed to her room and looked out the window at her St. Mark's neighborhood.

Craig came up behind her, slipping his arms around her waist.

"Yes," she said.

"Pardon?"

She turned in his arms. "I think I said 'yes' already, but I'm just reiterating. You asked me to marry you. Yes, of course. I love you. I could never even think about being with anyone else. We'll have a lot of planning to do. First —"

"A venue, of course," he said.

"No, first I get back to the firing range. I really need to know how to protect myself. I mean, neither of us is ever going to leave what we do. Then . . ."

"A wedding party!" Craig said, grinning.

"Then we get settled in your place, and see to it that we have a good alarm system."

He laughed. "No dress, huh?"

She shrugged. "Somewhere along the line. As for venue . . . well, the church where Sister Teresa is interred, of course, and the party after . . ."

"Finnegan's on Broadway. Where else?" he asked.

She nodded.

"First things first. The gun range. Beautifully romantic!" he said.

"No one ever said our jobs were full of glamour and romance."

"That's all right. I can work on the romance," he said.

He swept her up.

"I think you're working on the sex part of it."

"Your point? I mean . . . I think we're romantic. With sex."

She laughed.

Yes, for the moment, the sex part sounded

just divine.

Very romantic, indeed.

ABOUT THE AUTHOR

New York Times and *USA Today* bestselling author **Heather Graham** has written more than one-hundred-fifty novels and novellas, is published in approximately twenty-five languages, and has had over seventy-five million books in print. She's a winner of the RWA's Lifetime Achievement Award, and the Thriller Writers' Silver Bullet. She is an active member of International Thriller Writers and Mystery Writers of America. For more information, check out her websites: TheOriginalHeatherGraham.com, eHeatherGraham.com, and HeatherGraham.tv. You can also find Heather on Facebook.